To

Eyes on the Stars

May the stars always shine brightly in your universe

By

Lynn Ames

EYES ON THE STARS
© 2010 BY LYNN AMES

ISBN: 978-1-936429-00-4

This trade paperback original is published by

PHOENIX RISING PRESS
PHOENIX, ARIZONA
www.phoenixrisingpress.com

CREDITS
EXECUTIVE EDITOR: LINDA LORENZO
AUTHOR PHOTO: JUDY FRANCESCONI
COVER DESIGN BY: TREEHOUSE STUDIO

Dedication

To the WASPs—fearless women who risked their lives in the skies so long ago. They paved the way for all of us who dare to step outside the box.

Acknowledgments

Writing a novel based on actual events in history requires mountains and mountains of research. Much of what I know and learned about the Women Airforce Service Pilots (the WASPs) I gleaned from watching, listening, and reading dozens of interviews with many of the WASPs themselves.

The sources I found for these interviews are too numerous to mention by name. There are, however, two resources in particular I want to single out.

There is an incredible organization dedicated to keeping the memory of the WASPs and their wonderful contribution to the war effort alive. It is Wings Across America, and it was created by the daughter of a WASP. The web site address is www.wingsacrossamerica.org. I hope you will visit the site, and feel free to donate if you are so moved.

Chapter Fifteen contains references to and accounts of actual events that occurred in WASP history. Although I read dozens of accounts of the incidents I describe, my primary source was *Women in the Wild Blue*, by David S. Stallman.

I spent many weeks gathering information about the planes flown by the WASPS and actually seeing the planes in person. My thanks to the patient mechanics and pilots of the World War II-vintage Vultee Valiant for sharing their expertise.

Finally, to those individuals who assisted me along the way with this labor of love by reading/suggesting, or helping me with complicated mathematical calculations, you have my eternal gratitude.

Other Books in Print by Lynn Ames

Outsiders

What happens when you take five beloved, powerhouse authors, each with a unique voice and style, give them one word to work with, and put them between the sheets together, no holds barred?

Magic!!

Brisk Press presents Lynn Ames, Georgia Beers, JD Glass, Susan X. Meagher and Susan Smith, all together under the same cover with the aim to satisfy your every literary taste. This incredible combination offers something for everyone—a smorgasbord of fiction unlike anything you'll find anywhere else.

A Native American raised on the Reservation ventures outside the comfort and familiarity of her own world to help a lost soul embrace the gifts that set her apart. * A reluctantly wealthy woman uses all of her resources anonymously to help those who cannot help themselves. * Three individuals, three aspects of the self, combine to create balance and harmony at last for a popular trio of characters. * Two nomadic women from very different walks of life discover common ground—and a lot more—during a blackout in New York City. * A traditional, old school butch must confront her community and her own belief system when she falls for a much younger transman.

Five authors—five novellas. *Outsiders*—one remarkable book.

Heartsong

After three years spent mourning the death of her partner in a tragic climbing accident, Danica Warren has re-emerged in the public eye. With a best-selling memoir, a blockbuster movie about her heroic efforts to save three other climbers, and a successful career on the motivational speaking circuit, Danica has convinced herself that her life can be full without love.

When Chase Crosley walks into Danica's field of vision everything changes. Danica is suddenly faced with questions she's never pondered.

Is there really one love that transcends all concepts of space and time? One great love that joins two hearts so that they beat as one? One moment of recognition when twin flames join and burn together?

Will Danica and Chase be able to overcome the barriers standing between them and find forever? And can that love be sustained, even in the face of cruel circumstances and fate?

One ~ Love, (formerly The Flip Side of Desire)

Trystan Lightfoot allowed herself to love once in her life; the experience broke her heart and strengthened her resolve never to fall in love again. At forty, however, she still longs for the comfort of a woman's arms. She finds temporary solace in meaningless, albeit adventuresome encounters, burying her pain and her emotions deep inside where no one can reach. No one, that is, until she meets C.J. Winslow.

C.J. Winslow is the model-pretty-but-aging professional tennis star the Women's Tennis Federation is counting on to dispel the image that all great female tennis players are lesbians. And her lesbianism isn't the only secret she's hiding. A traumatic event from her childhood is taking its toll both on and off the court.

Together Trystan and C.J. must find a way beyond their pasts to discover lasting love.

The Kate and Jay Trilogy

The Price of Fame

When local television news anchor Katherine Kyle is thrust into the national spotlight, it sets in motion a chain of events that will change her life forever. Jamison "Jay" Parker is an intensely career-driven *Time* magazine reporter. The first time she saw Kate, she fell in love. The last time she saw her, Kate was rescuing her. That was five years ago , and she never expected to see her again. Then circumstances and an assignment bring them back together.

Kate and Jay's lives intertwine, leading them on a journey to love and happiness, until fate and fame threaten to tear them apart. What is the price of fame? For Kate, the cost just might be everything. For Jay, it could be the other half of her soul.

The Cost of Commitment

Kate and Jay want nothing more than to focus on their love. But as Kate settles into a new profession, she and Jay are caught in the middle of a deadly scheme and find themselves pawns in a larger game in which the stakes are nothing less than control of the country.

In her novel of corruption, greed, romance, and danger, Lynn Ames takes us on an unforgettable journey of harrowing conspiracy—and establishes herself as a mistress of suspense.

The Cost of Commitment—it could be everything...

The Value of Valor

Katherine Kyle is the press secretary to the president of the United States. Her lover, Jamison Parker, is a respected writer for *Time* magazine. Separated by unthinkable tragedy, the two must struggle to survive against impossible odds...

A powerful, shadowy organization wants to advance its own global agenda. To succeed, the president must be eliminated. Only one person knows the truth and can put a stop to the scheme.

It will take every ounce of courage and strength Kate possesses to stay alive long enough to expose the plot. Meanwhile, Jay must cheat death and race across continents to be by her lover's side...

This hair-raising thriller will grip you from the start and won't let you go until the ride is over.

The Value of Valor—it's priceless.

CHAPTER ONE

E mancipation Hall in the new Capitol Visitor Center was throbbing with activity. Jessie let it wash over her. The bright lights, the politicians, the young men and women in uniform—it was overwhelming, really. And then there were "her" girls—even so many years later, she had no trouble recognizing them. There was Shirley holding court, like always, and Annabelle, who still was a looker, with her flowing hair, and...

Jessie clutched at her throat and leaned heavily against her cane. It wasn't possible. It couldn't be. Sixty-seven years melted away, and she was standing on the tarmac at Avenger Field in Sweetwater, Texas, staring at the most beautiful girl she'd ever seen. Back then, her heart had thudded once—hard—and she was a goner. The same was true now. Jessie moved as quickly as her age would allow, threading through the throngs of people.

"Claude? Is that really you? Oh, Claude..." She reached out with her fingertips to touch that smooth cheek, and the woman in front of her flinched.

"Umm. I, I'm not..."

"You must be Jessie." A woman in her mid-sixties came up alongside and put her hand out for Jessie to shake. When Jessie stood frozen, the woman offered, "I'm Natalie, Claudia's daughter. And this," she put her hand on the young woman's shoulder, "is my granddaughter, Chelsea."

Jessie's eyes tracked from the younger woman to the woman who was speaking and back again. "What?"

"My name is Natalie. Claudia Sherwood is my mother. This is Claudia's great granddaughter, Chelsea."

The young woman who had shrunk from Jessie's touch smiled sheepishly and said hello.

"You're not..."

"She's the spitting image of Claudia, isn't she? I always tell her how lucky she is to favor her great grandma."

"I'm so sorry, what a silly mistake for me to make." Jessie attempted to gather her wits and regroup. "Pardon an old woman, will you, dear?"

Chelsea touched Jessie's hand. "I don't mind. Really. I've always admired Grandma Claudia."

The young girl's smile reached directly into Jessie's heart. "You are very like her. She had a smile like sunshine on a sweet summer's day." Jessie's eyes narrowed as she turned her attention back to Natalie. "How did you know who I was?"

"I've heard so much about you over the years, I feel as if I've always known you. I grew up hearing stories of your bravado and adventurous spirit. For a long time I thought you were the only person my mother knew." Natalie laughed.

"Claudia talked about me?"

"Incessantly. I think I was almost as in love with you as Mom was."

Jessie's eyes widened. "I'm sorry?"

"Grandma!" Chelsea elbowed Natalie.

"What? It's true."

"Claudia spoke of me to you." Jessie tried to wrap her mind around the words.

"Of course," Natalie said kindly. "She loved you with all her heart. Always."

"I don't understand."

"Mmm. Mom said you wouldn't." Natalie frowned.

There was a moment of awkward silence as Jessie took in the women before her. Finally, she asked, "Where's your father?"

"Never had one." Natalie waved her hand as if to dismiss the notion.

"You—"

"Never had a father. Don't even know who he was. Mom would never discuss it with me. She was a wonderful mother, so I never really felt like I was missing anything. She raised me all by herself. Worked two jobs and never missed a major occasion in my life. I can't complain." Natalie's eyes misted over.

Jessie swayed, and Chelsea immediately came to her aid.

"Here, we should sit down," Natalie said.

Jessie sat heavily. She worked her jaw, but words would not come. Tears hung on her lashes. She hid her face in shaking hands. When she had composed herself, she said, "Surely Claude married…"

Natalie shook her head. "Never married. Never even went on a date that I can remember."

"Oh, Claude," Jessie whispered. "Dear, dear Claude."

"Ladies and gentlemen, honored guests, please, take your seats. We're ready to get started. WASP members, please take the reserved seats in the first three rows."

Jessie looked around her. She knew she needed to get up and move to the front of the room, but she wasn't sure her legs would hold her. As she struggled to rise, Chelsea took her elbow.

"It would be my honor to escort you to your seat."

Jessie smiled. "I see impeccable manners run in the family."

Chelsea walked Jessie to a vacant seat in the first row and steadied her as she sat.

"Thank you, young lady. You do your great grandmother proud."

"Hey, Jess. Jessie Keaton, is that you? I'll be."

Jessie turned to face the weathered old woman as Chelsea slipped away. "Hello, Rebecca. Good to see you."

"The uniform still looks good on you, Jess."

"Thanks."

A politician Jessie recognized from the television stepped to the microphone. "Ladies and gentlemen, today has been a long time in the making. The one thousand seventy-four Women Airforce Service Pilots served their country with distinction in World War II, freeing up the male pilots for combat. Many of the three hundred surviving WASPs are here with us today to receive the Congressional Gold Medal, the highest civilian honor bestowed by this country. We want each and every one of you to know that you have the thanks of a grateful nation. Your journey began in 1942 in Houston, Texas, and continued in 1943 at Avenger Field…"

The voice faded into the background as Jessie recalled mustering on that first day at Sweetwater, in front of the legendary Jackie Cochran, founder of the WASPs.

"Listen up, you lot. I know the fly suits are ill-fitting, the cattle truck is uncomfortable, and it's hotter than your oven on Thanksgiving day. I know you had to pay your own way here, the parachutes are heavy, and the living arrangements are Spartan. I know that there are many men who want to see you fail. But I also know that you're here because you love to fly, and because you want to do something substantial to help the war effort..."

Jessie wiped her brow and looked around her. There were young women of all shapes and sizes. She was grateful the fly suit she'd grabbed fit her relatively well. Of course, she was as tall as most men, which helped considerably, since the suits were designed for the male combat pilots. Her eyes lit upon a tiny wisp of a woman—a girl, really—a few rows back and to her left. The suit swallowed the woman whole.

Jessie tried not to laugh as she watched her surreptitiously fuss with the sleeves, pull at the yards of extra material around her waist, and tug on the pant legs on which she was standing. Still, she wore a look of determination that told Jessie she was not easily discouraged.

"Okay, ladies, get settled in your assigned bays, stow your gear, and report back here at 0930."

Jessie and the other twenty-two women in her class broke ranks, hoisted their gear, and set off to find the assigned quarters where they would spend the next six months while they trained to fly every aircraft in the US Army Airforce fleet.

After several false starts, Jessie located her bay in the row of old Army barracks. Since she was first in, she had her choice of the six beds—cots, really. She peeked in the adjoining bathroom and was shocked to realize that the single commode, sink, and mirror would have to accommodate not only her bay but also an identical one on the other side of the bathroom.

"Well, this ought to be fun."

"I'm sorry, did you say something?"

Jessie whirled around to find the same tiny woman from the lineup. Her head was cocked inquisitively and, up close, Jessie could see that her eyes were startlingly green. Her hair, a pretty shade of auburn, hung in waves and shimmered in the dusty light from the only window.

Jessie dimly became aware that she was staring. "Um, I was just... Well, you see..." Jessie stopped talking. She had no idea what she wanted to say, which was a completely foreign experience for her. She knew her cheeks must be red because her face was hot.

The woman threw back her head and laughed. The sound was like birds singing in the early morning. "I'm Claudia." The woman put out her hand for Jessie to shake.

"Jessie." *Her hands are so soft.* After another awkward pause, Jessie realized she hadn't released Claudia's hand. "Oh, sorry." Jessie dropped her hand to her side, then, not knowing what else to do with it, stuffed it in her pocket.

"You were here first, you should get first pick. Which bed do you want?"

"It doesn't matter to me, you go ahead."

Claudia's smile was brilliant. She turned in a full circle as she surveyed the room.

"Before you make up your mind," Jessie rushed ahead, "you'll probably want to know that there's only one commode for twelve of us."

"Oh. In that case, I think I'd better take the bed closest to the bathroom." Claudia shrugged. "Weak bladder."

"Ah," Jessie murmured, not knowing what to say to that. She put her duffle bag on the bed next to Claudia's, trying for nonchalance. "Guess I'll just bunk here." She watched as Claudia struggled to lift her suitcase onto her cot. Jessie noted that the bag likely cost more than her entire wardrobe. "Here, let me get that." She reached over and hoisted the suitcase onto the bed, and was rewarded with another laugh from Claudia.

"You make that seem so easy, when I know full well how heavy that bag is." Claudia swept an errant strand of hair out of her eyes. "I had no idea what to pack."

"I can see that."

The door flew open and four other women burst in, all laughing and talking at once. Jessie winced at the noise level. Growing up in rural upstate New York, she was unused to a lot of extraneous chatter.

"They are a loud bunch, aren't they?" Claudia whispered conspiratorially.

"Wha?"

Claudia smiled. "Your expression gave you away. Remind me to play poker with you."

Before Jessie could respond, Claudia crossed the room and introduced herself to their new bunkmates. "That's Jessie over there." Jessie waved weakly as the other women followed Claudia's gaze to where she still stood rooted to the spot.

"I'm Janie."

"Rebecca."

"Shirley."

"Annabelle."

Jessie nodded in each of their directions, hoping she'd be able to keep them straight.

"Goodness," Shirley said, or was it Rebecca? "Look at the time. We'd better get going. Don't want to be late for ground school."

As quickly as they'd rushed in, Janie, Rebecca, Shirley, and Annabelle flew back out, leaving Jessie alone with Claudia once more.

"Whew, they're going to be a handful, aren't they?" Claudia remarked. She crossed the room and hooked her arm through Jessie's. "C'mon. We'd better get going."

"Right." Jessie looked down at their interlocked arms, and warmth spread through her. What was it she was being asked to do, again? Oh yeah, walk.

∽∾

"Please come with me, Jess? Please?" Claudia stood at the foot of Jessie's bed, looking pretty as a peach in a sleeveless sundress and slingback, medium-height heels. Her hair framed her face like a picture, and her makeup reminded Jessie of one of those big movie stars.

They'd been training for three weeks solid without a day off. It was Saturday night, and some of the girls were going into town to check out the action at the Blue Bonnet Hotel. Jessie's stomach twisted painfully as she envisioned some young buck putting his paws on sweet Claudia, even just to dance. She sighed heavily. "Okay, I'll go, but there's no way I'm setting foot on the dance floor."

"Deal." Claudia put her hand out and they shook on it, as had become their custom whenever she got Jessie to give in on something, which, Jessie noted, was often.

Jessie ran a comb through her hair and grabbed her jacket.

"You're going like that?"

Jessie frowned and looked down at her standard WASP-issued white shirt and khaki slacks. "What's wrong with this?"

Claudia smiled and patted her on the arm. "Not a thing. I think you look incredibly dashing. But I expect you might get hassled for wearing slacks."

Jessie shrugged. "Too bad."

"Okay, then. Let's go," Claudia said brightly, linking their arms.

The contact sent a shiver down Jessie's spine, as it always did.

When they arrived, the crowd at the Blue Bonnet was raucous and the music was loud. Cigarette smoke wafted through the air, men and women danced to the latest tunes, and others congregated near the bar.

"Want something to drink?" Jessie yelled close to Claudia's ear to be heard.

"Oh, I'm not much of a drinker. Just some pop, please."

"Okay, I'll be right back." Jessie fought through the throngs to get to the bar. By the time she'd gotten the drinks and returned, there was an enlisted man standing close enough to Claudia to count the dusting of freckles on her nose. Jessie's jaw set.

"No, I really don't want to dance."

"Come on, sugar. A pretty thing like you? We'd look perfect together."

"Thank you, but I'm just not interested."

The man took Claudia's wrist and pulled her toward the dance floor...and ran directly into Jessie, whose eyes showed fire.

"The lady said she wasn't interested."

"Yeah, but she really didn't mean it."

"Actually, I believe she did." Jessie didn't give any ground as the soldier tried to push past her. "Now let go of her and go on your way."

"Who do you think you are?" The man made a show of examining Jessie's shirt and slacks. They stood eyeball to eyeball.

"Jess, it's okay," Claudia said, putting her free hand on Jessie's arm. "Don't make a scene."

"Do you want to dance with this...person?"

"N-no, but..."

Jessie continued to stare daggers at the soldier. "Then it's not okay, is it?"

"Jess..."

Jessie heard the desperate, nervous plea in Claudia's voice but chose to ignore it. To the soldier she said, "Take your paws off my friend and go find someone else to pester."

The soldier hesitated, clearly weighing the blow to his ego against the effort this conquest was taking. Finally, he released Claudia's wrist and, with a disgusted look in Jessie's direction, faded into the crowd.

"Whew. Goodness," Claudia chattered, "I wasn't counting on that kind of excitement." She fanned herself. "Is that for me?" She pointed to the Coca Cola Jessie held in her hand.

Jessie wordlessly gave Claudia the drink as she tried to wrestle her temper under control.

After an uncomfortable silence, during which Claudia sipped her soda and swayed to the beat of the music, Jessie said, "I'm sorry, Claude. I shouldn't have come." She turned on her heel and hurried to the exit.

When she got outside, she took several deep breaths and stared at the stars. "Stupid, stupid, stupid," she mumbled to herself as she strode away from the hotel.

"Hey! Hey! Jess, wait up." Claudia came up alongside.

"What are you doing, Claude? Go on back inside and have a good time."

"It won't be a good time without you there, silly."

"Nonsense. You were looking forward to dancing and letting your hair down."

Claudia shook her head and chuckled. "You don't get it, do you?"

"Get what?"

"What I was looking forward to," Claudia linked her arm through Jessie's in a now-familiar gesture, "was spending time off-base with you, getting to know you better."

Jessie stopped short. "What?"

"For someone as sharp as you are, you can be so dense, sometimes." Claudia glanced around at the crowded parking lot. "Let's go for a walk, shall we?"

Jessie made a show of looking at Claudia's feet. "You're not really wearing the appropriate footwear for that, are you?"

"God, you can be so pig-headed." Claudia reached down, slipped her shoes off, and dangled them from two fingers. "Come on." She pulled Jessie forward, away from the lights of the town.

After a little while, Claudia stopped them and looked around. Jessie wrinkled her brow. They were in the middle of nowhere, inky darkness enveloped them, and there was not a soul in sight.

"This will do."

"For what?"

Claudia sighed exasperatedly. "You really are dense, you know?" She turned to face Jessie, stood on her tiptoes, and softly kissed Jessie on the mouth.

Jessie's brain froze, then melted, as Claudia slipped her arms around Jessie's waist and pulled her closer, deepening the kiss. When they broke apart, Jessie's eyes were still tightly shut.

Claudia cleared her throat and took a step back. When Jessie dared open her eyes, Claudia was smiling at her dreamily. "For that. This spot will do for that, which is something I've been wanting to do since the first time I saw you."

"Um. You did?"

"Yes, silly. Gosh, you are the dreamiest." Claudia chewed her lip. "You didn't mind, did you? I mean, if you did…"

Jessie tried to get her mouth to move so that she could speak, but her lips were still tingling. So instead, she pulled Claudia back to her and kissed her, gently at first, and then with more urgency when Claudia melded to her body.

"I guess that means you were okay with it, huh?"

Jessie laughed. Claudia linked their arms and began walking again. "That's the first time I've ever heard you laugh. I like it. I'll have to work on getting you to do that more often."

CHAPTER TWO

Jessie was sure she must have died and gone to heaven. It was their two-week anniversary—two weeks since that wondrous first kiss, and Claudia wanted to celebrate in style. Somehow she got permission for the two of them to borrow one of the BT-13s in which they'd been training. With the brass's blessing, they were flying to the Palm Springs Army Air Base in California.

She'd never been to California, but Claudia had spent a lot of time there growing up and promised to show her the sights. Two whole days alone with Claudia. Wow.

"Hey Jess," Annabelle called on her way to the bathroom. "You thinking about a fella?"

"N-no, why?" Jess fidgeted with the beret she held in her lap.

"You've got this queer expression on your face—all gaga-like." Annabelle studied her and Jessie shifted uncomfortably on her cot. "Sorta the way I felt when I'd kissed my first boyfriend." When Jessie remained silent, Annabelle shrugged and went on her way.

Jessie waited until the door closed and rushed outside. She didn't want to be around when Annabelle emerged. "Of all the idiotic…" Oof.

"You know, you really ought to watch where you're going. You might run into someone."

Jessie raised her gaze from her shoe tops and looked directly into Claudia's laughing eyes. When she realized that Claudia's arms were wrapped around her waist, she blushed and stepped back. "Sorry."

Claudia regarded her quizzically. "I'm not. Are you okay, Jess?"

"Yeah. Fine. Why?"

"You're acting like your pants are on fire."

"Am I? No. Everything's good."

Claudia took a step closer. "Listen, if you don't want to go tomorrow…"

Jessie saw the uncertainty in Claudia's expression and wanted to kick herself. She would've, in fact, if she were that flexible. "Of course I want to go. Are you kidding? I can't wait."

Claudia stared hard at her for a few seconds longer, then relented. "Okay, but if you change your mind—"

"I won't."

"Outstanding." Claudia's smile was as bright as the midday sun. "Now we'd better hurry or we'll be late for instrument training. Jess? Earth to Jess, come in, please."

"Huh? Oh. Right." Caught mooning again, Jessie gave herself a second mental kick for good measure.

Claudia was in the front cockpit, piloting the Vultee Valiant on the second leg of their trip, so Jessie took full advantage of her position in the rear to study her. Jessie noted the way she bit her lip in concentration every time she turned her head to check their surroundings, how her hands looked as they flew over the instrument panel, the way her hair curled at the base of her neck. "Damn, woman, you've got it bad."

"What's that?" Claudia shouted to be heard over the engine noise. "Did you say something?"

"No. We should be coming up on it soon."

"Yep."

"You do know how to land this bird, right?"

"Very funny. You can always take over from back there if you don't trust me."

"I'll keep that in mind." Jessie smiled. Claudia had logged nearly seventy-five more flying hours than her, and she was an excellent pilot.

When they touched down ten minutes later, they were guided in by two enlisted men. As they jumped down from the wing and removed their goggles and caps, one of the soldiers said, "Catch this, Solly. It's a couple of dames. A couple of dames flying one of our trainers. What is this world coming to?"

Jessie felt the hair on the back of her neck rise at his derisive tone, but before she could say anything, Claudia stepped forward, effectively blocking her path.

"Hi fellas. Just thought we'd drop by for a bit. You know, before we head back to hang the wash and cook our men dinner." She swept past the men, exaggerating the sway of her hips. There was nothing for Jessie to do except to follow. "Jerks," she heard Claudia mumble under her breath.

A little while later, they arrived at The Desert Inn and checked in to their room. "How did you know about this place?" Jessie asked, as she unpacked her bag and hung up her dress khakis.

"Are you kidding?" Claudia was sprawled across one of the two beds. "This place is legendary. We might even see Cary Grant at the pool. Clark Gable and Carole Lombard stayed here. Terrible about her death, wasn't it? And now I hear he's overseas flying missions. I wish he'd just make another movie."

"Are you a big movie fan?"

"Gosh, yes. Did you see Grant and Katherine Hepburn in *The Philadelphia Story*? What about Gable and Vivian Leigh in *Gone With the Wind*? That was epic."

Jessie looked back over her shoulder at Claudia. "Nope and nope. I like the movies. Just never had much time to go."

Claudia sat up, a determined look on her face. "Well, we'll just have to fix that. I noticed on our way in that *Casablanca* is playing in town. Maybe we could go tonight?"

"Sure, if that's what you want."

Claudia popped up off the bed and came to stand in front of Jessie, essentially pinning her in the corner. Her gaze was searching. "What do you want, Jess? I feel like we only ever do what I want to do. I don't want it to be that way." Her lower lip stuck out appealingly, and Jessie couldn't tear her eyes away. "Are you just going to stand there looking, or are you going to kiss me? It's been forever."

Jessie swallowed hard and wiped her sweaty palms on her pants as Claudia closed the few remaining inches between them. "Claude…"

"Mmm? You're not going to keep me waiting, are you?"

"Of course no—"

Claudia slid her arms around Jessie's neck and brushed her lips against her. "Stop"—Claudia pulled Jessie's lower lip into her mouth and sucked on it briefly—"talking."

Warmth spread throughout Jessie's body. She buried her hands in Claudia's soft curls and kissed her. Claudia's lips parted, inviting her inside, and Jessie was lost.

"Claude," Jessie murmured, when they stopped briefly for air. She licked her lips. Her legs were shaking. "If you keep kissing me like that, I won't want to stop."

"Who said anything about stopping?" Claudia ran her fingers down Jessie's arms and captured her hands. She kissed each of Jessie's palms. "I could kiss you forever."

"You won't get any complaints from me, but…"

"But, what?"

Jessie felt the blush creep up her neck. "I'm feeling a little out of my depth here."

"What are you talking about?"

Jessie examined a spot on the carpeting. "I-I've never kissed anyone before." She said it in a rush, as if pushing the words out fast would somehow make the admission less embarrassing.

"Huh. Not in your whole entire life? Not even a boy in high school?"

Jessie shook her head. She didn't need to look up. She could practically hear Claudia snickering at her.

"Hey." Claudia squeezed Jessie's hand. "That's nothing to be ashamed of. I think it's sweet. And you picked me as your first. Wow. I'm a lucky girl."

Jessie finally chanced a glance, and was surprised to discover the earnestness in Claudia's expression. "You really don't care?"

"Of course not, silly."

"You don't think less of me?"

"Gosh no. Do you think less of me because I *have* been kissed before?"

"What? No. I suppose one of us should know what we're doing."

At that, they both laughed.

"Come on," Claudia said, tugging on Jessie's sleeve. "Let's go see what kind of trouble we can get into."

◈◈

They rented bikes from the hotel and rode through town. Claudia pointed out various sites along the way—watering holes of celebrities, nifty dress shops, and the like.

"Oooh. That's dreamy." Claudia hit the brakes so hard Jessie nearly ran into the back of her bike.

"Hey!"

"Sorry, but oh, Jess, look."

Jessie turned her attention to the display in the store window, where a mannequin modeled a shimmering gown with a daring neckline. Taped to the window was a picture of Betty Grable wearing what looked to be the same dress. Claudia pulled her by the sleeve.

"Can we go inside? Please? I just want to try it on."

"Where would you wear that?"

Claudia punched her in the arm and rolled her eyes. "You're so practical. Nowhere, silly. I just want to see what it looks like."

Jessie couldn't see the sense in it, but she could tell that Claudia was determined, so she dismounted the bike.

"Thank you. You won't regret it."

When Claudia emerged from the fitting room wearing the dress, Jessie was grateful to be sitting. "Holy mother of God."

Claudia twirled around in place. "You like it?"

Jessie, who was sure her eyeballs must've fallen out of her head, blinked several times. "It's…um, it's out of this world." The front of the gown revealed a healthy expanse of creamy smooth skin, including a scandalous amount of cleavage. The back dipped low so that Claudia's upper back and shoulder blades were visible.

"Yeah?"

"Definitely," Jessie said.

Claudia twirled one more time, the smirk on her face a clear indication that she was enjoying the effect the dress was having on

Jessie. "Wish I had somewhere to wear it," she said wistfully, as she disappeared back into the dressing room.

"Wish I could afford to buy it for you," Jessie mumbled, painfully aware, not for the first time, of the disparity in their circumstances.

"Let's pick up some supplies for a picnic. What do you say?" Claudia asked, once they were back on their bikes. "There's a nice park a ways outside of town. It'd be fun."

"Sure." Jessie was starting to become more accustomed to Claudia's impulsiveness.

"We could get some cheese and crackers, fruit, and maybe a piece of pie. Does that sound okay?"

"Sure."

"I swear, you are so difficult."

"What?"

"Trying to have a conversation with you is like pulling teeth. All I get are one-word answers."

"Your choices are fine with me, so why would I need to say anything more than what I did?"

"Ugh. You are hopeless."

"I-I'm sorry, Claude." Jessie felt a sinking sensation in her gut. "I don't mean to upset you."

Claudia stepped on the brakes, and Jessie followed suit. "Listen, Jess. In case you haven't noticed, I'm really, really sweet on you. I just wish I felt like I knew you better."

Jessie searched Claudia's face. Reticence was a natural part of her personality. If she wanted Claudia in her life in a meaningful way—and boy, did she—then she was going to have to go against her nature. She swallowed hard. "I grew up in rural upstate New York—a little town called Indian Lake. I was an only child, and a girl at that. My father wanted a boy. So I became his 'son.' He was a state park ranger, so we fished, we cut brush, we hiked, we cleared trails... That was my life. He was a quiet man—didn't have any patience for small talk and didn't care about things like feelings. So I learned to keep to myself." Jessie cast her eyes downward and clicked her jaw shut. That was the most words she had strung together in, well, forever. "I guess I've never learned to have proper conversation."

Claudia was silent for so long, Jessie was afraid that if she looked up, she might be alone.

"Thank you."

Jessie's head jerked up. "For what?"

Claudia leaned forward and kissed her sweetly on the lips. "For sharing something about yourself. I can see that was hard for you, and I want you to know it means a lot to me that you did it anyway."

"Oh."

"Baby steps, I guess." Claudia laughed and shook her head. "We're here, by the way. Let's walk the bikes over by the water." She pointed to a pond a short distance away, on the other side of a grassy knoll.

They worked together setting out the tablecloth they'd purchased along with the spread of cheese, crackers, and fruit.

"It's pretty here," Jessie said, as they watched ducks floating on the pond.

"I thought you might like it." Claudia scooted herself closer and offered Jessie a bite of her apple.

Jessie searched her mind for something to say. Truth be told, she was just content to sit silently and have Claudia to herself. "So, have you been here many times?"

"My family used to vacation in Palm Springs, so I've ridden by here on my bike a bunch of times."

"Oh."

"Where did you go on vacation when you were growing up?"

"Um," Jessie felt the color creep up her neck, "my dad never took a vacation."

"You never went anywhere?"

Jessie heard the note of incredulity in Claudia's voice and shifted uncomfortably. "Not until I started flying. Then I would fly to New Hampshire or Vermont or Maine. One time I flew to Cape Cod."

Claudia ran her fingers over the back of Jessie's hand, sending shivers up Jessie's spine. Jessie looked around furtively.

"There's no one here but us, silly."

"How can you be sure?"

"Why do you think I picked this spot?" Claudia batted her eyelashes suggestively, then leaned forward and kissed Jessie long and slow.

Although she was uncomfortable with being so openly affectionate, Jessie couldn't keep her body from responding. After a while, she stopped trying to keep track of their surroundings and simply lost herself in the sensation of Claudia's soft lips on hers.

"Gosh," Claudia exclaimed when they finally took a breather, "I could kiss you forever and ever and never get tired of it."

"Have you—" Jessie paused to allow her pulse to slow. "Have you kissed many women?"

"Would you be terribly jealous if I said yes?"

Jessie considered. "Yes."

"You're so refreshingly honest. No, silly. You're my second."

"Who was the first?"

"Sandra Kenniston. We were fifteen and she was my best friend. We were doing homework upstairs in my bedroom. One thing led to another, and we just sort of leaned into each other and did it."

"Did you love her?"

Claudia laughed. "In a fifteen-year-old adolescent kind of way, I suppose. When she started going steady with Andrew Burson, I was a little bit crushed."

"Ouch."

"Well, it could've been worse. At least he was cute."

"Did you ever like boys?"

"I had a boyfriend in high school, if that's what you're asking. But it was mostly for show. I've always been more attracted to girls."

"You're so matter-of-fact about it."

"Why wouldn't I be? As far as I'm concerned, there's nothing wrong with it."

They fell quiet for a bit, and contented themselves with nibbling and watching the ducks.

"Does it bother you, Jess? I mean, I know you said you'd never kissed anyone before. Do you...well, do you fancy girls or boys?"

Jessie frowned as she tried to collect her thoughts. "It's true that I've got no experience to fall back on, but I've never wanted to kiss a boy. Never even been tempted."

"And girls?"

Jessie scratched her head. "I'd be lying if I said I'd never thought about it." She felt the blush stain her cheeks.

"You're so cute when you blush." Claudia kissed her temple. "I, for one, am glad you've thought about it."

"You are?"

Claudia trailed her fingers down Jessie's arm. "If you'd never thought about it, you probably would've slugged me the first time I made a move on you."

Jessie laughed. "Trust me, slugging you was the last thing I thought of doing. I'd been watching you since the very first time we stepped on the tarmac."

"Yeah?"

"Oh, yeah. You were irresistible in that flight suit. It was ten sizes too big for you, and there you were, gamely struggling not to drown in it."

"It's not my fault they only gave us men's clothes."

"Nope."

"And it's not my fault that I'm short, although I prefer to think of myself as petite."

"You're perfect," Jessie blurted.

Claudia perked up. "Yeah?"

"Absolutely."

"I'm glad you think so." Claudia rewarded her with another thorough kiss. "Jess?"

"Mmm-hmm."

"How come you never talk about your mom?"

Jessie stiffened and pulled back.

"I-I'm sorry. Did I ask something wrong?"

"No." Jessie averted her gaze. Talking about her mother was always painful. "She died when I was six. Boat capsized and I went underwater. She saved me, but…"

Claudia pulled Jessie into a hug. "Oh, honey. I'm so, so sorry. That's horrible."

"I think my dad always blamed me for what happened. It was like he couldn't look at me without being reminded of losing her. If he could've traded my life for hers, I know he would've."

"Jess! Surely that's not true. He loves you."

Jessie shook her head and swiped at a tear as it made its way down her face. "No. He loved her. He tolerated me." Misery flowed through her body.

"Well, any father who feels that way doesn't deserve you." After another minute, Claudia asked, "Why do you talk about him in the past tense?"

"He died last year. Heart attack while he was out chopping wood. I was in Vermont when it happened. I'd been ferrying some passengers to Burlington. Came home and found him on the ground."

"That must've been so hard."

"Yeah. He was always so strong. It was a shock, that's for sure."

"So it's just you now?"

"Yep." Jessie cleared her throat. "Enough talk about me. How about that piece of pie?"

CHAPTER THREE

A re you enjoying yourself?" Claudia leaned in close and whispered in Jessie's ear. On the screen, Humphrey Bogart was pacing in his office at Rick's Café.

Jessie felt the warmth of Claudia's breath on the side of her neck and the softness of her skin where their hands were surreptitiously joined between the seats. "Mmm-hmm."

"Good. I think you're much dreamier than Ingrid Bergman."

"You're crazy."

"You prefer her to me?" Claudia asked.

"Shh." Jessie tore her eyes away from the screen. "Of course not. But no one would ever choose me over Ingrid."

"Well," Claudia said huffily, "I would."

Jessie shook her head, even as her heart fluttered happily, and returned her attention to the movie. When it was over, everyone in the theater stood and clapped. Looking around, Jessie realized for the first time that the audience was comprised almost exclusively of boys from the base and their girls. She and Claudia were virtually the only two unaccompanied women in the place.

"What do you want to do now?" Claudia asked as they emerged on the street.

"How about some ice cream?"

"Mmm. We could share a sundae. Hey," Claudia said, looping her arm through Jessie's, "that's the first time you've ever picked something for us to do. I like it." She smiled, and Jessie knew she was grinning like a fool in return.

The ice cream parlor was packed with couples from the movie. Jessie and Claudia found a small booth in the corner and sat across from each other.

"What kind of ice cream do you like?" Claudia asked.

"Anything with chocolate."

"Okay. How about a hot fudge sundae with chocolate ice cream and extra whipped cream?"

"Deal."

Claudia gave the order to the harried waitress. Jessie jumped when something brushed against her pant leg.

"What's the matter?" Claudia asked, batting her eyelashes. "Nervous?"

The contact against her leg became more solid, and Jessie realized with a start that it was Claudia's foot rubbing against her, and that it was quite intentional. She swallowed hard. "What if someone sees us?" she asked, as her eyes darted furtively around to see if anyone was watching.

"They won't."

"You like to take risks, don't you?"

"Don't you?" Claudia challenged. "Why else do we fly?"

Jessie considered. "You've got a point there, but that's different."

"A risk is a risk. Unless, of course, you'd rather risk your life than risk being caught playing footsie with me."

Jessie didn't answer. In truth, she wasn't sure that she wouldn't rather risk her life. It wasn't that she was ashamed to be out with a girl as beautiful as Claudia—not at all. But the consequences if they got caught weren't something Jessie wished to contemplate. Girls dating other girls…it just wasn't done.

Claudia withdrew her foot and played with her napkin. Quietly, she said, "I'm sorry, Jess. I didn't mean to make you uncomfortable."

"It's not that. It's just…" Jessie wished with all her heart she could erase the disappointment in Claudia's eyes.

"It's okay. I won't do it again."

Jessie's stomach clenched painfully, and she started to apologize.

"Don't worry about it," Claudia said breezily. "It's no big deal."

"I don't believe you."

The waitress set the sundae down between them with two spoons. Suddenly, Jessie wasn't very hungry.

Claudia took the first spoonful. "Mmm. Yummy."

Jessie licked her lips as she watched the expression on Claudia's face. She would've given anything to have been the cause of that look.

"Why aren't you eating?"

"I'm not that hungry."

Claudia frowned. "You have to eat your share. C'mon." She reached across the table and briefly brushed her fingers over the back of Jessie's hand under the guise of grabbing Jessie's spoon. "Really. Everything's fine. Cross my heart." And she did with her free hand. "Please?" She scooped some ice cream and held out the spoon to Jessie.

"Okay." There was no way that she could resist a direct plea.

When they'd finished the entire bowl, they walked back to the inn.

Jessie finished brushing her teeth and washing her face. She changed into the pair of men's pajamas that for her were standard fare. She couldn't remember ever being so nervous. Would Claudia still want to be her girl after the incident in the ice cream parlor? If so, what would she expect from Jessie? Would they share one bed or each take her own?

A knock on the bathroom door made her spill the cup of water in her hand.

"Damn it."

"Everything okay? You've been in there an awfully long time. It's getting lonely out here."

Claudia's voice was seductive and compelling. *Guess that answers one question.* "Um, just finishing up. Be out in a sec."

"Good."

"Okay. You can do this." Jessie addressed herself in the mirror. "Maybe she'll just want to sleep."

"Did you say something, sugar?"

Jessie took one last peek in the mirror, squared her shoulders, turned, and opened the door. "Oh."

"You like?" Claudia twirled in place. She was wearing a sheer silk nightie that barely covered the essentials.

Jessie's mouth suddenly was very, very dry. She nodded dumbly. Claudia crooked her finger, beckoning Jessie forward. When she didn't move, Claudia took a step toward her and pulled her by the pajama shirt lapels.

Unbalanced, Jessie stumbled right into Claudia's arms. "That's more like it." Claudia ran her fingernails up and down Jessie's back, sending chills along her spine. "Mmm. Is that a shiver of anticipation, or are you cold?" Claudia pushed up onto the balls of her feet and lightly nipped Jessie's earlobe, then licked the spot. "Either way, I bet I've got a solution."

Jessie couldn't think. All of the blood that should have been powering her brain migrated south. She could feel Claudia's hardened nipples through the flimsy material.

Claudia must have known the effect she was having, because she chuckled low and deep and pushed harder into Jessie before relenting. She sauntered over to one of the beds, and Jessie noted for the first time that it already had been turned down.

Jessie remained immobile as Claudia sat on the edge of the bed, leaning back on one arm and crossing her shapely legs. When Claudia patted the spot next to her with her free hand, Jessie willed herself to move. She sat down but didn't meet Claudia's eyes.

"Is it that you're nervous, or aren't you interested in me? I'll leave you alone, if that's what you want."

"What? Gosh, no." Jessie fiddled with one of her shirt buttons as she tried to compose what she wanted to say. "Remember when I told you I'd never kissed anyone before?"

"Yeah."

"Well, in case you haven't figured it out yet, that also means I haven't—oh, heck. I haven't done anything else, either." Jessie finished in a rush. "There, I said it." She faced Claudia. "Geez, Claude, you're beautiful, and self-assured, and I'm neither of those things. I feel things for you I've never felt before, and I don't have the first idea what to do about it."

Claudia nodded knowingly. "Do you want to do something about it?"

"Uh-huh."

"Okay, then. Let's just start with what we know how to do and see where it goes from there." Claudia traced Jessie's jaw line with her fingertips, then leaned in and captured her lips in a leisurely exploration.

When Jessie felt air on her chest, she realized Claudia must have undone at least two of her shirt buttons. She gasped as warm fingers stroked her skin. Her heart hammered and her pulse jumped in her neck.

"Is this okay?"

"Uh-huh." Jessie gulped as Claudia's fingers moved lower. Heat spread throughout Jessie's body, and she was horrified to feel herself push forward into Claudia's hand. She moaned into Claudia's mouth.

"You like that, sugar?" Claudia asked against her lips.

Jessie's hands moved of their own accord. She caressed Claudia's face, neck, and shoulders. When Claudia guided her hands underneath the nightie, Jessie lost any restraint she might have possessed. Despite her inexperience, it was as if her body knew what to do. And for that, she was eternally grateful.

Jessie was vaguely aware of a breeze on her cheek. *A breeze?* Her eyes popped open. Claudia. She was fast asleep, her head resting on Jessie's shoulder, her face tipped upward, a smile on her beautiful lips. Claudia...her lover. The thought made Jessie giddy and, as a disbelieving laugh bubbled up in her throat, she fought to stay quiet. As gently as she could, she reached over and brushed away a lock of hair that was covering one of Claudia's eyes.

Claudia shifted minutely but didn't wake. Instead, she snuggled closer in Jessie's embrace. Jessie's heart tripped. How was it possible that this sophisticated, intelligent, desirable woman had chosen her?

"What are you thinking about?" Claudia's voice was thick with sleep.

"Nothing."

Claudia pushed up and leaned on her hand. "Liar."

Jessie shushed Claudia with a kiss and guided her back down onto her shoulder.

"You're trying to distract me."

"Is it working?"

"No. So give."

"You need to sleep. It's the middle of the night."

"I'm not going to stop pestering you until you tell me what's going on in there." Claudia tapped Jessie's forehead with a well-manicured fingernail.

Jessie debated with herself briefly before acknowledging that if she didn't answer, Claudia would likely keep them both up the rest of the night. Since they had to fly back to Sweetwater in less than ten hours, they really needed to get some rest.

"I love you," she whispered.

"What?" Claudia shot straight up in the bed, dislodging the covers.

Jessie swallowed hard, then cleared her throat. "I said, I love you, Claude."

Jessie didn't know what she had expected, but seeing tears in Claudia's eyes startled her. "Did I... Geez, Claude, did I say something wrong?"

Instead of answering, Claudia simply shook her head and sniffled.

"But you're crying." Jessie used her fingertip to wipe away moisture from Claudia's cheek. "I knew I shouldn't have said anything. I'm sorry. I'm an idiot." Jessie felt an overwhelming urge to flee. She struggled to disentangle their bodies and was surprised to meet resistance.

"Where do you think you're going?" Claudia's arms and legs wrapped around her like a vise.

"Get out of my way, Claude." Jessie's face flamed with embarrassment and shame. "It's bad enough, don't make it worse for me. I-I can quit the program, and you won't have to see me again."

"What are you talking about?" Claudia released her grip. Jessie could feel her body shake. "Why would you say such a thing?" Claudia poked her hard in the chest. Their faces were inches apart.

Jessie pulled her head back to create a little distance. "You—you cried because I said I love you. It's obvious you don't feel the same way. My mistake, and I won't trouble you again."

Claudia took her by the shoulders and shook her. "You *are* an idiot, Jessie Keaton." She cupped Jessie's face in her hands and forced eye contact. "Now you listen to me! I…love…you…too. I was crying tears of joy. You have heard of those, haven't you?"

Jessie nodded dumbly.

"You're not going anywhere without me. You're stuck. Period. I love you, and that's all there is to it."

Jessie knew she should say something, but her mind was still busy processing what Claudia was saying. She blinked a few times. "So, you do love me? You don't want me to leave?"

Claudia rolled her eyes. "That's what I said, isn't it?"

"For real?"

"For real." Claudia leaned forward and stroked Jessie's face as she kissed her.

"Oh," Jessie said when they broke apart. "Oh," she said, in an entirely different tone of voice, when she felt Claudia's hands begin to roam over her body.

"What are we going to do when we get home?"

"Hmm?"

They were in the park where they'd picnicked the day before. Jessie was sitting with her back against a big oak tree. Claudia's head was resting in Jessie's lap, and Jessie was contentedly stroking her hair, noting the varying hues of burnished copper as they glinted in the midday sun.

"When we get back to Sweetwater."

"Fly planes, of course." Claudia stretched and crossed her legs at the ankle. Her eyes remained closed.

"I know that." Jessie snapped off the last "t."

"What are you getting so irritated about?" Claudia half-rose on an elbow to face Jessie.

"I mean, what are we going to do about us?"

"Oh." Claudia scrunched up her face in a look Jessie quickly was coming to recognize as her "thinking" pose. She shrugged. "We'll just have to find time to be alone."

"You say that like it's going to be a simple thing."

"We'll just have to make it that way." Claudia captured Jessie's hand and kissed her palm.

"But— How am I supposed to act like nothing's changed?" Jessie was having a hard time not jumping up to pace, which was what she normally would have done when faced with a problem that was vexing her.

"Are you worried about what the girls will think?"

"Aren't you? We could get kicked out of the WASPs for having an inappropriate relationship. Then where would we be?"

Claudia sat all the way up and faced Jessie fully. "We're not going to let that happen. We'll just have to be careful, that's all."

"I don't think you're understanding the full import here, Claude. I can't just treat you like you're any of the other girls. I'm sure they'll see my love for you written all over my face, just like your feelings are written all over yours right now."

"Why?" Claudia licked her lips seductively. "Just because I want to kiss you?" She tipped forward and did just that, until Jessie pushed her back.

"I'm serious. It won't take Shirley or Annabelle thirty seconds to put two and two together and get four. You know how they gossip about everybody. They're like hawks, those two."

"Janie and Rebecca aren't much better."

"Exactly. So, what are we going to do about us?"

Claudia leaned into Jessie. "What do you want to do about us, Jess?"

"I keep going over it in my mind, but I can't come up with any good answers. All I know is I'm not willing to go back to the way things were." Jessie cupped Claudia's face in her hands and caressed her cheeks, marveling yet again at the softness of her skin. "I can't lose you."

"You won't. I promise. I love you, Jess."

"I love you too. You're right—we'll find a way to make it work."

❧❧

It was 1450 hours, and Jessie and Claudia were back at the Palm Springs Air Base. They were running through the final visual inspection on the Valiant. Jessie would fly the first leg to their refueling stop in Alamogordo, New Mexico. Then Claudia would take over, just as they had done on the way out.

"Everything looks to be okay."

"Except for them." Claudia subtly jerked her head in the direction of the handful of flyboys and mechanics lurking just inside the hangar.

"What about them?"

"I can't put my finger on it. They just look like my little brother used to look when he'd been up to mischief."

"I wouldn't know anything about that. But I can't see that anything's amiss here."

"Yeah, I guess."

"But you still don't like it." Claudia looked uneasy, something Jessie had never seen before.

"Not a bit."

"What do you want to do about it?"

"Nothing we can do. Just make sure your parachute is in good order."

Jessie nodded grimly. They'd both heard stories of WASP planes intentionally being sabotaged. "Off we go, then." She helped Claudia into the rear cockpit and climbed into the front. She ran through the instrument checks. Everything seemed fine. She turned and gave Claudia the thumbs up.

Claudia returned the gesture and mouthed a silent "I love you."

Jessie nodded back at her.

A few minutes later, they had the all-clear. Jessie accelerated down the runway and pulled back on the control stick. The Valiant lifted off effortlessly, and Jessie took her into a gradual ascent. Their eventual cruising altitude would be 12,000 feet.

"Beautiful day for a sightseeing cruise." Claudia's voice crackled over the airwaves of their internal communications system. "You do know how to fly this bird, right?"

"Who me?" Jessie responded, keying her mic. "Nah. Just making it up as I go along."

"I suspected as much. Never trust a woman who won't wear a dress."

That startled a laugh out of Jessie.

"That's the sound I adore."

The love in Claudia's voice brought a smile to Jessie's lips. She remained deeply concerned about how they would handle their relationship at Sweetwater. Being in such close quarters and not looking at Claudia like she wanted to get her alone every second was going to be a challenge. As Claudia herself pointed out, Jessie was no poker player. Her feelings were always written all over her face. But up here, all alone so high above the earth, it was hard to care about such things.

The sky was a brilliant blue, the clouds puffy and sporadic. It was, indeed, a perfect day to fly.

"Leveling her off now." Jessie said, more out of habit than anything else. It's what she would have told her instructor had he been in the plane with her.

"Roger. We'll be home in time for the sunset if the refuel doesn't take too long."

"Not sure I'm all that happy about that."

"About what, watching a glorious sunset together on our descent?"

"No, about sharing you once we arrive back in Sweetwater." Jessie frowned. From the time she'd become aware of Jackie Cochran's program, she'd set her sights on getting accepted. Flying planes was her greatest love—until now. Would she put Claudia before flying? She didn't know, and that frightened her more than words could say. Nothing and no one had ever mattered to her as much as being in the air.

"I know what you mean. Wish we could've stolen a few more days alone—" Claudia stopped talking mid-sentence when the engine coughed, sputtered, and quit.

"Jess?"

Claudia's voice held all the alarm that Jessie felt as everything suddenly went deathly quiet around them.

Jessie watched the instrument panel, cursing when the indicator predictably showed the oil pressure rapidly dropping.

"Hang on. I'm going to put us into a shallow dive and try to get her back." Jessie pushed down on the stick and attempted to restart the single engine. Nothing happened.

"Switch to the other fuel tank."

"Roger." Jessie flipped the toggle to switch from the left fuel tank to the one on the right wing. "That one's no good, either."

"Dandy. I knew those idiots were up to something. Bet you a million dollars they put water in the fuel lines."

"Bastards."

"Never mind that. How are you at flying gliders?"

Jessie appreciated Claudia's obvious calm, despite the dire nature of the situation. "Haven't done it in a while, but there was this one time…"

"Now you want to get all loquacious on me?"

"All what?"

"Talkative. Now you want to get talkative?"

"Sorry. Thought it might lighten the mood." Jessie noted the falling RPMs, and the fact that they were still at 11,500 feet. If everything went right, they would have a maximum of thirty minutes to land the plane. "Check the map, will you, Claude? Find a place for us to put down."

"You know map-reading isn't my strongest suit, right?"

"Now you tell me." Jessie turned her head from side to side to lessen the tension in her neck. There was nothing for it now, except to bring the Valiant down safely. If anything happened to Claudia while she was flying the plane, Jessie would never forgive herself. "Okay, risk-taker. You said you like adventure. Hang on, this ought to be one for the books."

CHAPTER FOUR

J essie worked desperately to keep control of the powerless plane. She feathered the prop, putting just the leading edge of the blade into the wind, and began a gradual, controlled descent.

She and Claudia jointly determined that the safest place to put the Valiant on the ground was the Kingman Army Air Base in Arizona, some two hundred miles to the east.

After radioing their distress call and getting the go-ahead to land, Claudia fell silent, and Jessie was grateful. She didn't need to be reminded of the many perils they faced on the way down, or that their calculations could be thrown off by shifting winds or any number of other factors.

Sweat dripped into her eyes, and she used her sleeve to wipe the moisture away. She had, indeed, flown gliders before, but never for this distance or under these circumstances. And never with someone else's life at stake—never mind that she was in love with that someone else.

"Land ho, darling." Claudia's voice crackled over the radio. Twenty minutes had passed.

"And here I thought we'd been over land all this time."

"True, but in this instance I do believe this spit of land is Kingman, Arizona."

Jessie looked off to the left side of the aircraft, and spotted a runway in the near distance. "Roger." She keyed the radio and requested clearance from the tower to land.

"Bravo-four-zero-niner, all clear for your bird. All other traffic has been diverted. Nothing in your way now," a male voice informed her. "Happy landings."

"Roger," Jessie replied. "Here we go," she said to Claudia. "In case—"

"In case, nothing," Claudia cut her off. "We'll tell each other over a pop after we're on the ground."

Jessie smiled thinly at Claudia's forced bravado. She reviewed in her head procedures and possibilities. *Lower the flaps until they're lined up with the runway, reduce speed, land normally.* It sounded so simple in theory. Jessie took in a deep breath through her nose and let it out through her mouth. She did the same thing two more times for good measure. "I love you, Claude," she whispered, as she maneuvered the crippled plane over the runway. She could see a pair of fire trucks moving into position nearby. The sight did nothing to steady her nerves.

She wasn't one for praying, but she made an exception in this instance. *God, I just found love, please don't take it away now. But, if I can't save myself, at least let me save Claudia. Let her have a full and happy life.* "Brace for impact, Claude." Jessie pushed the words out through the tightness in her chest and throat. There were so many more things she wanted to say. Would she ever get the chance again? Brief memories from the night before flitted through her mind. Claudia's head thrown back in rapture. Claudia calling her name in passion. Claudia—

"Looking good, bravo-four-zero-niner." The disembodied voice in the tower interrupted Jessie's train of thought.

"Roger. One dead stick landing coming up." Jessie put both hands on the control stick and pulled back until the Valiant leveled off. The front wheels bounced once hard off the ground, shoving Jessie forward into the control panel. She fought to keep the stick steady as it vibrated wildly in her hands. It seemed the plane might flip over as the front wheels pounded the ground again. A second later, the back wheel hit and the plane skidded sideways. Jessie stubbornly held onto the stick, steering as best she could.

Seconds seemed like hours as dust flew everywhere. Jessie momentarily was blinded. Her head hit something, hard. She blinked but refused to let go of the controls. When the plane came to rest off the side of the runway, miraculously still right-side-up,

Jessie slumped back into her seat. She was dimly aware of the sound of wailing sirens coming closer, then of hands grabbing at her safety harness. Then her world went black.

◈◈

The first thing Jessie was aware of was a blinding light. She blinked quickly, and closed her eyes again. "Claude?" she mumbled. "Claude!" Jessie shouted. Her eyes flew open as her mind clicked into gear, and she remembered what had happened.

"Shh. I'm here, darling."

Claudia's hand pressed into hers, warm and soft, and Jessie immediately subsided. She tried to turn her head in Claudia's direction, but a white-hot lance of pain behind her right eye forced her to abort the motion.

"Stay still, Jess. The doctor says you suffered a bad concussion, and you shouldn't move around just yet."

"Where am I?"

"Kingman Army Air Base Hospital."

"Are you okay?"

"I'm fine."

Jessie detected a note of…something…in Claudia's voice. "I don't believe you. Come here where I can see you."

"Really, I'm okay."

Claudia's face came into focus as she moved into Jessie's line of sight, and Jessie gasped. "Oh my God. Oh my God, Claude." She reached out with gentle fingers and traced the contours of a bandage that covered part of Claudia's left eyebrow. "You're hurt."

"It looks worse than it is."

Jessie swallowed back tears. The sight of Claudia injured was almost more than she could take. "You've got a gash over your eye and a shiner."

Claudia squeezed Jessie's hand harder. She looked back over her shoulder, then leaned over and quickly brushed her lips against Jessie's. "I'm alive, and I'm here with the woman I love. A woman who just happens to be a hero."

"I'm—" Jessie started to protest.

"You brought that bird down safely and kept it from doing a cartwheel on the runway. Not many pilots could've done what you did. You saved our lives."

Jessie opened her mouth to speak again, but Claudia silenced her with two fingers on her lips.

"The cut will heal, and the shiner will give me a good story to tell. It's nothing compared to what could've happened."

Jessie was surprised to see tears swimming in Claudia's eyes. She pushed up in the bed until she was sitting, ignoring the pain in her head. All she wanted to do was take her lover into her arms and hold her. She opened her arms in invitation.

"Ah, I see you're awake."

Jessie froze in mid-motion as a nurse bustled into the room. Jessie felt her cheeks flame red. She leaned back against the pillows to create distance from Claudia, who had yet to move.

"She just woke up. I was adjusting her pillows to make her more comfortable."

If Claudia was flustered, Jessie sure couldn't detect it. Apparently, neither could the nurse, who seemed to accept the explanation without question.

"Are you in pain?"

"My head only hurts when I'm awake," Jessie muttered.

"Okay. Well, I'll go see about getting you something for your headache. Be back in a jiff."

When the nurse was gone, Claudia reached over and kissed Jessie softly on the mouth. "You have got to learn not to blush, sugar. You look guilty even when there's no reason to be."

"I was about to put my arms around you. What if we'd gotten caught?"

"I would've talked our way out of it." Claudia waved a hand dismissively. "You were overcome—distraught over the accident. I needed to console you."

"You treat everything so cavalierly."

"Not everything," Claudia said.

Jessie noted that her eyes were wet again. "What's the matter?"

"When you were out cold, I couldn't stop thinking how I would feel if I lost you. It would've been unbearable." Claudia ran her fingertips over the back of Jessie's hand.

"As you said, it didn't happen. I'm going to be fine—you said so yourself."

"So I did." Claudia sniffled once, dabbed at her eyes, and straightened her shoulders. "Right. So let's see about getting you out of here."

⊰ॐ⊱

As it turned out, it was two days before the doctor released Jessie from the hospital. Claudia already had spoken with Jackie Cochran, who was spitting nails about the obvious sabotage and the danger to "her girls." Jessie and Claudia weren't under any pressure to get back before they were physically ready.

And then there was the issue of the plane, itself. After what had happened in Palm Springs, neither Jessie nor Claudia was willing to trust anyone to work on repairing the plane without supervision. So while the mechanics drained the fuel tanks, cleaned out the fuel lines, and changed the fuel pump and carburetor, Jessie and Claudia stood a silent vigil.

"Are you feeling all right?"

"Mmm-hmm." Jessie pushed the sunglasses up higher on the bridge of her nose. Even in the shade of the open hangar, her head throbbed. Still, that was less disconcerting than the dizziness and the blurriness at the edges of her vision. She didn't dare say anything, because she didn't want to worry Claudia, who was already hovering protectively.

Claudia was fixing her with that pinpoint-laser gaze, and Jessie made a conscious effort not to squirm.

"Remember when I said I wanted to play poker with you?"

"What does that have to do with anything?"

"You're a terrible liar, that's what." Claudia bumped Jessie gently with her hip. "You need to go lie down."

"No." Jessie didn't budge when Claudia tugged on her arm.

"Jessie Keaton. Don't be stubborn. You're clearly hurting and you need rest."

Jessie spread her feet a little wider to stabilize herself. She stared meaningfully at the group of flyboys who had been eyeballing Claudia for the last forty-five minutes. Then she shifted her gaze to her lover. "There is no way on God's green earth that I'm leaving you alone with that bunch."

Claudia huffed out a breath and put her hands on her hips. "Surely you know that I can take care of myself."

"I'm sure you can. But I'm not chancing it."

Claudia held her indignant pose. "I don't know whether to be insulted or grateful."

"Um, let's stick with grateful? Besides, I think they're almost done." Jessie gave a barely perceptible nod toward the young mechanic headed in their direction.

"Ma'ams. She's all set to be checked out." He ducked his head and fiddled with the cap in his hands. "I'm real sorry for what happened to y'all. That was a bad business. I give you my word, I'll personally guard her," he gestured at the Valiant, "until you're ready to go."

Claudia gave him her most brilliant smile, the one that melted Jessie's heart every time. "Well, aren't you sweet?"

For a terrified heartbeat, Jessie thought Claudia would kiss him on the cheek.

"How about I take her for a checkout ride, and then we'll take you up on your offer."

"Claude—" Jessie started to protest.

"You aren't in any shape to take her out, and we need to be sure she's air-worthy."

"I don't like you going up there alone."

Claudia raised her eyebrows. "I'm sure one of those nice flyboys over there would go up with me if I asked." She blinked disingenuously.

Jessie was sure the mechanic heard her growl. "You can go by yourself, but don't showboat up there. Check the instruments, check the handling, and get back down here."

"As if I need your permission." Claudia laughed and patted her on the cheek. "Be back in a jiff."

Jessie watched as Claudia jogged off to don her gear, wishing that she were going with her.

Ten minutes later, Jessie was shielding her eyes and watching as the Valiant climbed. When Claudia took her into a slow roll and stalled the engines, Jessie clenched her fists at her sides. She'd never felt more ineffectual. Although it seemed like hours, it was really a matter of seconds when Claudia restarted the engines as she completed the maneuver. Several minutes after that, she landed the plane and taxied back to the hangar. Jessie stood at the wing to greet her.

"Fancy meeting you here." Claudia hopped down off the wing as Jessie took her hand to steady her.

"Speaking of fancy, what the hell was that?"

"What?"

"You know what."

"The roll? I had to do that. You know we needed to know if the engines would re-engage."

"And you needed to flip over to see that." Jessie's nostrils flared. "That was irresponsible."

"Pfft." Claudia waved her hand dismissively, which only added to Jessie's anger.

Claudia must have realized her mistake, because she stopped short and turned to face Jessie fully. "I wanted to know that we could trust her. Are you angry because of what I did, or because you felt helpless down here?"

Jessie opened her mouth to respond, then closed it again. Claudia was right. Standing on the ground, knowing there was a possibility that the plane wouldn't respond and Claudia would be in peril, was horrifying. Jessie was shocked to feel a single tear track down her cheek.

"Aw, sugar. It's okay." Claudia wiped the moisture away with her fingertip and drew Jessie into a hug. "Everything's going to be okay."

Jessie stiffened in Claudia's embrace. Cognizant that there were many eyes on them, she disentangled herself. "Let's get going."

"In a sec." Claudia moved over to where the mechanic was standing in the shadows, said something to him, laughed, then returned to Jessie. She looped her arm through Jessie's in a now-familiar gesture as they walked away.

Jessie flinched, but did not pull away. She didn't have the energy.

⤳⤳

Jessie and Claudia's footfalls echoed off the barren walls in the empty barracks where they'd been assigned to stay for the night. The building was on the other side of the base from the male pilots and mechanics.

Claudia spun in place. "It isn't the Ritz, but at least we'll have our privacy."

"Mmm." Jessie leaned over and tested the bed with her hand. It was as unforgiving as the beds at Avenger Field. "It'll do, I guess. Nothing we're not used to."

Claudia grabbed one corner of the bed closest to the bathroom and dragged it toward the bed next to it.

"What're you doing?"

"What does it look like I'm doing? I'm pushing two beds together."

Jessie looked back at the door.

"There's nobody here but us. Relax." Claudia came over, wrapped her arms around Jessie's waist, leaned up on her tiptoes, and kissed her briefly on the mouth. "Gosh, I've been dying to do that for days."

Jessie jumped back as if she'd been bitten by a snake. As wonderful as it was to be close to Claudia, she couldn't shake the feeling that someone could come walking through the door.

"Good Lord, Jess. It's our last night alone together, and this is how you want to spend it? Avoiding me like I'm the plague?" Claudia plopped down unceremoniously on the bed she hadn't quite finished moving. She hid her face behind her hands and began to sob.

Jessie stood motionless for several heartbeats, but the sight of Claudia's misery trumped whatever misgivings she had about being discovered in a compromising position.

"Hey." Jessie sat down and put her arm around Claudia's shaking shoulders. "Hey, now. None of that." She pried one of Claudia's hands away from her face and captured a tear on her fingertip. With a little goading, she managed to get Claudia to drop her other hand, as well, and pulled her fully into an embrace.

They silently rocked together, until Claudia's sobs became sniffles and then an occasional hiccup. She straightened up and patted Jessie's shirt where her face had been resting. "Sorry about that. I got you all wet."

"S'okay. It'll dry. I'm the one who's sorry. You wouldn't be crying if I hadn't hurt your feelings."

Claudia slowly shook her head. "It wasn't just that." She played with a button on Jessie's shirt. "It's like I said in the hospital room—when..." She stopped to clear her throat. Her haunted gaze came to rest on Jessie's eyes.

"What is it, Claude?"

"When you were lying there, so still and pale, I-I didn't know if I'd ever get a chance to make love to you again. What if I couldn't tell you I loved you? What if you couldn't hear me? I cut you off when you tried to tell me before we crashed. I thought we'd always have time later. What if I'd been wrong?"

Claudia began to sob anew. Jessie pulled her against her chest and kissed the top of her head. "Shh. But you weren't wrong."

"I c-could have b-been. I nearly was."

"As I said before, we can't worry about things that didn't happen. I'm here, you're here, and we're both fine."

"You're...not...f-fine," she managed between sniffles.

"Sure I am, honey."

"N-no, you're n-not. I can tell your head still hurts, you're not all that steady on your feet, and you were squeamish about me doing a routine slow roll."

"I'm feeling much better now that we're inside and sitting, and my symptoms are just temporary. I'll be good as new in no time flat." Jessie intentionally ignored the comment about flying, since she still hadn't processed what happened on the tarmac as she watched Claudia intentionally stall the engine. She knew her evasion wouldn't fool Claudia for long, but for right now, she just wanted to restore Claudia's good humor. "C'mon, let's finish getting these beds moved."

"Not if you're going to be jumping like a cat at every sound."

"I've got a solution for that." She stood and pulled Claudia up with her. "Help me out." Jessie led them across the room and over to the bed closest to the only exterior door. She grabbed one end of the bed.

"What're you up to?"

"Take hold of the other end, will you?"

Claudia's mouth fell open. "You want to barricade the door?"

Jessie, who was already lifting her end of the bed, said, "Yeah. You want to get cozy and not have me be jumpy. The only way that's going to work is if I know no one can get in."

"But isn't that a fire hazard?"

"You, who are always so willing to take a risk—you're going to worry about something as unlikely as a fire? Are you planning to smoke in here?"

"No."

"Light any matches?"

"No."

"Then pick up your end and help me move this thing."

Claudia grumbled something Jessie couldn't quite make out, but she did hear the words, *pig-headed, unreasonable,* and *ridiculous.*

After the bed was in place, Jessie added two empty foot lockers on top of the mattress for good measure.

"Are you satisfied, yet, Miss Paranoid?"

Jessie pulled on the door knob. The door only moved a fraction of an inch. She closed it again. "Yep."

"Are you going to wake up in time for morning muster to undo all of this?"

"Yep."

"Even if I keep you up all night?" Claudia's voice took on a sultry tone as she snuck her hand underneath the collar of Jessie's uniform shirt.

Jessie glanced one more time at the door before giving in. "Be gentle with me. As you said, I'm not in tip top shape at the moment."

"I promise to go easy on you."

Jessie thought that the sound of Claudia's laughter might just be all the medicine she needed.

CHAPTER FIVE

I can't get her restarted. Brace for—" Jessie awoke in mid-sentence and shot straight up in bed, dislodging Claudia and the covers. She was drenched in sweat. Her heart and head were pounding in a quick, staccato rhythm. She looked around wild-eyed, half expecting to find herself mid-flight and in a nosedive.

Claudia, having been tossed aside, scrambled to her knees on the bed and put her hand against Jessie's heaving chest. "Shh. Hey, sugar. What's going on?"

"I-I couldn't get us out in time. We were going down and there was nothing I could do about it." Jessie wiped angrily at the tears now falling freely from her eyes. She didn't want Claudia to see her like this. When Claudia tried to wrap her arms around her, Jessie twisted away. She threw her legs over the side of the bed. "I'm going to get a glass of water."

"O-okay."

Jessie could hear the uncertainty in Claudia's voice, but she kept walking. Once she was in the bathroom, she shut the door behind her, leaned her back against it, and slid to the floor. The images from the nightmare still were vivid in her mind—the sound of the engine choking and dying, the whine of the wind as the plane picked up speed in a free fall.

Jessie clasped her shaking hands together. How could she possibly fly again? There was no place for fear in the cockpit—only certainty and the ability to stay calm under pressure. What if she couldn't do that anymore? What if—

"Hey. You okay in there?" The door standing between them muffled Claudia's voice.

"Fine."

"Can I come in?"

"No. I'll be out in a minute." The words came out harshly, and Jessie knew that Claudia deserved better. But she felt so lost and out of her depth, and she had no idea what to do about it. Flying was her life. Up until she met Claudia, it was the only thing that mattered to her. Now, without flying, not only would she lose the one thing she was good at, but she likely would lose Claudia too.

Jessie pushed herself up until she was standing and looked at her face in the mirror. Claudia was right—she should never play poker. Fear and anxiety were writ large in her eyes. She turned on the faucet and splashed cold water on her face.

She opened the door expecting to find Claudia standing just outside. Instead, Claudia was visible only as a lump in the bed, facing the other way. Jessie felt miserable. She slid carefully under the covers. "Claude?" She brushed her fingers over the smooth skin of Claudia's exposed shoulder. Claudia didn't answer. "Claude?" Jessie tried one more time. When she received no reply, Jessie whispered, "I love you, Claude. I'm sorry."

She was relatively certain that Claudia wasn't asleep, and she hoped that in the light of day, Claudia would forgive her for being so rude.

∽෧෨

"We'd better get going."

Jessie stared bleary-eyed at Claudia, who was partially dressed and shifting from foot to foot at the side of the bed. "Surely it's not time for muster yet."

"No. But we have to move everything back to its place. That's going to take time."

Jessie couldn't stand to hear the coolness that was so foreign to the Claudia she knew. "Claude," Jessie sat up in the bed, "I'm sorry about last night."

"Don't worry about it." Claudia bustled to the other end of the room and lifted one of the footlockers off the mattress blocking the door.

Jessie got up, threw on her uniform shirt without buttoning it, and followed. "Wait."

Claudia grabbed for the second footlocker, her back still to Jessie.

"Wait a cotton-picking second." Jessie reached around and stilled Claudia's hands. She pulled Claudia against her chest. The scent of their lovemaking permeated the air. That had been before the nightmare, before Jessie's panic. She swallowed hard. "I lost it, and I didn't want you to know. I was afraid you would see it in my eyes."

Claudia turned slowly to face Jessie. "Of course I would see it in your eyes. What of it?"

"I didn't want you to think less of me." Jessie looked at a point over Claudia's shoulder.

"What makes you think I would think less of you? Because you had a nightmare that frightened you?" Before Jessie could answer, Claudia pushed on. "Because you're not infallible? Because you crash-landed a plane three days ago and it's haunting you?"

"Well, yeah."

"News flash, sugar, I know all those things and I love you anyway."

"You do?"

"I do. But if you insist on shoving me away and shutting down every time something emotional or uncomfortable comes up, this is never going to work out."

"I'm sorry, Claude. I've never done this relationship thing before. I'm no good at it."

"How can you know if you're any good at it if you've never done it before? And what makes you think I've got so much practice?"

"You're more worldly than me. You've dated before."

"Not like this." Claudia indicated the two of them. "Never like this."

Claudia's voice was thick with emotion, and it cut right through Jessie's armor.

"I've never given myself to anyone before you, Jess. Never. I never wanted to. Now I'm desperately in love with you, and I'm afraid you'll cut and run at the slightest hint of trouble."

"I won't leave you, Claude. I won't." Jessie cradled Claudia's head against her bare chest. "But what if I can't get over this? What if I can't fly? What if I'm too afraid?" There, she'd given voice to her worst fears.

"You *will* get over this. We'll make sure of it. We'll go up and practice until you're back to your normal self. You're one of the best pilots I've ever seen up there, Jess. When that engine quit and there was nothing around us but air, I was relieved."

"Relieved?"

"Yes, relieved that you were the one at the controls. I wouldn't have trusted anybody else to get us out of that jam. Probably not even myself. I knew you would get us down safely, and you did. And you'd do it again given the same circumstances."

"You don't know that."

"I know it in my heart."

"Your heart is biased."

"Maybe. But my heart is also right. There won't be a next time, but if there is, I want to know you're in the cockpit flying that bird. Out of all the pilots at Sweetwater, I'd pick you every time."

There was nothing Jessie could say to that, so instead, she lifted Claudia's chin and kissed her. "How did I get so lucky, again?"

"Right place at the right time, I guess."

"We really do have a little more time before daylight, right?"

"Half an hour."

"Then why are we standing here talking?" Jessie steered Claudia back to their bed. They had time to make love one last time before the rest of the world would intrude again.

"Follow my finger," the doctor instructed Jessie. "Okay. Eyes straight ahead. I'm going to hold up fingers in your peripheral vision. I want you to tell me how many you see."

"Two."

"Now?"

"Three. No. Four."

"Which is it, three or four?"

Jessie bit her lip. Her vision remained blurry around the fringes. "Four."

"Weren't too sure about that, were you?"

"I'm fine, sir."

The doctor pulled out a flashlight and shone it first in Jessie's right eye, and then her left. "Mmm-hmm. Okay." He clicked off the light and stepped back.

"Okay, what?"

"Okay, I don't mind you sitting in a plane, but you are not fit to fly one just yet."

"What?"

"If you want to get out of here and back to Sweetwater, it'll have to be with a conditional release."

"Meaning?"

"Meaning you can be a passenger but not a pilot until you get clearance from a doctor when you get back to Texas."

"But—"

"There are no 'buts' here. I'm not clearing you to fly that plane, and that's final. I understand you have a co-pilot who is equally qualified, is she not?"

"Of course she is, but—"

"What did I just say?"

"No 'buts,' sir."

"Exactly."

The doctor wrote something on a slip of paper and handed it to his nurse. "Good luck to you, Miss Keaton."

"Thanks," Jessie mumbled on her way out the door.

"What did he say?" Claudia asked, when Jessie came outside.

"He said I can go home, but only if you take me."

"What does that mean?"

"I'm not cleared to pilot the plane."

"Don't worry, sugar." Claudia looped her arm through Jessie's. "I promise to take good care of you."

"Now I'm really worried."

"Hey!"

They took off at 0800 hours, Claudia at the controls in front, and Jessie relegated miserably to the back cockpit. When they were less than one hundred miles from Avenger Field, Claudia keyed her microphone. "Hey, you awake back there?"

"Of course I'm awake. You don't think I'd trust you to fly this rust bucket without someone keeping an eye on you, do you?"

"Very funny. Now don't get mad at me, but I have an idea."

"How can I get mad at you when I don't know yet what it is?"

"You have a point there."

"Well, are you going to tell me sometime today?"

"Maybe if you're nice to me."

Jessie rolled her eyes, even though she knew Claudia couldn't see her.

"I know the doc said you weren't cleared to fly, but it's just the two of us up here."

"And?"

"And this would be a great time for you to get rid of your jitters."

"No way."

"Hear me out before you answer. No one's watching except for me, so no one will ever know. You're safe with me, and if something happens I'll take over from you."

"Absolutely not."

"C'mon, Jess. This is the perfect opportunity. It's like riding a horse—if you fall off, you have to get right back up on it again."

"First, a plane is not a horse. Second, my vision still isn't right."

"All I want you to do is a slow roll with an engine stall and restart."

Jessie's palms started to sweat. "Is that all? Claude, do you have any idea what could happen if the brass found out that I violated a direct order?"

"How are they going to find out? I'm sure not going to tell."

"Which is great, except if something goes wrong."

"Nothing's going to go wrong."

"You don't know that. And, even if I were willing to risk my own life, I'm not willing to risk yours."

"I'd be as safe as a bear cub with its mama with you in control."

"I won't do it."

When Claudia didn't respond again, Jessie assumed the matter was settled. That lasted about fifteen seconds, until she felt the right wing dip and the air speed slow.

"Don't you dare."

"Pilot to co-pilot. Initiating roll. I'm turning over control to you."

"No!" By now they were more than halfway into the roll. Jessie realized the engine would stall any minute. "Claudia!"

"Save us or don't, Jess. The choice is yours."

Jessie grabbed hold of the controls in front of her. "Of all the bone-headed, asinine things to do..." Moisture dotted her forehead. She blinked hard, but the fuzziness that had plagued her since the accident remained. The engine cut out, and tendrils of fear snaked up Jessie's spine. For what seemed an eternity, she sat motionless.

"You can do this, sugar. I believe in you."

Jessie wondered if Claudia really had said the words, or if she merely imagined them. "Right." Her mind shut out all non-essential thought, and her hands moved of their own accord. Jessie completed the gradual roll, leveled the plane, and restarted the engine.

"Take it, Claude." Jessie hated that her voice shook. She slumped back in her seat and closed her eyes. Her heart had yet to return to its normal rhythm, her shirt was damp with sweat, and her breathing was erratic.

Jessie had no idea how much time had passed when she heard Claudia tell the tower at Avenger Field that they were on approach for the landing. She opened her eyes as the wheels touched down.

They taxied to a halt, and Jessie undid her harness. She swung out of the cockpit and onto the wing, then hopped down onto the tarmac. She could see the women running toward them.

Claudia put her hands on Jessie's shoulders and squeezed. "Aren't you going to help me down?"

Jessie looked up at Claudia, who was standing on the wing. Automatically, she put her hands on Claudia's waist and helped her down.

"You did it, Jess. Told you."

Jessie clenched her fists at her side. "If you ever pull a stunt like that again, you'll be flying alone."

Claudia's face registered shock. She opened her mouth to speak…

"Hey, we heard what happened. Gosh, thank goodness you're okay. Wicked shiner, though, Claudia." Annabelle was at the front of the pack of WASPs who seemed to be descending upon them from all sides. "Tell us all about it."

Jessie fought through the throng, turned on her heel and stalked away.

"What's the matter with her?"

Jessie heard Rebecca's question but didn't catch the response. She could feel Claudia's eyes on her back, but she was too angry to care.

∽≈∾

As she had been since returning from Palm Springs, Jessie rose before the sun. She showered, brushed her teeth, combed her hair, put on her uniform, and left the barracks before any of the other girls, especially Claudia, awoke.

She walked the grounds, listened to the birds sing, and watched the sunrise from a perch atop a grassy knoll she'd discovered two days earlier. She skipped breakfast to avoid any chance of contact with Claudia, and when she lined up at muster, she stared straight ahead, studiously ignoring Claudia's confused glances and pained expression.

Jessie missed Claudia terribly, but she was not ready to forgive her for thrusting her into a position she wasn't prepared for and which, she admitted to herself, scared the pants off her.

"Penny for your thoughts."

Jessie jumped at the sound of Shirley's voice so close to her. She hadn't even heard her approach. "I don't have any."

Shirley held up her hands in mock surrender. "Just trying to start a friendly conversation here. You've been awfully scarce. Me and the girls are worried about you. Claudia won't even touch her food, and you know how Claudia eats."

Jessie looked at Shirley sharply. If she was fishing for information, Jessie couldn't discern it.

"There's nothing to worry about."

"You haven't been cleared to fly, you're up before the birds, you don't come to meals. You're the first into the classroom and the last one out. What about all that behavior should make us stop worrying? None of that is like you. Not one bit of it."

Jessie kept her expression blank. "Maybe I'm turning over a new leaf."

"And maybe pigs fly," Shirley scoffed. "All right. Have it your way. Be all mysterious. But if you're not going to come clean with me, at least you should talk to Claudia. She hasn't been the same since you came back from your adventure."

After Shirley was gone, Jessie walked quickly behind the nearest building and leaned heavily against it. Claudia was hurting. She wasn't eating. She wasn't herself. Jessie kicked at the dirt. She was being a heel. But Claudia had put her in an untenable position and hadn't apologized for it in the least. In fact, she'd seemed rather proud of herself when they landed.

"Mmph." Jessie pushed off the wall. If she didn't hurry, she would be late for ground school. In the afternoon, while the others were off flying, the base doctor would examine her for flight-readiness. If he cleared her, she would have her sixty-hour checkout flight on the PT-17 before the end of the week.

Jessie exited the examination room and ran directly into Claudia.

"Fancy meeting you here." Claudia's body language indicated there was nothing fancy about it. Clearly, she'd been waiting, and, judging from the wrinkles in her uniform trousers, she'd been sitting for a while.

"How'd you know I'd be here?"

"What, no 'hi, it's great to see you'?"

Jessie looked around, noticed two women she didn't recognize sitting in the waiting room, and grabbed Claudia's arm to steer her outside.

"Don't want to be seen with me, Jess?"

"There's no reason to make a scene."

"Seems that might be the only way to get your attention."

Jessie stopped short and pivoted to face Claudia. "What do you want from me?" Even as she finished the sentence, Jessie regretted it. The hurt in Claudia's eyes was palpable.

"Apparently, I want more than you're willing to give. I'm sorry I bothered you. I'll leave you alone from now on." Claudia pulled free and broke into a run.

"Aw, hell." Jessie took off after her. "Claude, wait. Claudia. Claude, wait!" Jessie screamed as she struggled to keep up and fought for breath. Claudia was a lot faster than Jessie would have guessed. She cursed as Claudia disappeared around a corner between two buildings.

Jessie rounded the turn and skidded to a halt. There was Claudia, bent over double, her hands covering her face, her whole body shaking.

"Darn it all, Claude," Jessie wheezed out. She put a tentative hand on Claudia's back and rubbed circles. "Calm down. Shh. It's okay."

"How can you s-say that?" Claudia asked, between sobs. When she looked up, Jessie could see the tracks where her tears continued to fall.

"Please, stop crying. It seems like I'm always making you cry. C'mon, Claude. It's not that bad. Everything's going to be fine." Jessie reached into her pocket for her handkerchief and pushed it into Claudia's hand.

Claudia straightened up and blew her nose. "No, it's n-not." She shuddered. "You don't want anything to do with me. You won't even look me in the eye. You leave before I wake up in the morning, go to sleep before I get out of the bathroom…"

Jessie was about to ask again what Claudia wanted from her but thought better of it. "I was just mad at you, that's all. It's not the end of the world. I'll get over it eventually."

"Yeah? When? After we've graduated and been sent to opposite ends of the country?"

"Of course not."

"What are you so mad about?" Claudia's eyes were red-rimmed and glassy. The sight melted Jessie's heart.

"I didn't like being forced to do something I wasn't ready for. I felt like an incompetent ass, and all you could do was congratulate yourself for being clever."

"What are you talking about? I was so proud of you I could've burst a button. You handled it like a pro."

"I felt like a rookie. My palms were sweating, my heart was racing, and I came close to panicking."

"But you didn't. You righted the bird, leveled her out, and restarted the engine like you could do it in your sleep."

"It was embarrassing."

Claudia's eyes grew wide. "You were embarrassed in front of me? Jess Keaton, you don't ever need to be embarrassed in front of me. I love you."

"You tried to humiliate me."

"I did no such thing!"

"Well, it sure felt like that."

"Good heavens. That's the last thing I wanted to do. I wanted to restore your confidence, that's all."

"Yeah, well that wasn't the way to do it."

"I can see that now, sugar."

They were face-to-face, inches apart, both breathing heavily. In the end, Jessie couldn't say which one of them moved first, but it didn't matter. Once their lips met, everything else ceased to exist.

"We…" Jessie cleared her throat and looked around. There were no windows on either of the two buildings, but she was acutely aware that they were standing outside where someone could come around the corner any second. "We'd better get going." She trailed her fingers down Claudia's gaunt cheek. "I love you, Claude."

"I'm sorry I put you on the spot. I shouldn't have done that."

"You were just trying to be helpful."

"True."

Jessie caught the ghost of a twinkle in Claudia's eye, and she was very glad to have put it there. "We okay?"

"You tell me, sugar." Claudia leaned into Jessie, and Jessie felt herself grow wet with desire.

"We're good. Maybe—" Jessie momentarily lost her train of thought when Claudia's pelvis pushed against the zipper of her slacks. "Um. Maybe we could find someplace to go later?"

"Now you're talking. I'll find us a spot." Claudia patted Jessie's cheek and jogged away.

"Yeah," Jessie said to Claudia's retreating form, "you do that."

CHAPTER SIX

W hat are you two up to? Giggling like schoolgirls with your heads so close together—makes me think y'all are up to no good."

"Nothing. We were just talking." Jessie scooted away from Claudia, aware even as she did so that she was acting like a kid caught with her hand in the cookie jar. She knew her face was flushed and she fanned herself. "Gosh, it's hot in here, isn't it?"

"It's always hot in here," Janie complained.

"Hey, Janie. We were sharing the latest juicy gossip. Didn't want anybody walking by to hear, that's all." To Jessie's eye, Claudia was relaxed and nonchalant.

"Yeah?" Janie sat down on Claudia's other side and leaned in close. "What'd you have? I bet it's something really good."

"You know Iris Stavinski?" Claudia asked, her voice barely above a whisper.

"The nail-biter? Always looks nervous?"

"That's the one. Well, it seems she just got a letter from home. She opened it at lunch and ran out crying hysterically."

"Really? What was in the letter, I wonder."

"No need to wonder. I know what it was."

"Spill." Janie moved in closer still.

"You know she's Jewish, right?"

"Yeah. So?"

"She has family in Poland. The letter said they'd been sent to a place called Auschwitz. Nobody's saying much officially, but the scuttlebutt is that it's some kind of death camp or something."

"Oh, my God! That's horrible."

"I know. Poor girl."

"I can't imagine being her. What's she going to do?"

"I don't know. Rumor is she's thinking about quitting and going home to be with her folks, but it's not a sure thing yet."

Jessie watched the exchange in amazement. She had no idea if the story Claudia was telling was true or not. When Janie walked in, Claudia had been describing exactly what she wanted to do to Jessie later that night, punctuating the description by running her fingers lightly along the inside of Jessie's upper thigh.

"I'm going to go find Shirley. I bet she'll know all the details right down to who licked the stamp on the envelope." Janie took off out the door like a whirling dervish.

Claudia collapsed back on the bed laughing. "Woo, that was something, huh?"

Jessie shook her head. "Was any of that tale true?"

"Every bit of it. Rebecca told me after Annabelle told her while we were waiting to go up this afternoon." Claudia rolled over on her side until she was facing Jessie. She reached out and tugged at Jessie's belt. "Now, where were we? Oh, yes. I believe I was telling you what I had planned for you tonight."

Jessie slapped her hand away. "Do you have any idea how close we just came to being discovered? We can't even be sure Janie didn't see where your hand was."

"Trust me, Janie didn't see anything. My back was in her way."

Jessie got up and paced back and forth in front of the bed. "We've almost gotten caught at least three times in the last three months. I swear I'm getting gray hair from worrying. I hate this."

Claudia got up and came to her. "What do you want to do about it? Stop seeing each other?"

Jessie grabbed Claudia's hands and squeezed. "Never. I love you, Claude."

"And I love you, sugar. We've done all right so far. Another two months, and we'll be through the training. Then we can put in for the same assignment and live off-base together wherever we go, just like a married couple."

Jessie sighed. Claudia was right—if they could make it through the next sixty days without being found out, they'd practically be home free. There had been close calls, but it had been worth it.

She gazed at the woman she loved with all her heart. "I can't wait."

"Me, either." Claudia kissed her briefly on the mouth. "So I'll meet you back here after dinner, right?"

"Wild horses couldn't keep me away."

"That's my girl."

≪≫

"You two are moving like your pants are on fire. Where're you off to in such an all-fired hurry?"

"Hiya, Annabelle." Claudia gave her one of her megawatt smiles as Annabelle caught up to them near the entrance to the base.

Jessie grumbled under her breath. "Here we go again."

"There's a new record I need to pick up in town. I wanted to get there before they're all sold out."

"Yeah? What're you hot for now?"

"Glenn Miller. He's got a new one out called 'That Old Black Magic.' It's dreamy."

"I don't think I've heard that one yet."

"You will as soon as I can get my hands on it." Claudia waved in dismissal as she looped her arm through Jessie's and propelled them forward. "See you later," she called.

"Yeah. See ya."

When they were out of earshot, Claudia said, "Geez. We could've been stuck there for hours. You know how Annabelle likes to talk."

Jessie rolled her eyes. Annabelle, whose penchant for long-windedness and vapid conversation was well-known at Sweetwater, had trapped her on many occasions. "Let's get a move on before anyone else spots us." Jessie began walking faster. It had been a whole ten days since she and Claudia were able to steal away and make love. If she had to wait any longer, Jessie was sure she would combust.

They managed to get off the base and into town without further incident. "Mrs. Dunphy? Are you here?" Claudia called, as she knocked on the door of the little, unassuming house just off the main strip. She peered through the curtain on the front door.

"Who is this lady, again, and how do we have use of her home?"

"I met her when I was getting my hair done last week. We got to talking, she mentioned that she was going to be away this week visiting her sister in Abilene, and I offered to bring in her mail and water her flowers. She's a widow—lives here all by herself. I was just being helpful." Claudia winked.

"If she arranged for you to take care of her house, why are you knocking and asking if she's here?"

"It's polite to ask before barging in, silly."

"Oh." Jessie was quiet before asking a question that had been plaguing her all the way over here. "She doesn't mind us using the guest bedroom?"

"I explained to her that the beds we sleep in aren't beds at all, but pieces of cardboard masquerading as cots. She felt sorry for me and said I could sleep at her house any time, and bring friends with me."

"Convenient." Claudia opened the front door and Jessie followed her inside. "I don't suppose you explained to her that we have a curfew and a bed check and that we have to be back on base on time or we face disciplinary measures."

"Must've slipped my mind."

The house was spotless and filled with family photos. Jessie picked up a framed photograph from the top of the piano in the living room. A handsome young man in an Army Air Forces uniform stared back at her. He portrayed an air of cockiness.

Claudia looked over Jessie's shoulder. "That must be her son. She said he's overseas flying missions."

"Good-looking guy."

"If you like that sort of thing." Claudia's voice held that seductive quality that made Jessie wild.

She pulled Claudia to her and kissed her deeply. "I want you so much. I've missed you."

They stumbled down a hallway, stopping to kiss and touch more along the way. "I think the bedroom is this way," Claudia breathed against Jessie's lips. Together they moved through a doorway.

Jessie backed Claudia over to a bed with a homemade quilt. Without breaking the kiss, she leaned over and pulled back the covers. Deftly, she unbuttoned Claudia's blouse and slacks, lowered the zipper, and slipped her hand inside the waistband. Her now-experienced fingers found the spots she knew would make her lover beg for more.

"Too many clothes." Claudia struggled to free herself from the sleeves of her blouse. Jessie paused to help. She unbuttoned the cuff of one sleeve, brushed the material off Claudia's shoulder, kissed the exposed skin, released her breasts from the constraints of her bra, and bent to taste the sweetness underneath.

For the next two hours, they touched, tasted, marveled, and exulted in each other. Jessie memorized the scents, the flavors, the murmured words, the meaningful sighs, the textures, a plea here, an exclamation there, a fervent prayer answered. For her, each time they were together this way was more special than the last.

"You have to give me time to recover, sugar."

"I'll give you exactly two minutes." Jessie kissed Claudia's collarbone, then the side of her neck as she swept aside her tousled hair. She laughed when Claudia groaned.

"I do believe I've trained you too well."

"Are you saying I'm too much for you?"

Claudia sighed contentedly and rolled over on top of Jessie. "Oh, no, darling. You're just enough."

"How long do we have?"

Claudia lifted her head to glance at a bedside clock. "Mmm. Not enough time, lover. We've got to be back in forty-five minutes. We've got to put this place back in order, and I've still got to bring in the mail and water the flowers."

A thought occurred to Jessie. "How are you going to explain to Annabelle that you didn't get the record?"

Claudia smiled. "But I did get it."

"Claude, I know my powers of observation aren't always the best, but I'm sure you haven't snuck out to a record store since we got here."

"Didn't have to. I bought the record last weekend. I've been keeping it in my footlocker."

"Oh, you sneak."

"A girl's got to do what a girl's got to do."

"Yes, she does," Jessie agreed, her voice muffled as she buried her face between Claudia's breasts.

❦❧

"Another day in paradise," Rebecca remarked, passing first Jessie's bed, and then Claudia's on her way to the bathroom. "I swear, if we get one more dust storm, I'm going to start looking for camels."

"Maybe we can all get out to the lake this weekend," Shirley said, as she sat on the edge of her bed, spit-polishing her shoes.

Claudia, who was busy pinning up her hair, grunted noncommittally. "What's on your schedule this morning, Jess?" Claudia asked.

"After calisthenics and drill, I've got time in the Link trainer."

Claudia scrunched up her nose. "Eww. It's 100 degrees and you're going to be cooped up in a simulator for two hours? Why? You're already the best pilot here."

"It'll only be one hour fifteen minutes, and I'm working on my bad weather instrument flying."

"If I didn't know any better," Janie threw in from across the room, "I'd swear our girl Jessie has a crush on her Link instructor."

"Well, he *is* a good-looking man," Annabelle said. "Anybody would have to be blind not to notice. So, if that's the case, I say good luck to you, Jess."

"Cut it out," Jessie said, her face turning bright red. She chanced a glance at Claudia to make sure she didn't think any of it was true.

"Relationships on base are prohibited, ladies. And we all know our Jessie would never go against regulations." Claudia winked at Jessie.

Rebecca, who was just exiting the bathroom, said, "If I didn't know any better, I'd say it was Claudia Jessie was having a relationship with. The two of you spend every free minute together. I don't know if there's enough space between you for a man."

Jessie's hands began to shake.

"If we were having an affair, at least we wouldn't have to worry about getting pregnant!"

"Claudia Sherwood, how completely, deliciously scandalous," Annabelle said, laughing heartily.

Jessie felt her face flame an even brighter shade of red, and she grabbed a towel and rushed into the bathroom to prevent anyone from seeing. Through the closed door, she heard Janie say, "Don't ever change, Claudia. You are the bee's knees, I swear. You always have the most up-to-the-minute music and magazines, and the most wicked sense of humor. I never know what will come out of your mouth next."

"Me either," Jessie mumbled, as she turned on the water to wash her face.

≼≽

"Go to the canteen with me and split a lemonade?" Claudia asked, coming up alongside Jessie as she walked across the grounds.

"I don't have time right now, Claude. I'm going up in the AT-6 in a couple of hours." Jessie noted Claudia's pout and steeled herself. When Claudia pouted, Jessie almost always gave in. "Besides, you heard what Rebecca said this morning. Maybe we should lay low for a while."

"Rebecca doesn't know what she's talking about. Besides, I took care of that."

"By nearly admitting that it was true? My God, Claude, what were you thinking?"

"The best way to deal with speculation is head-on. If we really were seeing each other, nobody would expect that I'd come right out and admit it. What I said throws off suspicion."

"I'm not sure I agree with your logic. Not only that, but you know I'm no good in those situations. I just about incinerated on the spot."

Claudia laughed. "I know, sugar. Boy, was I glad the bathroom was free. You'd have given away everything."

"It's not funny, Claude. I really could've blown our cover, and then what?"

"Relax. No one's got any proof. Let them gossip."

Jessie stopped walking and faced Claudia. "You don't really mean that. What if we got called in by Cochran?"

"We won't."

"You don't know that."

Claudia sighed heavily. "Why must we always have this conversation?"

"Because we constantly seem to be living on the edge."

"What do you want me to say, Jess? We'll cross that bridge when we come to it. But I don't believe it's as big an issue as you do."

"You don't think it'll be a big deal if we get caught?"

"I don't intend for us to get caught."

"Nobody intends to get caught. It just happens."

"Well, it's not going to happen to us." Claudia brushed past Jessie and stalked off.

"Great. Just great." Jessie kicked at the ground, throwing up a cloud of dust. It would be a relief to get up in the air, where everything was so much simpler.

๛๏

"Jerk. I swear he's going to get someone killed." Janie ripped off her goggles and hat on her way into the flight prep area.

"What's going on?" Jessie asked, as she geared up for her second flight of the day.

"Achison."

"Mmm. Say no more," Jessie sympathized. Of course, she knew Janie wouldn't let it lie there. Gerald Achison was the most reviled instructor at Sweetwater. Almost every girl in the program had a Gerald Achison story. Every morning when the girls checked the flight schedule for the day, they all prayed together that Achison's name would be missing from the instructor list. So far, no such luck. There were other instructors who merited a deep dislike, but none who inspired fear the way Achison did.

"First, he rushes me through the pre-flight check. Can't be bothered with the checklist. Forget the fact that I wouldn't put those tires on a tricycle. Then, we're at max altitude, and he wants to take it up another two thousand feet. Has the nerve to accuse me of being a chicken. He says, 'You're just afraid because you're a girl. The boys wouldn't hesitate—they'd take her right up.'"

"You didn't fall for that line of garbage, did you?"

Janie straightened up. "I couldn't very well let him brag that we girls aren't as brave as those silly boys, could I?"

"You did it?"

"You bet. That damn bird was shaking like she was going to come apart at the seams. I was frightened out of my mind."

"You shouldn't have done that. You're lucky to be alive."

"No kidding. Jerk." Janie threw her gear in her locker. "You're not going up with him, are you?"

"Not this time," Jessie said, as she checked the fastenings on her parachute. As she walked out to the tarmac, she couldn't help but think about the fact that Claudia was scheduled to go up with Achison that night for her checkout flight on the AT-6.

CHAPTER SEVEN

P romise me you'll be careful up there." Jessie pulled Claudia to her. They were in the bay, locked in the bathroom. Everyone else was still socializing over dinner.

"I'm always careful, sugar. What's eating at you about this trip?"

Jessie debated how much she should say. She wanted Claudia to be prepared for anything, but she didn't want to spook her to the point where she would be thinking instead of flying instinctually.

"Well?"

Jessie looked into the eyes she loved more than flying. In the months they'd spent together, she'd come to crave Claudia with an intensity she'd never thought possible. "It's Achison."

"I know that. It isn't like I haven't flown with that moron before. I can handle it." Claudia leaned into Jessie's body. "Right now, all I want to handle is you." She kissed Jessie, slowly at first, then with wild abandon.

Jessie nearly forgot what she was worried about. Nearly. She pulled back when she felt Claudia's hands undo her belt buckle and pull the blouse free of her slacks. "Claude." Warm fingers played at her naval. "Claude," she pleaded. "I'm serious."

"So am I, lover."

"Damn it, hold on a minute." Jessie tried to reverse the flow of blood in her body. At the moment, all of it seemed to be below her waist.

"Tell me you don't want me."

Jessie knew she couldn't say that.

"Tell me this doesn't feel good."

She couldn't say that, either.

"That's what I thought." Claudia resumed her exploration, finding a particularly sensitive spot.

Jessie groaned and took Claudia's mouth with a savage need she hadn't known was within her. Before she could resist, Claudia was inside her, urging her forward, rocking against her to increase her pleasure. Jessie lost track of where they were and what they'd been discussing. The only point of orientation was the delicious pressure building within. Even if she'd wanted to, she couldn't have stopped the explosion that consumed her.

She leaned heavily against Claudia, gasping for breath.

"That's more like it." Claudia continued to stroke her.

"Claude. You have to stop." It took all Jessie's restraint not to succumb again. She stilled Claudia's hand with a vice grip. "Please. The girls will be back any minute."

"You know I hate when you get all practical on me, don't you?"

"One of us has to be." Jessie said, panting between the words as she tried to recover.

Claudia withdrew her hand, pouting all the while.

Jessie tucked her blouse back in, buttoned up her slacks, and adjusted her belt. "Will you promise me you'll be extra careful up there tonight?"

Claudia was looking in the mirror, fussing with her hair where Jessie had run her fingers through it. "I promise, sugar." She looked at Jessie in the mirror and winked. "You want to walk out first, or do you want me to?"

"I'll go." Jessie knew that if she stayed any longer, she would be tempted to kiss Claudia again. Or make love to her. The girls really would be back any second, and it wouldn't do to push their luck any more than they already had.

∽·≈

Jessie looked at her watch for the third time in as many minutes. Reluctantly, she had let the girls drag her to the canteen for some refreshments. She figured it would be a good way to distract herself from thinking about...

"Got a date?" Shirley asked.

"What?"

Shirley picked up Jessie's wrist and dropped it. Her eyebrows were raised in question.

"Oh. No."

"You seem on edge tonight, Jess."

"Even more than ususal," Rebecca chimed in.

Jessie frowned. In this case, the truth would work just fine. "Claudia's on her checkout ride."

"So? She's a great pilot. Should be a piece of cake for a girl with her skills," Annabelle said. "Gin, by the way."

"You have to be the luckiest card player ever," Janie complained. She shoved her chair back from the table. "I'm going to get another pop. Anyone want one?"

A chorus of "no thank yous" greeted her offer.

"She drew Achison," Jessie said, picking up the thread of the conversation.

"Man, that's bad luck."

"The pits."

"Yeah."

Jessie bit her lower lip as the girls' sympathetic comments washed over her. She had a sinking feeling in her gut, and her gut was seldom wrong.

"Why don't you play a hand, Jess?"

"No thanks. I'm terrible at cards." *Remind me to play poker with you.* Isn't that what Claudia was always saying to her? That train of thought made Jessie's stomach clench anew.

Rebecca shuffled the deck. "Guess I'll just have to clean Annabelle's clock myself, then."

As Rebecca dealt the hand, a horrible noise pierced the air. All of them jumped up and ran outside. Janie, who already had been standing, was first through the door. Jessie was right on her heels.

In the distance, they could see showers of sparks. The unmistakable sound of metal screeching on pavement tore through Jessie's body like shrapnel. A siren sounded. She doubled her pace.

As she rounded a corner, the runway came into sharp focus. The landing lights cast an eerie glow on a macabre scene. A mangled engine sat by itself off to the side. The plane, sheered in two, erupted in flames in front of Jessie's eyes.

"Claude!" Jessie closed the last twenty feet separating her from the cockpit. Flames shot up in the air. Jessie ripped off her bomber jacket and threw it over her head. She scrambled up on the twisted metal. She could see the outline of a pilot still strapped into the seat. The canopy was hot to the touch, and Jessie recoiled as the metal seared the flesh on her hands.

She looked around wildly. "Give me that," she yelled, as she spied a mechanic spraying the fuselage with a fire extinguisher. When he didn't immediately respond, she jumped down and grabbed it from him. She climbed back up, the flames licking at her boots, and rammed the canister hard into the canopy. On the third strike, it shattered, showering fragments everywhere. Covering her hands with her sleeves, she reached inside and released the catch, then shoved the canopy back.

She felt intense heat on her legs and looked down to see her pant legs on fire. She aimed the extinguisher and sprayed herself, then the area all around Claudia's unmoving form. She dropped the canister and used both hands to unfasten the straps that held Claudia hostage. Hands joined hers as she struggled to lift her lover out of the cockpit.

"We've got her. You can let go now."

Jessie heard the words, but her body and heart refused to obey. She cradled Claudia's head and shoulders.

"Dave, take her legs."

Jessie glanced up to see the instructor she had flown with that morning shouting instructions to one of the other instructors. The man lifted Claudia's legs and together, he and Jessie lowered her to the ground.

Gently, Jessie removed Claudia's leather cap and goggles and disengaged her parachute, peeling it off her back. "Ah, Claude. I'm right here, baby. Don't you go anywhere on me. Don't you dare." Jessie's tears mingled with the ash that smudged Claudia's face. Gently, she stroked Claudia's cheek with trembling fingers.

"Excuse me, miss. We need to take her now." A medic hovered over them.

Jessie blinked up at him but did not move.

"Get her out of the way, we've got work to do," a man with a stethoscope instructed gruffly.

"Please, miss. We need to assess her condition."

Jessie felt herself shoved aside, and she lost contact with Claudia. "No!" She fought against the arms that came around her to restrain her.

"It's okay, miss. You have to let us get her to the hospital."

"I'm going with her."

The man ignored her, and Jessie screamed it again. "I'm going with her!"

A stretcher arrived and Claudia was loaded onto it. Jessie thrashed wildly in an effort to break free. "Let me go. I have to go with her."

"If you don't let her go, she'll likely tear your arms off," a voice said weakly from the stretcher, as two men lifted it off the ground to carry it toward a waiting ambulance.

"Claude? Oh, God. Claude." Jessie stomped down on the man's foot and he loosened his grip, cursing her roundly. She ducked under two other men and reached Claudia's side.

"Fancy...meeting...you here," Claudia managed, coughing between words.

"Don't try to talk, Claude." Jessie grasped for Claudia's hand, and cried out.

"Wh—what is it?" Claudia asked.

Jessie looked down at the seared flesh. "It's nothing."

One of the medics who was accompanying the stretcher grabbed Jessie's wrist and shined a flashlight on her hand. "Bad burns you've got there, miss. We'll have to treat those."

"Just worry about her," Jessie indicated Claudia with a nod of the head.

"Guess we'd better take you with us, after all," the medic said.

❧❧

Jessie could have sworn she felt fingers combing through her hair. She opened first one eye, and then the other. After a moment's disorientation, she remembered where she was. She lifted her head off the edge of Claudia's hospital bed.

"About time you woke up, sleepyhead."

Jessie straightened up gingerly. Falling asleep slumped over in a chair left her feeling stiff and sore. She moved to rub her eyes, only to realize that both of her hands were swathed in bandages. Claudia was propped up against some pillows, smiling at her. "What time is it?"

"0500."

"Oh." She stood up and hovered over Claudia. "How are you feeling?"

"Right as rain, thanks in large part, I understand, to you."

"I don't know what you're talking about."

"This cute little medic kept going on and on about how you risked life and limb to get me out of that cockpit. He said you even ignored your pants being on fire."

"Did not." Jessie blushed. "I put that fire out."

"Oh, that's much better." Claudia laughed, which set off a coughing jag. Her voice was raspy from having inhaled smoke.

"What happened up there, Claude?"

"The damn engine failed. Probably the wrong octane in the tank, and it was that bird's seventh flight of the day. Poor thing must've been tuckered out."

"Why didn't you bail out?"

"Achison insisted that we could pull off a belly landing. By the time we finished arguing about it, we were too close to the ground to use the parachutes."

If Jessie could've gotten to the asshole, she would've strangled him with her bandaged hands.

"Where is he, anyway? What happened to him?" Claudia asked.

"Don't know, don't care," Jessie responded.

"That's not very charitable of you."

Jessie's nostrils flared. "That idiot nearly killed you."

"I'm tough to kill, sugar."

"Not funny, Claude. I'm not laughing."

"So I see."

Before Jessie could respond, the doctor walked in. "Oh, hello. I didn't know you still had company."

Jessie shuffled from foot to foot but made no move to leave. The memory of being separated from Claudia hours earlier was too vivid.

"You really ought to go get some sleep, miss. Miss Sherwood is in good hands."

"What's wrong with her?"

"Just some smoke inhalation and a few bumps and bruises. Nothing a little bed rest won't cure. Now, if you'll excuse us, I really need to examine the patient."

Although she didn't want to, Jessie knew that she had no good reason to object.

"Go ahead, Jess. You can come by and see me later."

Jessie reluctantly parted the curtain surrounding the bed and left.

When she arrived back at the barracks, she was surprised to find all the girls already awake.

"How is she?" Rebecca asked, before Jessie even had a chance to close the door.

"Doctor says she'll be fine. Lungful of smoke and she got banged around pretty good."

"God, Jessie, you were a force of nature out there," Shirley said.

"I've never seen anything like it," Annabelle agreed. "You were like a mama bear with her cub. You weren't going to let anything or anyone get in your way."

"I thought you were going to deck that one instructor," Janie said.

Not knowing what to say, Jessie simply shrugged.

"I don't think anybody's crying over Achison," Rebecca said.

"What do you mean?" Jessie asked.

"Didn't you know? He's a crispy critter."

"Shirley!"

"What? It's true. They couldn't get his canopy to release in time. He burned to death."

Jessie remembered standing on the fuselage, unable to open Claudia's canopy—those desperate seconds when she feared she'd lose her love. She looked down at her bandaged hands, and tears sprang to her eyes.

"Jessie? Earth to Jessie, come in, please," Annabelle said. "Hey? Where are you? Don't tell me you're shedding tears for that jerk."

"Huh? Who? Achison? Not a chance," Jessie said, recovering her equilibrium.

"Did you stay by Claudia's side all night? Or did they keep you for observation too?"

"Hmm? Oh. It was really late when they finished with my hands. I decided to sit with Claudia for a bit to make sure she was okay, and I must've fallen asleep." Jessie marveled at how easily the explanation tripped off her tongue. She decided Claudia must be rubbing off on her after all.

Jackie Cochran, herself, investigated the accident. In the end, she concluded that the plane was suffering from metal fatigue, was cobbled together with worn parts, had the wrong octane fuel in the tanks, and shouldn't have been flown that night. In addition, she found fault with the instructor's decision-making. If he had chosen to deploy parachutes instead of attempting a difficult belly landing in the dark, he likely would still be alive.

All of which was well and good, Jessie thought when she read the report, but it didn't change the fact that she almost lost her beloved Claudia. Every time she passed the charred wreckage, as she just had done, she experienced the horror all over again—the smells, the sounds, the sight of Claudia, motionless in the cockpit, looking completely defenseless, the shattered canopy, the arms restraining her, keeping her away from her lover...

Jessie entered the administration building, stopped in front of a partially open door, and knocked.

"Keaton, you're late."

Jessie snapped to attention in front of Lucinda Hutchins, Cochran's handpicked pit bull. "Yes, ma'am. I'm sorry ma'am." Jessie wanted to sneak a peek at her watch. She was positive she was on time and this overblown windbag was just jerking her chain.

Hutchins didn't acknowledge the apology. In fact, she didn't look up at Jessie at all. She was reviewing paperwork on her desk. Jessie stood stock-still and waited. She recognized this as one of Hutchins tricks to throw her prey off balance.

A full five minutes after Jessie had entered, Hutchins raised her eyes. "You've been a busy girl."

"Ma'am?"

"Putting out fires, rescuing damsels in distress, running back and forth to the base hospital for visits... Anything you want to share with me?"

"I'm sorry, ma'am, I'm not sure what you're getting at." Jessie resisted the urge to fidget.

"I hear the scuttlebutt around the base, you know. Folks are raising questions about the nature of your relationship with Miss Sherwood. Care to comment?"

The intimation didn't come as a complete surprise to Jessie, but hearing it spoken out loud brought the peril she and Claudia faced into sharp focus. "No, ma'am."

"No? *No?*" Hutchins shoved her chair back as she rose and slammed her palms down on the desk.

Jessie narrowed her eyes and stood up a little straighter. If Hutchins's aim was to intimidate her, she would have to do better than that. Jessie was a good six inches taller. She held her silence.

"Sure as hell something is going on, and I'm going to get to the bottom of it."

"Respectfully, ma'am, I don't know what you're talking about."

"I'm talking about something unsavory, that's what I'm talking about." Spittle formed at the corners of Hutchins's mouth, and Jessie tried not to stare.

"Miss Sherwood is my best friend. We started in the program together, and we enjoy each other's company. Do you have a best friend, ma'am?"

"What does that have to do with anything?" Hutchins thundered.

Jessie started to bite her lower lip but stopped herself. "Best friends stick together. They protect and defend each other. They spend lots of free time together. That's just what best friends do."

Hutchins sat down again and shuffled through the papers on her desk. "There's a report here from someone at the scene of the crash that swears he heard you call Miss Sherwood by a term of endearment generally reserved for a sweetheart."

Although Jessie didn't react outwardly, inwardly she frantically reviewed what she might have said to Claudia as she pulled her from the wreckage. Nothing was coming to her, but she'd been out of her mind with fear that night. She hadn't cared about being judicious with her words. Under the circumstances, it hadn't mattered. All she cared about was Claudia. Then she focused on what Hutchins said. She used the pronoun "he." So, it wasn't one of the girls who was ratting them out, it was an instructor, or a doctor. *Well, screw them.*

"I have no idea what I might've said that night, ma'am. I was only focused on saving lives."

"One life, Keaton. You were only interested in saving one life. Sherwood's."

"With all due respect, ma'am, I am only one person, and I could only reasonably be expected to help one victim at a time."

"Cute, Keaton. Very cute. And the sleeping with your head on Sherwood's hospital bed? I suppose you have an explanation for that too?"

"As I said, ma'am, Miss Sherwood is my best friend. It was a traumatic event for both of us. I just wanted to be sure she was okay."

"And you didn't trust the doctors to see to that?"

"Would you, if it was your best friend?"

"Don't sass me, Keaton." Hutchins looked as though she would explode.

Several minutes of silence ensued, and Jessie prudently decided to wait Hutchins out.

"I'm putting you on notice. You are on very thin ice, Keaton. If you so much as blink wrong, I'll have your can on the next train out to whatever hole you crawled out of. Now get out of my sight."

Jessie turned on her heel and marched out without looking back. She hustled behind an empty hangar and slumped against the building. Her hands were shaking badly, and she thought she might be sick.

She and Claudia hadn't been caught, but they might as well have been. Claudia would be getting out of the hospital in less than an hour. All Jessie wanted was to take her in her arms and hold her close. Now even looking at Claudia wrong might get her thrown out of the program. What was she going to do? Giving up Claudia would be like giving up breathing. But they couldn't go on as they were.

Jessie clutched her stomach. What would Claudia want to do? Would she take the threat seriously, or just dismiss it? Jessie was afraid of the answer. *Oh, Claude. What are we going to do now?*

CHAPTER EIGHT

Hey, look who's back," Shirley said, as Claudia entered the bay. All the girls gathered around her, except for one.

Jessie looked up from her bunk, where she was mending a tear in her flight suit. She fought desperately against the urge to run to Claudia and take her in her arms. "Welcome back, Claude," she managed, around the lump in her throat. "Ouch! Damn it!"

"What's the matter, Jess?" Rebecca asked.

"Poked myself with the damn needle."

Claudia shooed the girls away and came to stand directly in front of Jessie. "You never were any good with that thing." She sat down next to Jessie on the bed. "Give me that." She took the needle and thread and pulled the flight suit onto her lap. "Your hands are shaking, sugar," she said under her breath.

Jessie made eye contact briefly, then, unable to maintain it, looked away.

"You're upset. What's the matter, Jess?" Claudia rested her hand on Jessie's thigh.

Jessie felt the touch all the way to her toes—it only made her more miserable. "I'll be right back." She jumped up and hustled the few feet to the bathroom, closed the door behind her, stood over the sink, and wept. A knock on the door startled her. "Be out in a sec."

"Honey, it's just me," Claudia's muffled voice carried through the wood. "Everyone's gone. They went to get milkshakes at the canteen."

"Oh."

"Please, Jess. Come out?"

Jessie ran her sleeve across her eyes and opened the door to find Claudia leaning against the wall. "Hi."

"Hi yourself." Claudia captured an errant tear as it dropped from Jessie's lashes. "Want to tell me what this is all about?"

Jessie wanted to speak, but the words wouldn't come, so she nodded.

Claudia took her by the hand and led her back to the bed. "I thought you'd be there to pick me up at the hospital and walk me back here."

"I meant to," Jessie whispered. "I wanted to."

"Look at me, sugar." Claudia lifted Jessie's chin with two fingers. "Your eyes are all red, and you look like someone just killed your sister, except we both know you don't have one of those. What on earth is going on?"

"Oh, Claude." The thought of having to distance herself from her lover was too much to bear. It was as if a dam broke, and Jessie couldn't stop the flood of tears. She fell into Claudia's open arms.

"Shh, it's okay. Aw, c'mon baby, what's so bad? I'm here, and I'm fine. Good as new."

"It…it's not th-that," Jessie said between sobs.

"Then what is it? Honey, I've never seen you like this. Whatever it is, we'll fix it."

"I don't think w-we c-can."

"Of course we can. Together we can do anything. C'mon, sugar. Tell me what's got you so bent out of shape."

Jessie struggled to take a deep breath and regain control of her emotions. After several aborted attempts to speak, she finally said, "I got summoned by Hutchins." She felt Claudia stiffen.

"What did that witch want with you?"

Jessie closed her eyes as Claudia ran her fingers through her hair. God, that felt good. "She wanted to warn me off."

"Warn you off what?"

Jessie swallowed hard. "It wasn't a 'what,' it was a 'who.'"

"Sorry?"

Jessie reluctantly disentangled herself from Claudia's warm embrace and straightened up to face her. "You." She searched Claudia's eyes. "She told me to stay away from you."

"She what?" Claudia's shout echoed off the walls.

"Shh. Keep it down. She raked me over the coals about our relationship—said she'd heard rumors of 'unsavory' behavior between us."

"Nobody's seen anything," Claudia said, indignantly.

"She didn't say they had, exactly. Just that there was talk, and that one of the guys at the scene of the accident overheard me use a term of endearment after we got you out of the cockpit."

"Oh, come on. That's what she's got? She jerked your chain for that?"

Jessie shook her head. "That and the fact that I slept in a chair with my head on your hospital bed."

"So what? I was a friend who'd been in a harrowing situation. You were concerned and offered support."

"That's what I told her. I asked her if she'd ever had a best friend."

"Her only friends are probably crocodiles."

Jessie laughed. "Nah. They'd probably reject her."

"Yeah, you're right."

"Anyway," Jessie said, sobering up again, "she told me if she caught wind of anything else, she'd personally kick me out of the program and ship me home."

"I see. I guess that explains why you didn't come get me from the hospital. She tried to frighten you, and it worked."

Jessie could sense Claudia's rising ire. "Claude, she's serious."

"I'm sure she is."

"What are we going to do?"

"Do?"

"We can't keep going the way we've been—she'll have me out of here before I can pack my bags."

"She wouldn't dare. You're one of the best pilots here."

"Doesn't matter, Claude. She's just itching for an excuse, I could tell."

Claudia picked up one of Jessie's hands and kissed it. Jessie rested her palm against Claudia's smooth cheek.

"I love you."

"I love you too, sugar. Hutchins can't change that."

"No, but she can make our lives hell. She can banish me and send me home. Then what?"

Claudia frowned. "We're not going to let that happen. That's all there is to it."

Jessie felt herself tearing up again. "The only way to stop it is not to see each other anymore."

Claudia recoiled as if she'd been slapped. "Perish the thought."

"I don't see any other way."

"There has to be another way." Claudia's voice shook.

Jessie took Claudia's hand in hers. Exhaustion was etched in her face, and Jessie silently cursed herself for being so insensitive. "You need to rest. Here you are barely out of the hospital, and I've dumped all this on you. I'm a clod."

"You are no such thing. I'd have been really mad if you'd kept this from me."

"I couldn't. As it is, it didn't take you two seconds to know something was wrong. I can't keep anything from you."

"I'm glad of that. I wouldn't want you to." Claudia leaned in and kissed Jessie sweetly on the mouth. "Mmm. There's no way I'm going to live without that."

"Which brings us back to the point. What are we going to do?"

Claudia yawned. "We'll figure something out. Right now, I think I need to lie down."

"Of course you do." Jessie stood and pulled Claudia up with her. Holding her with one arm, she used the other to turn down Claudia's bed. She helped her to sit down again and knelt to pull off Claudia's boots.

"I ought to get into accidents more often if it gets me treatment like this."

"Don't even say that," Jessie said, as she guided Claudia into a prone position. She itched to lie down alongside her and hold her.

As if reading her mind, Claudia said, "Gosh, I wish you could crawl in here with me."

"Yeah. Me too."

"Someday," Claudia said, as her eyes began to close.

Jessie stood over her and watched her sleep for a long time, gently sweeping a lock of hair off her forehead and listening to the deep, even sounds of her breathing. It was a sight she wished she could witness every day for the rest of her life. Before emotion could overcome her again, she turned away and busied herself with sewing.

❦

"Are you sure you're up to this?" Jessie asked Claudia for the fifth time as they approached the entrance to the Blue Bonnet Hotel.

"How many times are you going to ask me the same thing? Yes, I'm sure. Frankly, I'm less sure that you're up to this."

"What the heck does that mean?"

"As I recall, the last time we tried this, it didn't go so well."

Jessie thought back to that first outing and smiled. "No, but I sure enjoyed the walk home."

Claudia smacked her playfully in the arm and laughed. "If someone makes a play for me in there, you're going to have to trust me to handle it. You can't go all King Kong on me."

"You gals coming, or what?" Janie called, as she disappeared inside.

"I hate this," Jessie muttered.

"Me too, darling, but we agreed that we can't keep turning down invitations—it looks bad."

"I want to be clear that I only said yes to this to get Hutchins off our backs."

"No kidding. Well, here we go," Claudia said as she guided them inside.

The music was loud, the booze was flowing, and the dance floor was jam-packed. Jessie fought her way to the bar and ordered two sarsaparillas. As she waited, she spied Annabelle on the dance floor with a boy in uniform. She was flirting shamelessly, and Jessie wondered if Annabelle knew the boy, or if this was the first time they were meeting. She realized with a start that she knew next to nothing about the personal lives of her bunkmates. She was willing to bet that Claudia knew everything.

"Here you go, Miss." The bartender handed Jessie the drinks.

"Thanks." Jessie had to concentrate hard to avoid spilling as she navigated through the crowd. Eventually, she found Claudia standing against the wall. She wasn't alone. Jessie's nostrils flared, but she clamped down on her temper.

"Ah, here's my friend I was telling you about," Claudia said to the boy, who looked vaguely familiar, although Jessie couldn't quite place him.

Jessie handed Claudia her drink without comment.

"Jessie Keaton, this is Matt Dunphy. He's just back from flying missions overseas."

Reluctantly, Jessie shook his hand. He was wearing the uniform of the Army Air Forces. Jessie narrowed her eyes. Dunphy. Dunphy. Where had she heard that name before? And then it struck her—the picture on the piano.

"Are you sure you don't want to dance?" Matt was asking Claudia when Jessie refocused on the conversation.

"Positive. I'm still recovering from my injuries. Jessie here saved my life."

"Then I should thank Jessie for making it possible for me to gaze upon such a pretty face." Matt glanced dismissively at Jessie, then returned his full attention to Claudia. He shifted his body as if to shut Jessie out. "How about getting some air with me, then? Since you can't dance."

"No, thank you, Matt. Don't be rude. Jessie is my friend. I'm not leaving her."

Matt mumbled something Jessie couldn't hear. Then again, she was pretty sure it wasn't meant for her ears. "What if I find a friend for her too? Would I stand a better chance with you then?"

Claudia batted her eyelashes. "Maybe."

"Be right back," Matt said. "Don't go anywhere."

When he was gone, Claudia turned to Jessie. "I know what you're thinking."

"I bet you don't," Jessie said, under her breath.

"I heard that, sugar. You want me to tell him to get lost."

"Something like that."

"He's harmless."

"And you know that from five minutes of conversation?"

"C'mon, Jess. You promised to behave."

Jessie pursed her lips. "He turned his back to me—practically told me to skedaddle."

"Okay. I'll admit that his manners could use a little work, but honestly, he could be the answer to our problem."

"What do you mean?"

"If I feign interest in him, and you agree to spend time with one of his buddies so we can double date, we can throw off suspicion and still spend time together."

Jessie felt as though she might throw up. Share Claudia with a boy? Sit by and watch him manhandle her? She couldn't see how she could do it. She looked up from her shoes to see Claudia watching her, a knowing expression on her face.

"Please, Jess? It won't have to be for long. We've only got a couple of weeks left. Then we can be together, just us. We'll find a place to live off base wherever we end up. I promise."

Before Jessie could answer, Matt was back, with a friend in tow. He was a few inches shorter than Jessie—a redhead with freckles.

"Claudia Sherwood, Jessie Keaton, may I introduce Jordan Escher. Jordan, this is Jessie." Matt virtually shoved him in Jessie's direction.

Jessie thought the boy looked frightened.

"Um, wanna dance?"

"No, thank you."

"Oh. Okay." Jordan stuffed his hands in his pockets and shuffled his feet.

Where Jordan was bashful and deferential, Jessie noted that Matt was smooth and aggressive. He had positioned himself too close to Claudia, his hand resting against the wall just over her shoulder so that he easily could lower it and have his arm around her. Jessie thought that Claudia didn't seem to mind in the least, which made her want to bodily drag her lover out of there.

"So, Matt, how is it you're home? I thought it was all hands on deck over there," Jessie said. If she couldn't keep him away from Claudia, at least she could knock some of the cockiness out of him.

"Got strafed over Berlin. Barely made it back to safety. Took some shrapnel in my leg, so I'm on temporary leave. I'm itching to get back and kill me some more Nazis, though, so I'll only be here long enough to let my mother see that I'm fine and get back to it."

Jessie wasn't convinced that his story was true, but she didn't want to call him on it. The best news she heard was that he would be gone shortly. It couldn't come soon enough for her.

"You're not a little bit afraid to get back in the cockpit after that?" Claudia asked.

"Nah. No big deal."

"Wish I felt the same. I have to admit, I'm a little nervous about going back up."

"You are? You didn't tell me that." Jessie said.

Claudia shrugged. "After how brave you were on the way back from Palm Springs, I feel like a chicken. I didn't want you to be disappointed in me."

"I could never be disappointed in you, Claude. It's natural to be gun shy after what you went through."

"I could go up with you if it makes you feel better," Matt offered.

Jessie clenched her fists at her sides to keep from hitting him. It was her job to protect Claudia. Her job to help Claudia get her confidence back. Who did this jerk think he was, anyway?

"I don't know if the brass would approve that," Claudia said, "but it's a really sweet gesture."

"Well, I mean it, so you just go back and ask whoever you need to get permission from. Tell them a real flyboy is ready and willing to help."

Jessie wanted to stick her finger down her throat, but refrained. She was surprised that Claudia could keep a straight face. Surely Claudia could see through this idiot's bluster. Couldn't she?

"Speaking of the brass, we'd best be getting back. Don't want to miss lights out," Claudia said.

"Already? Aw, come on," Matt countered, "we're just getting to know each other. The night is young."

"Sorry, fellas. Rules are rules," Jessie added, happy that this lousy night was about to end.

"Let me walk you out."

"That's really not necessary, Matt."

"Jordan will come with us to escort your friend. Won't you, Escher?"

"Um, yeah. Sure."

Jessie wanted to tell them both to stuff it, that she could get her and Claudia back to base just fine, but Claudia gave her a warning look.

The four of them walked out together.

"You really shouldn't walk around in the dark without someone along to protect you," Matt said when they were outside.

"We're tougher than we look," Claudia said. "We do just fine on our own."

"Still, it's not right, two women out wandering around by themselves, is it Escher?"

"N-no. I suppose not."

"We could walk you back to the base."

"No, thank you. We came with friends. One of them has a car, so we won't be walking," Claudia said.

"Really, where are they?" Matt made a show of looking around.

"They'll be out any second. We agreed to meet out front."

"We'll wait with you in case they don't show."

Fortuitously, right then Rebecca and Shirley stumbled out, laughing and chatting.

"Here are our friends now. Well, see you fellas."

"Wait," Matt said. "Can I see you again?" he asked Claudia. "How about my offer to take you up?"

"We'll see about that," Claudia said, breezily.

"I warn you, I'm not going to take no for an answer."

"Somehow, I believe you," Jessie muttered.

"It was nice to meet you," Jordan said, holding up his hand in a semi-wave.

"Yeah," Jessie said, without conviction. She pulled on Claudia's sleeve to get her to move, afraid that, at any moment, Matt would try to kiss her goodnight.

They caught up to Rebecca and Shirley, who were weaving a few feet ahead. "Where's Annabelle? And what about Janie?" Claudia asked.

"Who?" Rebecca asked, overly loud.

"You know, our bunkmates," Jessie said.

"Oh, them. Annabelle's with some boy, and Janie was on the dance floor last I saw," Shirley said.

"Shouldn't we wait for them?"

"Nope." Rebecca giggled.

"When I told her we were leaving, Janie said to go ahead without them—one of the guys has a car and will take them back to the base," Shirley said. "Speaking of cars, where did I leave that thing?"

Jessie pointed to a row of cars. "It's over there. But maybe you should let me or Claudia drive."

"Okay, s'long as you don't wreck it." Shirley handed Jessie the keys.

"I think there's far less chance of me wrecking it than you."

"Probably right about that."

They all climbed in, and Jessie drove them back to Avenger Field.

"Those seemed like nice fellas you two were with," Rebecca said, as they walked back to the barracks after parking the car.

"Nice enough," Claudia agreed.

"Gonna see them again?" Shirley asked.

Claudia squeezed Jessie's hand to keep her from answering. "Maybe," she said.

Jessie didn't like the sound of that. She wished she could get Claudia alone so they could discuss it. She didn't know which depressed her more—the thought of Claudia seeing Matt again, or the fact that she hadn't had any private time with her lover in days.

CHAPTER NINE

It was the middle of the night and Jessie lay awake staring at the ceiling. She replayed the night over and over in her head—the way Matt immediately assumed that Claudia would return his interest, her feelings of impotence when she thought he might kiss her girl. Jessie groaned out loud and pulled the pillow over her head. The idea of someone else kissing Claudia made her want to scream.

True, it hadn't happened...yet. But Jessie felt the ground shifting beneath her, and she had no idea what to do about it. Hutchins's warning was clear as a bell. Any hint or whisper of anything inappropriate between her and Claudia would result in Jessie's being sent home. But to sit idly by and watch...

Someone grabbed her hand, and Jessie nearly levitated off the bed. "Easy, sugar, it's only me," Claudia whispered. "Move over."

"What? What are you doing?"

Claudia lifted the covers off Jessie and slid in next to her.

"Are you crazy?"

"I'm crazy about you."

"Claude, if we get caught it'll be lights out for us." Jessie lifted her head to make sure the other girls were asleep.

"Shh. I just need to feel you next to me, to hear your heart beat in my ear. I won't stay long, I promise. I love you, Jess."

Jessie closed her eyes as a tear leaked out. "I love you too, baby."

"God, I miss you even when I'm with you."

"I know." Jessie wrapped her arms around Claudia and spooned her.

"He's just a boy, you know."

"Hmm?"

"Don't pretend you weren't laying awake fretting about Matt Dunphy and what happened tonight."

Jessie frowned. It amazed her how often Claudia knew exactly what she was thinking. "He's not 'just a boy.' He's the boy who wants to take my girl away."

"Well, there's no chance of that."

"He wanted to kiss you, for goodness sake. If Shirley and Rebecca hadn't come along when they did, he probably would have."

"But he didn't."

"What about next time?"

Claudia scooted back even further into Jessie. "Anyone ever tell you you worry too much?"

Jessie chuckled. "Yeah. You."

"I must be one smart girl." Claudia took Jessie's hand and placed it on her breast. "Mmm. That feels good." Claudia squeezed Jessie's hand, silently urging her to use more pressure. "Jordan seemed like a decent fella."

"Don't try changing the subject."

Turning her head, Claudia brushed her lips against Jessie's jaw. "Even if he did kiss me, it wouldn't mean anything."

Jessie dropped her hand and tried to find her voice. Her throat suddenly seemed dry as parchment. "It would mean something to me."

"I know, sugar. I know." Claudia took Jessie's hand again. "You're the only one for me, now and always. Nothing changes that. Not Matt, not Hutchins—nothing and nobody. Got that?"

Jessie didn't respond for several heartbeats. She wanted so badly to believe Claudia.

"Got that, sugar?"

Jessie sighed heavily. "Yeah, I got that."

Claudia turned fully and kissed her deeply. "Say it like you mean it," she said, against Jessie's lips.

"I'm the only one for you, Claude." Jessie knew her voice was trembling. "I'll always be the only one for you."

"Don't forget that," Claudia said, kissing Jessie one last time before she slipped out of bed and back into her own.

❧❧

Claudia, Jessie, Janie, and Annabelle were on their way to shower and change after calisthenics when Jessie spotted Hutchins heading directly toward them.

"Witch at two o'clock," she whispered under her breath to Claudia.

"Yep, I spotted her too. Just keep your cool—she's got no beef with us."

"Hello, girls," Hutchins said as she effectively blocked their path. "Sherwood, Keaton, I'd like a quick word."

"We'll catch up with you gals in a bit," Claudia said to Janie and Annabelle. "Don't use up all the cold water."

It was a running joke in the bay that there was never any hot water with which to shower.

When the girls had moved on, Hutchins said, "I had an interesting visit today." She paused for effect. "An officer in the AAF. He says he's a friend of yours, Sherwood."

"Matt," Jessie said, trying hard to keep the misery out of her tone.

"As a matter of fact, his name *was* Matthew. Matthew Dunphy, I believe he said. He fed me some nonsense about you being afraid to fly after your accident, Sherwood. Said he was coming over to volunteer to take you up."

Jessie stuffed her hands in her pockets to hide her balled-up fists. Matt was going to be the one to help Claudia over her fears, not her. It was all she could do not to stomp away. Claudia must have sensed this, because she surreptitiously nudged Jessie.

"What did you tell him, Miss Hutchins?"

"Why, I told him the truth—our gals don't need help from any flyboys to do our jobs. I thanked him for the offer and told him he'd have to find another way to spend time with you." Hutchins looked from Claudia to Jessie and back again. "This doesn't mean you two are off the hook, but for now, it looks as if you've taken my warning seriously. A very wise choice."

Hutchins turned on her heel and walked away, and Claudia burst out laughing.

"What are you laughing about?"

"Hutchins. Did you see how disappointed she looked that she couldn't pin anything on us?"

"Aren't you skipping over the part where that 'harmless' boy marched over here and tried to talk his way into a flying date with you?"

Claudia patted Jessie's arm. "It didn't happen. You heard Hutchins. She told him to go fly a kite."

"He's not going to let it rest there, Claude."

"Didn't we go through this last night, sugar? He's no competition for you."

"I should be the one to take you up for your first time back in the cockpit." Jessie knew she sounded petulant, but she didn't care.

"I'm pretty sure they'll make me go with one of the instructors."

"Probably." Jessie rubbed her toe in the dirt. "Still, I wish it could be me."

"I wish that too, sugar."

"Have they told you when you're scheduled next?"

"Tomorrow night."

"A night flight?" Jessie's eyes flashed angrily. The idea of sending Claudia back up in the dark instead of letting her get her confidence back in the daylight was outrageous. "Whose bright idea was that?"

"Cochran, apparently. Said it would show my character."

"That's poppycock."

"It's okay, Jess. I'll have to go up at night again sometime. It might as well be sooner rather than later. Less time for me to worry about it."

"Who's the instructor?"

"Don't know yet. I'll find out tomorrow. Hey, I was thinking I would go into town later and get my hair done to take my mind off things. Come with me?"

"You're kidding. You want me to come with you to get your hair done?" Jessie thought she would rather be tortured by the Germans.

"It's a way for us to spend time together, silly."

"I guess."

"It's not like I'm asking you to stand in front of a firing squad, or get your own hair done, heaven forbid."

"True. Okay, I'll do it."

"That's more like it," Claudia said, as she opened the door to the bay.

ళ\ఉ

Jessie couldn't remember the last time she'd seen so many elderly ladies in one place at one time. The incessant chatter was enough to drive her crazy. She waited while Claudia gave her name to the receptionist, then sat down with her in the waiting area, where she picked up a copy of the latest *Life* magazine.

"Oh, goodness," Claudia said, looking up from her crossword puzzle.

"What is it?"

"Mrs. Dunphy. She must've just finished getting her hair done."

Jessie followed Claudia's line of sight to a slight, white-haired woman with an oversized purse walking in their direction. She wore a look of determination that told Jessie she was used to getting what she wanted.

"Claudia Sherwood," Mrs. Dunphy said in a tremulous voice. "Just the girl I wanted to see."

"Hello, Mrs. Dunphy. What a lovely surprise." Claudia stood up and beckoned Jessie to stand along with her. "Might I introduce my best friend, Jessie Keaton?"

"Oh, yes dear." Mrs. Dunphy shook Jessie's hand. "How nice to meet you. Any friend of Claudia's is a-okay in my book. And my, aren't you a tall one."

Jessie had no idea how to answer that, so she simply said, "Very nice to meet you, ma'am."

"What's this I hear about you and my boy Matt hitting it off? He told me he met you at the Blue Bonnet the other night. He was quite taken with you, you know." Mrs. Dunphy winked at Jessie. "Well, of course he was, she's beautiful, isn't she?"

"Pretty as a picture," Jessie agreed. *And mine.*

"Matt tells me you were in a very serious accident, my dear. Why I had to hear such dreadful news from him is a mystery. You should have come and told me. Are you all right?"

"I'm fine, Mrs. Dunphy, really."

"Say, I've got a splendid idea," Mrs. Dunphy said, her face lighting up. "Why don't you girls come over for dinner tonight? It'd be wonderful to cook for a gathering, and I'm sure what they're feeding you over at the base is worse than what I'd feed a cat, if I had one. Matt can rustle up a friend for Jessie here, and we'll have a grand old time. What do you say?"

Jessie wanted to say no, wanted to scream it, in fact, but before she could get a word in, Claudia said, "Gee, I'm so sorry. I'm sure it would be delicious, but we have to be on base tonight."

"How presumptuous of me. Of course you can't come on such short notice. How about day after tomorrow? I warn you, I won't take no for an answer."

Jessie couldn't see a way out of it, and apparently neither could Claudia, who agreed that they would have dinner at Mrs. Dunphy's house on Thursday night.

The prospect obviously made Mrs. Dunphy very happy, since she was whistling as she walked out of the beauty parlor.

Jessie remained mum, her head buried in the magazine, as Claudia got her hair done. The last thing in the world she wanted to do was to share a meal with Matt Dunphy and make polite conversation.

"You're brooding," Claudia said, as they left the shop.

Jessie didn't answer.

"It's only a dinner, and Mrs. Dunphy will be there."

"Mrs. Dunphy seems only too happy to play matchmaker between you and her son."

"That's only because Mrs. Dunphy doesn't know that I'm madly in love with you."

Claudia's voice had taken on that sexy timbre that made Jessie wild, but she was currently too single-minded to succumb.

"Are you planning to declare your love for me to Mrs. Dunphy, or to Matt, for that matter? No. So it isn't really of any consequence, is it?"

"It is to me, Jess. I've promised you that you are my one-and-only true love. Why can't that be enough for you?"

"Because some cocky, hot-shot flyboy wants to make a meal of you, and there's not a thing I can do about it, that's why."

"You don't have to do a thing about it, sugar. I can handle Matt, and I will." They walked in silence for a short distance. "Do you trust me, Jess?"

"What kind of question is that? Of course I do. Claude," Jessie said, bringing them both to a stop and looking directly into Claudia's eyes. "This isn't about you. It's about him—I don't trust *him*. I can't explain it. There's just something about him that makes the hair on the back of my neck stand up."

Claudia seemed to consider this. "Are you sure it's him, in particular, you have a problem with? Or would it be any boy who was interested in me?"

Jessie had been wondering the same thing. She owed it to Claudia to be honest. "I don't know. There hasn't been any other boy to come in between us, so I can't really say, now can I?"

"Matt isn't going to come in between us, sugar. Remember? Nobody can come between us. We won't let that happen."

A thought suddenly occurred to Jessie. "What if Jordan wanted to kiss me? How would you feel about that?"

Claudia chuckled. "That's not realistic."

"No? How come?" Jessie felt her temper start to boil. "Aren't I attractive enough or good enough to be kissed by a boy?"

"I didn't mean that," Claudia said quietly. "It's not realistic because you'd probably punch his lights out if he tried."

Jessie felt the blush creep up her neck. What Claudia said was true. Still… "Okay, you might be right about that, but if I did let him make out with me, how would you feel?"

"It'd make me a green-eyed monster—"

"Exactly."

"Let me finish. It'd make me really, really jealous, but I'd know in my heart that it didn't mean anything to you."

"And that would make it all right?"

"No! That would make it tolerable. It would never be all right. Now, can we stop talking about this? We have so little time alone together these days, I don't want to spend it talking about boys." Claudia looped her arm through Jessie's, something she hadn't done since Jessie's meeting with Hutchins. "I love you, Jess."

"I love you too, Claude."

"We need to think about where we want to put in for when training is over."

"What if Hutchins refuses to let us go together?"

"She wouldn't dare."

"I wouldn't put it past that witch."

"You're too right about that. I guess I'd just go over her head to Cochran."

"What makes you think Cochran would give us a better shake?"

"She's smart and she likes to take care of her girls. She wants us to be happy, not miserable. You're the best, so she's going to go out of her way to give you what you want."

"I disagree. I think that means she'll put me wherever she thinks there's the greatest challenge."

"You'll have some bargaining power, I'd be willing to bet. You could say we're a package deal."

Jessie pursed her lips. "I don't know how that would go over."

"It doesn't matter anyway," Claudia said, waving her hand dismissively. "Nobody's going to give us a hard time. We're going to go wherever we want—together—and we'll live happily ever after."

Jessie laughed. "I hope the real world mirrors your fairy tale, princess."

"It will, for I decree it so," Claudia said, imperially.

"Since you're feeling so royal, where's our carriage?"

"In the shop, I'm afraid. We'll just have to travel the rest of the way on foot."

"Pity."

"Uh-huh. Anyway, when you're done being silly, we still have to figure out what posting we want. We could tow targets, or test-fly repaired birds, or move planes from base to base, or fly VIPs around, or instruct newbie flyboys…"

"Do you want to pick our spot by the location, or by the function?"

"Oh. Good question. Very practical. Hmm… Which do you want?"

Jessie considered. "We need someplace where we can live off base and be inconspicuous, so I'm guessing that means we should stay away from isolated or small bases."

"Makes sense."

"How about if we look at the list and narrow it down that way, and then look at what's left and pick a function that suits both of us?"

"Sounds like a good plan to me."

They were getting close to Avenger Field. "Claudia, I…"

"You sound serious. What is it, sugar?"

"I want you to know how much it means to me that we're looking at a future together, that's all."

Tears sprang to Claudia's eyes as she turned to face Jessie. "You're everything to me. You're my heart. My home. There's no future for me without you, Jess."

"I know what you mean." *Boy, do I.*

Jessie could see that Claudia was nervous. She donned her gear, checked and re-checked her parachute, and fiddled with her bootlaces.

"You're going to be fine. You're a great pilot, Claude. There's nothing to worry about."

"Right." Her voice was tight.

Jessie placed a hand on either arm and made Claudia look at her. "I believe in you, Claude. I wish I were the one going up there with you. I trust you with my life. You brought that plane in when no one else could've."

"That's not true. You could've, and it probably wouldn't have broken in two or caught fire. Your instructor wouldn't have died because you—"

"Stop right there, missy. Achison didn't die because of anything you did. He died because he was a jerk. If he'd followed your advice to bail out, he'd most likely still be alive. Not only that, but the crash didn't kill him. It was a malfunctioning canopy release latch. So stop blaming yourself."

Claudia blew out an explosive breath and waggled her shoulders to loosen them.

"I need you to be confident and focused on the here and now. You've got to have your head on right, Claude. You hear me?"

"Loud and clear."

"Okay, then. Cochran will be here any second."

"I know. I can't believe she wanted to go up with me, herself."

"Obviously, she trusts you. I'm sure she's also sending a message to the mechanics that that bird better be in tip-top shape."

"Or it could be that she's planning to save my bacon up there."

"You ought to listen to Keaton, Sherwood, she's sharp." Jackie Cochran stood in the doorway, one hand on her hip, the other holding her cap and goggles.

"Yes, ma'am," Claudia said.

"Let's go. We don't have all night." Cochran disappeared into the darkness.

"You heard her, Claude. She believes in you as much as I do. You can do this. I promise you, I'll be watching and waiting for you."

"In that case, I'll be right back." Claudia smiled brightly, winked, and walked out the door.

Jessie climbed up to the tower and borrowed a pair of binoculars to watch. She really did have complete faith in Claudia—it was the war-weary AT-6 she was flying that worried her.

CHAPTER TEN

Claudia went up in the AT-6 last night. She was amazing." Jessie looked directly at Matt, who was sitting next to Claudia, across the dinner table from her. Jessie hoped he understood her unspoken message—she doesn't need you.

Matt glared at Jessie.

"I'm sure she was splendid," Mrs. Dunphy said, oblivious to the tension between Matt and Jessie. "Good for you, dear." She patted Claudia on the hand. "Goodness, the thought of a little thing like you operating that big machine. I never thought to see the likes of it in my lifetime."

Claudia chuckled. "Planes don't care about gender, Mrs. Dunphy. As long as I can see out the windshield, that's all that matters."

"Claudia is an excellent pilot," Jessie said.

"Not as good as you."

Jessie was acutely aware of Matt watching the interaction between her and Claudia with more than a little interest.

"No woman can hold a candle to me and my crew," Matt said.

"You don't know that," Jessie countered.

"Men have better, quicker reflexes, make better decisions, and are more fearless."

"Where are you getting your information?" Claudia challenged. "There's no data to prove that."

"It's obvious, right Escher?"

Jordan, who had been quietly enjoying his supper, made a non-committal sound. Jessie thought he looked like he'd rather be anywhere than caught in the crossfire at the table.

"Y'all ought to leave the flying to us. It's a man's job," Matt continued, undeterred by Jordan's lack of support. He stretched and casually put his arm around the back of Claudia's chair.

It was all Jessie could do not to launch herself across the table. Although Claudia tensed minutely, Jessie couldn't detect any other outward sign that Matt's familiarity bothered her.

"Without us, you'd be undermanned in battle. What we do frees up more male pilots to go overseas. Besides," Claudia added, "I'd put Jessie here up against the best male pilot in the AAF. There isn't anybody I'd rather fly with when the chips are down." Claudia shot Jessie a look that Jessie was certain was meant to reassure her of her place in Claudia's heart.

"That so?" Matt made a show of looking Jessie over. "Well, she's about as close to a man as you can get without actually being one."

Jessie's ears flamed bright red. Claudia jumped up from her chair and threw down her napkin.

"Matthew Dean Dunphy," Mrs. Dunphy said. "That was very rude. I didn't raise you to talk to a lady that way. You apologize right this minute."

"What? It's true."

"I'm sorry, Mrs. Dunphy," Claudia broke in. "I simply can't sit here and listen to my friend be insulted in this manner. Dinner was lovely. Thank you." Claudia motioned to Jessie that they were leaving.

"Please, don't go," Mrs. Dunphy pleaded. "Matt. Apologize… now."

Matt stared at Jessie with pure dislike. "Okay, already. Sorry."

"There. Please, Claudia, Jessie, sit. We haven't even had dessert yet. I made a pie especially for the occasion. Let's not let one instance of ugliness"—she shot a disapproving glance at her son—"spoil an otherwise wonderful evening."

Jessie felt thoroughly humiliated. She wanted nothing more than to be done with this debacle. Still, Mrs. Dunphy had gone to a lot of trouble to prepare a delicious meal, and Jessie was loathe to punish a kind old lady for her son's boorishness.

"I'll only stay if it's all right with Jessie," Claudia said, still standing next to her chair. She looked at Jessie, waiting for her cue.

"Pie sounds good," Jessie said. "Let me help clear the table, ma'am."

"Oh, such impeccable manners," Mrs. Dunphy said, clearly relieved.

"I'll help too," Claudia added, as she picked up her plate and Matt's, without so much as a glance in his direction. When they were through the doors into the kitchen, Claudia came up alongside Jessie. Mrs. Dunphy, standing at the sink, had her back to them. "I'm so sorry, Jess," she whispered.

"I don't care what he thinks," Jessie answered.

"What he said hurt you. I could see it in your eyes, sugar. He was very wrong. You're beautiful, and every inch a woman."

"Let's get this over with," Jessie said, unwilling to continue the conversation and unable to look Claudia in the eye.

They ate hot apple pie with vanilla ice cream in awkward silence.

"Can I get you anything else?" Mrs. Dunphy asked, when they were done.

"No thank you, ma'am. That was yummy," Claudia said.

"Won't you stay for coffee?"

"I'm sorry, but we have to get back to the base," Jessie said.

"Of course you do. Boys, walk the ladies home."

"We'll be fine on our own, ma'am," Jessie said.

"Nonsense. The boys will see you back to the base like the gentlemen they are. Right, Matthew? Jordan?"

"Yes, ma'am," Jordan said.

Matt didn't answer; he simply stood up and took Claudia's arm.

The gesture set Jessie's teeth on edge.

Once they were outside, Matt said to Jordan, "She's all yours." His tone was derisive. "I'll take this pretty little thing, here, and don't bother waiting for us."

"We'll all walk together, or Jessie and I will continue on our own, thank you," Claudia said, before Jessie could say a word.

It was crystal clear to Jessie that Matt wasn't happy, but there wasn't much he could do about it. They walked on in silence until the gates at Avenger Field came into sight.

"I suppose if I want to kiss you goodnight I'll have to kiss her too," Matt said, sarcastically.

Jessie, who was a few steps behind with Jordan, increased her pace. Maybe if she was standing next to Claudia, she could prevent what was surely coming next.

"Who said anything about letting you kiss me goodnight after the way you behaved at dinner?"

"Come on. I apologized for that."

"Not sincerely, you didn't," Claudia said.

Before Jessie could reach them, Matt grabbed Claudia and crushed her to him. Jessie froze. It was as if everything faded away except for the sight of this arrogant son-of-a-bitch kissing her lover. Her stomach flipped and Jessie had to concentrate to keep her dinner down.

"You okay?" Jordan asked, beside her. "You don't look so good."

Jessie closed her eyes and ignored him.

"Jess, come on, let's go." Jessie opened her eyes at the sound of Claudia's voice. How much time had passed? She had no idea. Claudia pulled on her sleeve, and Jessie put one foot in front of the other.

Jessie didn't talk; she couldn't. What was there to say? If what happened at dinner embarrassed her and fed her insecurities, then watching Matt manhandle Claudia made her wish the earth would swallow her whole.

"It didn't mean anything, sugar," Claudia said, quietly. When Jessie didn't say anything, Claudia went on. "I didn't even want him to do it, I swear."

Jessie rubbed the center of her chest. Her heart hurt.

"C'mon, Jess. Say something."

"What do you want me to say? 'Gee, Claudia, what a swell evening?' What, exactly, do you want from me?" Jessie hated that her voice shook and that tears were flowing down her cheeks. She couldn't take it anymore. It was all too much. So she ran. She ran until her lungs burned and she had no air left in her. She ran until she couldn't hear Claudia calling after her anymore.

She bent over to catch her breath. When she straightened up, she realized she was standing in front of one of the hangars that housed the Vultee Valiants. She wandered inside and walked amongst the planes. She ran her hands along the steel and traced the contours of the fuselage. This was where she belonged. Airplanes and flying—these were things she understood.

The fact that she had picked the Valiants on this night, well, she thought, that just figured. It was the first plane she and Claudia flew together, on that trip to Palm Springs. Jessie's mind strayed. The first time they made love. The first time she admitted that she loved Claudia, and Claudia professed to feel the same way. The first time Jessie knew—really knew—where she belonged. Perhaps the only place she truly belonged other than in the air. And now that was being taken away from her.

Jessie rested her forehead against the cold steel. They were less than a week away from graduation. If she fought back now and made an issue of Claudia seeing Matt, it could very well jeopardize her place in the program and ruin everything. If they could somehow get through this week, Matt would be nothing more than a distant memory, and she and Claudia would be alone together, at last, hopefully on a base far away from here.

If only she could erase from her mind the image of Claudia's body pressed against Matt, of him devouring her mouth, of... Jessie shut her eyes tightly and shook her head, as if doing so would clear away the memory. She grabbed handfuls of hair and pulled—hard. Self-inflicted pain surely would be better than what she'd been through tonight.

Eventually, Jessie became aware that all had gone silent. She wasn't wearing a watch, so she stepped outside to see the position of the moon. "Damn." It was late, very late. Jessie had never missed a bed check before, but she was in serious danger of missing one now. She sprinted halfway across the base to the barracks and skidded to a halt in front of the door. The bay was dark; she'd missed it.

As quietly as she could, Jessie crept inside. She hadn't gotten three steps before she heard a voice whisper, "Don't worry. We all covered for you." It was Annabelle. "So, you were with a boy, huh? I want to hear all about it."

"A boy?" Jessie tried to kick her brain into gear.

"Yeah. Claudia said you were out on a date."

"Oh. Um, yeah."

"So?"

"Not much to tell, really."

"You miss your first bed check ever and there's not much to tell?"

"Nope." Jessie shrugged and walked toward her bed. When she got there, she could see the outline of someone in it. She paused, unsure what to do. She tapped her on the shoulder, except that it wasn't a her—it was a mannequin. Jessie had no idea which of the girls dreamed up the idea, or where they found the mannequin, but she was grateful that the ruse worked.

She closed herself in the bathroom, brushed her teeth and washed her face, donned her sleepwear, and turned out the light before heading to bed. She stowed the mannequin in her footlocker. As she did so, she was sure she felt Claudia watching her, but she couldn't face her tonight. She turned and walked around the other side of her bed, the side away from Claudia, crawled under the covers, and prayed for sleep to take her.

"Where did you go last night?" Claudia asked Jessie, as the girls lined up for drill to practice for graduation.

"I was with you or have you already forgotten I was there."

"Cute. I mean when you ran away. Where were you?"

"Why do you care?"

"Why do I...? Great. That's just great. I stick my neck out to keep you from getting into trouble for missing bed check and all you can do is be surly."

Of course it had been Claudia who came up with the mannequin. Jessie should have known. "Thanks for saving my bacon," she mumbled.

"You're welcome."

Any further conversation they might have had was cut off when the drill instructor began shouting commands. Two hours later, all of the girls walked off the parade grounds tired and dusty.

"Sakes alive," Shirley said, "I can't wait until this is over with."

"Me either," Janie agreed. "Hey Jessie, have you figured out yet where you want to be stationed?"

"I haven't really thought too much about it," Jessie answered.

"How about you, Claudia?"

"Not yet. Have you picked your spot?"

"It's between Camp Davis and Tyndall. Shirley and I are going to put in together. That way, we'll both know someone when we get where we're going."

"That's an excellent idea," Claudia said.

"We figured you and Jessie would be doing the same thing, seeing as how you two are so close," Shirley said. "Of course, now that you've both got fellas, maybe that changes things."

Jessie shut her eyes against a stab of pain in her chest. Did last night change anything for Claudia?

"I'm not going anywhere unless Jessie has my back."

Jessie's eyes popped back open. Relief coursed through her.

"Figured that," Annabelle said.

"What about you?" Claudia asked Annabelle.

"Rebecca and I are planning to stick together for the same reason. We all ought to be watching out for each other. Things are tough enough without having to go it on our own."

Jessie nodded. Getting her and Claudia stationed in the same place would be easier if other pairs of girls were trying to do the same thing.

Claudia must have been thinking along the same lines, because she shot Jessie a sideways glance and winked as she peeled off toward one of the hangars.

Hours passed before Jessie saw Claudia again. "How was your flight? Were you okay up there?"

"Yeah," Claudia smiled, "thanks for asking, and thanks for caring."

"Surely you don't doubt that I care, Claude."

Claudia pivoted to face her so quickly Jessie took a step backward. "Ah ha! So, it's a given that you care, but it's not clear to you that I feel the same about you."

Jessie studied her boots. "That's different."

"How is that different, Jess? Explain it to me. Why do you suddenly think I've stopped caring?"

Jessie's eyes welled up, and she turned her head so Claudia wouldn't see. "It wasn't me you were kissing last night," she said, her voice strangled and strained.

"Oh, sugar. I didn't kiss Matt." Jessie opened her mouth to point out the obvious, but Claudia put her fingers over Jessie's lips. "He kissed me. If that's what you want to call that...that...assault." Claudia made a face. "I didn't ask for that, you know. He didn't exactly request my permission."

"You didn't stop him."

"I pushed him away as soon as I could, but you probably didn't see that, did you?"

"No."

"Do you really think so little of me that you believe I'd welcome his attention, even while I'm in love with someone else? And that I'd invite that kiss while that someone else was watching? Doesn't say much for me, Jess, now does it?"

Jessie sat down heavily on a nearby bench. "I think the world of you, Claude. It's just...I had a really, really bad night, and by that time I wasn't feeling too good about myself. So when the kiss happened..."

"You thought I'd be tempted, that I might enjoy it."

Jessie nodded.

"Well, you thought wrong. Dead wrong. All I could think about was how much I wanted it to be you. How much I wish you and I could kiss like that in public, without worrying about anyone seeing or what anyone else thought."

"Really? Cross your heart?"

"And hope to die." Claudia crossed her heart with her hand and sat down next to Jessie. "Where did you run off to? I was so worried about you."

"I didn't know where I was going. I ended up in one of the hangars with the Valiants. After a while, I realized it must be getting late, so I ran back to the barracks. Thanks for covering for me." She bumped Claudia with her shoulder. "The mannequin was genius."

"You're welcome." Claudia wagged a finger at her. "Now don't let that become a habit—unless I'm with you."

Jessie smiled for the first time in what seemed like days.

"That's a sight I love to see. So"—Claudia pulled a sheaf of papers out of her flight suit—"where would you like to settle together? I've been studying the options." She spread the papers out between them.

Jessie scanned the pages. "How about Las Vegas or Love Field in Dallas? Vegas is growing by leaps and bounds, and Dallas is hopping. I'm sure we can live together without creating too much of a fuss, and the flying would be challenging."

Claudia studied the choices. "Las Vegas could be fun. We'd be flying B-17s, B-26s, AT-10s, and AT-6s—nothing we can't handle. They're looking for instrument instructors and safety pilots. We're certainly qualified for that."

"Mmm-hmm. Flying the Widowmaker might be a kick."

"Easy, champ. There'll be no widows here. At Love we could fly fighters. Bet that appeals to you, huh, hotshot?"

"I wouldn't turn down the opportunity."

"What's our fall back?"

"Hmm… How about Victorville in California or Randolph in San Antonio? They're probably not as big, but the assignments might be interesting."

"True. So the plan is to take our requests directly to Cochran, right?"

"Right. You do it."

"Me? Why me?"

"Because, Claude, you have a way with people, and Cochran obviously likes you. After all, she was willing to risk her life going up with you the other night."

"Oh, all right." Claudia gathered up the papers. "I'll put it in writing and deliver it in person."

"That's my girl."

"Yes, I am, and don't you forget it."

Jessie wished more than anything that they could go somewhere so that she could hold Claudia close, feel their bodies slide together, reconnect. It had been too long. "Claude—"

"I know, sugar. Soon, we'll be living alone together, and we can hold each other all night long, every night."

"How did you know what I was thinking?"

Claudia's eyes sparkled. "Like I always say. I want to play poker with you—for a lot of money."

"Never going to happen." Jessie pulled Claudia to her feet.

"That's a crying shame, sugar. I could use the dough."

"Tell it to someone who has some, because that sure as shooting isn't me."

"So much for marrying for money."

CHAPTER ELEVEN

Graduation Day dawned sunny, hot, and windy. All the girls were chattering excitedly as they donned their uniforms and shined their boots.

"Hey Claudia, are your folks coming today?" Janie asked.

"Sure are, but only for the ceremony. My dad has to be back to work early tomorrow morning."

Jessie winced. The thought of meeting Claudia's parents made her so nervous her palms were sweating. Claudia said it was no big deal, but Jessie was deathly afraid that Mr. and Mrs. Sherwood would take one look at her and find her wanting. She'd never met anyone who had the kind of money the Sherwoods did. She was just a hick from the sticks.

"Is that dreamy boy you were kissing the other night coming too?" Rebecca asked.

Claudia and Jessie both looked up sharply.

"Don't think we didn't see that, little miss innocent. Oh, is he a looker."

"He can kiss me anytime," Shirley said, as she danced around the bay with a pillow.

Claudia cast a glance at Jessie. "I don't know. He didn't say."

"What about you, Jessie? Is that sweet, red-headed boy coming to see you march?"

"Search me."

"Say, we're all planning to have a picnic at Sweetwater Lake after the ceremony. Why don't you invite the boys along? We've got fellas coming too," Annabelle said.

Jessie busied herself polishing the buttons on her jacket.

"I don't know," Claudia said. "The boys probably have plans. Matt is due to ship out tomorrow."

"You'll never know unless you ask," Janie said. "What have you got to lose?"

Everything. Jessie swallowed hard. It wasn't enough that she had to contend with Claudia's parents, now she would have to worry about Matt too.

"Step lively, girls. It's show time."

The six women joined the rest of their class on the parade grounds. As they marched in formation, crowds cheered from either side. There were friends and family, an incoming class of WASPs, other WASP classes that were at various points in their training, instructors, and townspeople.

Jackie Cochran pinned on Jessie's silver wings, and for the first time in a long time, Jessie missed her mom. She wished she could have been there to see her standing tall and strong in her dress uniform. She hoped her mom would have been proud.

When the class was dismissed for the last time, everyone threw their berets up in the air and let out a whoop. There were hugs, pats on the back, and tearful goodbyes.

Jessie looked for Claudia but didn't see her. She started to walk toward the barracks, when she heard someone call her name.

"Jessie? Over here."

Jessie turned in the direction of the voice and spotted Mrs. Dunphy waving an American flag. *Perfect.* Jessie didn't want to be rude, so she waved.

Mrs. Dunphy motioned her over.

"Hello, dear. You look splendid. I'm so proud of you and Claudia. Oh. Matt and Jordan are here too. I sent them off to find Claudia."

Although Mrs. Dunphy's mouth continued to move, Jessie stopped listening. She excused herself and jogged off to find Claudia herself, hopefully before the boys did.

It didn't take her long. Claudia was standing with a striking woman who looked like an older version of her, a dashing man in an expensive business suit, and... Jessie's heart sank. Matt, in all his spit-shined, AAF-uniformed glory.

"Jess," Claudia called when the crowd around them thinned. "Come meet my folks."

Jessie took a deep breath, painted a smile on her face, and straightened her already-perfect uniform jacket.

"Mom, Dad, this is Jessie Keaton. She's the best pilot this program has ever known, except for maybe Jackie Cochran, herself. Jessie, this is my mom and dad."

"It's a pleasure to meet you," Jessie said, stiffly.

"Claudia's been raving about you," Mrs. Sherwood said. "She tells us you'll be stationed together in Las Vegas."

"Yes, ma'am."

"Take good care of our daughter."

"I will, ma'am."

"Enough of that, Elizabeth," Mr. Sherwood said. "Matt, tell us about what's going on with our boys in the war."

Jessie faded into the background as Matt blustered on about fighting the Germans in the air and facing off against the vaunted Luftwaffe. Mr. Sherwood seemed to hang on every word. Jessie had never felt more superfluous.

As soon as she was able, she made her excuses and headed back to the barracks. On the way, she encountered Jordan.

"Congratulations, Jessie. I think it's neat."

Jessie wanted to dislike him, but it was hard. He was so innocuous. "Thanks." After an awkward silence, she said, "I'm a little surprised to see you here."

"Yeah, well, Matt promised me a piece of his mother's apple pie if I came, so…"

"Ah, that explains it." Jessie started to walk away, but Jordan put a hand on her arm.

"I, um, I really do like you, Jessie. I think you're swell. It's just…I'm shy, you know?"

"Yeah. That's okay, Jordan. You're a nice guy, and I appreciate that you're not…" Jessie searched for the words.

"Obnoxious like Matt?" Jordan supplied.

Jessie laughed. "Something like that."

"He's not as bad as you think. Really. I've known him since we were in diapers. He watches out for his buddies…doesn't let anybody take advantage of us or anything."

"That's nice."

"Sort of like what you do for Claudia, if you think about it."

Jessie didn't want to think about it. "I've got to run, Jordan."

"You know Matt is shipping out tomorrow, right?"

"I heard."

Jordan shrugged. "So Matt heard about the picnic at the lake this afternoon, and he's pushing me to come along."

"I bet." Jessie narrowed her eyes as she imagined Matt trying to get her out of the way so he could be alone with Claudia.

"I won't go if you don't want me to."

Jessie looked at Jordan. He was so earnest, so honorable. "Nah, come along. It'll be fun."

"Okay." Jordan's face brightened. "I'll see you there. Thanks, Jessie."

"You're welcome." Jessie shook her head and continued on her way to the barracks. She tried to convince herself that if they could make it through today, tomorrow she and Claudia would be on their way to Las Vegas and home free.

She quickened her pace. "Man, I wish it was tomorrow already."

⋟⋞

"I wish you would've stayed longer, Jess."

"Your parents weren't interested in me, Claude. They were too interested in Matt."

Claudia sat down on Jessie's bed. "Daddy, maybe…you know, that man-to-man stuff. But Mother really wanted to get to know you."

"I'm sorry. I just felt like an outsider."

"I wanted my folks to get used to you being around. You know, so that it seems natural when I invite you home with me."

Jessie shook her head. "Someone like me doesn't belong in that kind of environment."

"Nonsense," Claudia said. "What does 'someone like me' mean, anyway?"

Jessie fiddled with one of her buttons. "Come on, Claudia. I'm the girl who chops your wood and starts your fire, not the one you invite in for afternoon tea."

"First of all, you can start my fire anytime, sugar," Claudia's voice dropped to that melodious, deep register that set Jessie on fire. "Second, we don't have afternoon tea."

"You know full well what I mean. Don't pretend you don't."

Claudia stood swiftly, hands on hips. "Do I strike you as being elitist, Jessie Keaton?"

"No, but—"

"But nothing. You're not being fair to me, my parents, or yourself. So stop it right now."

"Matt and Jordan are planning to be at the picnic," Jessie said, deliberately changing the subject.

"I heard."

"I wish we could skip it."

"Everybody's going to be there, Jess. It will look really bad if we don't show."

"We could tell them we have to leave early for Vegas."

"We have train tickets for tomorrow. Where would we spend the night tonight? You're not being realistic."

Jessie sighed. "I know."

"It won't be so horrible. It's the last chance to spend time with all the girls in one place, there'll be sandwiches, cookies, and pies, and we can go swimming together."

"But I can't touch you."

"Not today, no. But tomorrow night when we get to Las Vegas…"

Claudia didn't have to finish the sentence for Jessie's imagination to run wild. Now, if they could only get through today.

❧

The gathering was in full swing by the time Jessie and Claudia arrived. Picnic blankets were spread out everywhere, bodies were bobbing in the water, the girls were singing songs, and everyone seemed to be enjoying a last hurrah.

"Hey girls, over here." Rebecca, Shirley, Annabelle, and Janie and their dates had commandeered an area under a shade tree not far from the water's edge.

"Isn't this grand?" Janie asked.

"Swell," Claudia said.

"Dig in, we've got enough food to feed the entire Army Air Forces."

Jessie was famished, so she was only too happy to accept the invitation. She was halfway through a bologna and cheese sandwich when Matt and Jordan came strolling over.

"Hiya, girls. Mind if we join you?"

"No, of course not," Shirley said. "Get yourselves something to eat and have a seat." She patted the spot next to her, even though she already had a boy sitting on her other side. "You don't mind, Claudia, do you?" She playfully batted her eyelashes.

Claudia laughed and formally introduced Matt and Jordan to the girls and the other guys, leaving Shirley for last. "Watch out for that one."

"I can see that," Matt said. "Sorry…Shirley, was it? I've only got eyes for that pretty little thing." He pointed to Claudia.

"Too bad," Jessie muttered under her breath. She nodded a greeting to Jordan and ignored Matt completely.

After a while, Rebecca suggested they all take a dip in the lake to cool off. "We can all run in at the same time and see who gets there first."

"No fair, the boys have an automatic advantage," Annabelle complained, as they all stood up and readied themselves to go in.

"Actually," Matt said, grabbing Claudia's arm. "We're going to take a walk around the lake."

"Ooh, a nice, romantic stroll. You two love birds have fun," Shirley said, before Jessie could get a word out.

Jessie tried but failed to catch Claudia's eye as Matt pulled her in the direction of a wooded path.

She started after them, but Janie called, "Come on, Jessie. Let them go."

Jessie was torn. More than anything, she didn't want to let Claudia and Matt out of her sight. But there really was no plausible excuse to follow them. With a heavy heart, she waded into the water.

While everyone else was splashing around and having fun, Jessie kept her eyes trained on the tree line. The path around the lake wasn't visible from the water, but still she strained to catch a flash of clothing, a shadow—anything that might reveal the whereabouts of her lover.

"Aren't you going to play with us, Jessie?" Rebecca asked. "Jordan here isn't having much fun without you."

"I'm not much of a swimmer." It was a lie, but Jessie was in no mood to play.

Just when she decided she couldn't stand it anymore, Claudia emerged from the trees alone. Even from her vantage point in the water, Jessie could see that something wasn't right. She dashed out of the water and met Claudia before she reached the blanket.

Claudia had a far away, dazed look that frightened Jessie. "What's wrong? Claude?" Jessie moved to touch her on the shoulder, but Claudia shied away.

"Take me home, Jess." Her voice was shaking and her hair was disheveled.

"Where's Matt?" Not that Jessie cared about him, but she couldn't help wondering why Claudia had returned alone. "Did he do something out there? Did he hurt you?" Jessie narrowed her eyes and curled her hands into fists. "If he touched you, I swear I'll tear him limb from limb."

"N-no." Claudia absently straightened her blouse. "Please, Jess. No more questions. Just take me home."

"Okay. I'll get our things and tell the other girls we're going."

Claudia didn't answer or react.

Jessie thought about saying goodbye to Jordan, but she was too worried about Claudia to bother.

She ran to the water's edge and yelled to Annabelle that they were leaving. Then she jogged to the blanket and gathered up their towels and her clothes. She fumbled with her pant legs before managing to get dressed and put her shoes on. When she looked back, Claudia was staring straight ahead. Something was very wrong. Apart from Matt hurting Claudia, Jessie couldn't imagine what it might be, but she'd already asked that, and Claudia had denied it. Whatever it was, Jessie wanted to get to the bottom of it. "Are you okay?" she asked, when she returned to Claudia.

"I need to go home."

"Okay, I'll take you there right now. Here we go."

Jessie tried to sort through the possibilities in her mind. She noted that Claudia walked slowly, stepping carefully—a definite contrast to her usual energetic pace. She kept her eyes straight ahead, never once glancing at Jessie or engaging in conversation.

"Everything okay?" Jessie asked, when they were halfway back to the base.

Claudia moved off to the side of the road and vomited.

When Jessie started rubbing soothing circles on Claudia's back, Claudia jumped at the contact. "All right, Claude." Jessie turned Claudia to face her. "What's going on?"

"Nothing."

"This is not nothing." She made a sweeping gesture to encompass Claudia's appearance. "Look at me, Claude." Jessie waited until Claudia made eye contact. "I'm going to ask you one more time, and this time I want a straight answer. Did that jerk do anything to you? Did he hurt or manhandle you? Force you—"

"No!" Claudia cried. Her eyes were wild and wide as saucers.

Surprised at her vehemence, Jessie took a step backward.

"I already told you no, why can't you just believe me? Why must you push me?" Claudia touched a trembling hand to her blouse.

"I just—"

"Well, don't just. Asked and answered." Claudia closed her eyes.

"I'm sorry, Claude. I only—"

"Take me home, Jess." Claudia's voice shook as she pleaded. "I'm not feeling well. Please, just take me home."

Jessie's heart ached to see her girl in such a state, so she relented. "We're almost there, honey."

When they got back to the barracks, Claudia said she needed to take a shower. She gathered up some fresh clothes and a towel and disappeared into the bathroom.

Jessie heard the shower turn on, and she busied herself packing her duffle bag for the long train ride ahead. She smiled to herself. By this time tomorrow night, she and Claudia would be settled into The Last Frontier temporarily while they found a place to rent off base.

Jessie was folding her last uniform blouse when she realized the shower was still running. She checked the time. Claudia had been in there for nearly twenty minutes—far longer than the usual seven to ten it took her to shower.

"Claude?" Jessie knocked on the door. "You okay in there?"

There was no answer.

"Claude, hon? It's me, Jessie. Everything okay?"

Still no answer. Jessie started to get nervous. What if Claudia had fallen and hit her head? Jessie chewed her lip. "To heck with it, if she wants to be mad at me, she can."

She cracked open the door. Claudia was sitting on the floor of the shower, still fully clothed in the outfit she wore to the lake. "Claude!" Jessie entered the bathroom and closed the door behind her. She turned off the faucet and squatted next to Claudia.

Claudia didn't move.

"Claude? You're scaring me. Talk to me, honey."

Claudia's teeth were chattering, and her lips were blue. Jessie grabbed the towel.

"Can you stand up? You want me to help you? Are you feeling light-headed?"

Slowly, Claudia rose.

"Let's get you out of these wet clothes." Jessie reached for the top button of Claudia's blouse, but Claudia took a step back. Stung, Jessie dropped her hands.

"I'll do it," Claudia said, her voice so soft Jessie barely heard her. She turned away from Jessie and unbuttoned her blouse. "Go ahead back out there. I'll be out in a minute."

"This is a heck of a time to get modest on me, Claude. What if you throw up again or faint?"

Claudia reached back and took the towel from Jessie. "I'll call you if I have a problem."

"You're sure?" There was something dead, something foreign in Claudia's eyes. It was unsettling.

"Yes."

"Okay. I'll be right outside."

Claudia nodded but made no other move, and Jessie realized with a start that she was waiting for her to leave before getting undressed the rest of the way.

Jessie paced the length of the bay. She'd never seen Claudia act like this. Then again, she told herself, it had been a long and emotional day—first the graduation and her parents, then the picnic and Matt... Where had Matt gone? Jessie figured he'd be stuck to Claudia like glue. But then, if she'd gotten sick on their walk, it wouldn't be the least bit surprising for an oaf like him to abandon a damsel in distress.

Damsel in distress—wasn't that the term Hutchins had used? This was all her fault. If she hadn't stuck her nose in, there never would've been a Matt, and Jessie would've been the one walking in the woods with Claudia when she fell ill. *Damn.*

Maybe Claudia had the flu or food poisoning, or maybe it was just nerves about the move. Whatever it was, Jessie hoped she'd be feeling better soon; otherwise, it was going to be a difficult trip tomorrow.

As Jessie got closer to the bathroom once again, she could have sworn she heard the shower turn off. Hadn't she done that when she went into the bathroom earlier? She stood in front of the door, debating whether to knock again, when Claudia opened the door and emerged.

Her hair was shiny like she had just washed it, and her skin was pink as if she'd rubbed it too hard.

"Feel better?"

Claudia nodded.

"Where are your wet clothes?"

"They were ruined. I threw them out."

"You…" Jessie took a step into the bathroom.

"Where are you going?"

"You don't just throw clothes away. We'll wash and dry them, and they'll be good as new."

"No!" Claudia seemed on the verge of panic. "They're ruined. Leave them alone."

"Okay." Jessie held up her hands in surrender. "The girls will be back soon. Do you want a hug before they get here?"

Claudia ignored the question. "I'd better pack." She removed her suitcase from under her bunk.

"Claude? Did I do something wrong?" Jessie sat down on her own bed.

"Of course not. Why would you say that?"

"Well, it seems like you don't want me anywhere near you, so…"

"I'm just not feeling well. I'm sure I'll be better by tomorrow."

"Is it something you ate? Or the flu?"

Claudia paused in her packing and bowed her head. Her shoulders were shaking, and Jessie could hear her sobbing.

"Claude?" She stood and started to take Claudia in her arms but stopped mid-motion when Claudia held up a hand to stop her.

"I'm fine."

"You are a lot of things, but fine isn't one of them."

"It's been a long day, and I'm sick to my stomach. I just can't handle being touched right now, okay?"

"Sure. I was only trying to help."

"I know. I'm sorry, Jess. I'm just a mess. You're right—it's probably the flu."

Jessie lay down on her bed and put her hands under her head. "Okay. I'll be right here if you need me."

"Yeah. Thanks."

Jessie watched Claudia pack out of the corner of her eye. After a while she said, "Matt left you out there by yourself when you weren't feeling well? The guy really is a jerk."

Jessie could have sworn Claudia's hands shook, and then she ran into the bathroom. Jessie heard her throwing up again. She would have given anything to be able to hold Claudia's hair away from her face and rub her back, but she didn't think her efforts would be welcome.

If Claudia wasn't feeling better by morning, the train ride was going to be hell for her. Jessie supposed they could postpone the trip a day or two if they had to, but they were due to report to the base at the Las Vegas Army Air Field at 0800 sharp on Monday morning. She wasn't sure what the consequences would be if they were late for their assignment, but she was sure they wouldn't be good.

CHAPTER TWELVE

Jessie woke several times during the night to check on Claudia. At one point, she could've sworn she heard her crying.

She whispered, "Claude, are you awake?" She got no response. She asked one more time, and again was met with silence. Jessie guessed she must have imagined the sobbing, and went back to sleep.

At first light, when Jessie stirred, Claudia already was up, showered, and dressed. She sat on the edge of her bed, watching Jessie.

"Hey. How long have you been awake? It's barely dawn." Jessie yawned.

"Awhile."

"I can see that much." Jessie sat up and stretched. The other girls were still asleep, since none of them were due to leave until later in the morning. "You feeling any better?"

"Yes, thanks."

But she didn't look that much better. Her eyes were red and puffy and her skin was unnaturally pale.

"You sure?"

"Uh-huh."

"Because if you're not feeling up to it, we could probably stay a day or two longer and still make Vegas in time for—"

"No! I want to leave today."

"Okay. That's settled, then. Why don't you give me a few minutes to get ready, and we can go over to the mess and get some breakfast? That is, if your stomach is up to it."

"Fine."

"Be out in a jiff." Jessie gathered her toiletries and headed for the bathroom. Claudia still didn't seem right, but at least she was upright and talking, which was an improvement.

"How about some oatmeal?" Jessie asked, as they moved through the breakfast line. "That might be easy on your stomach."

"Okay."

They ate mostly in silence, except when some of the other girls in their class dropped by to say farewell.

"You can stop watching me like a hawk, Jess. I'm better."

"I just worry about you, that's all. It's my job, you know."

"Is it?"

"Your mother specifically told me to watch out for you. I sure wouldn't want to cross her."

"You, intimidated by my mother? That's a joke."

"Ah ha!"

"What?"

"I got a ghost of a smile out of you. Now I feel better."

Claudia made a face at her.

"What time do you want to leave for the train station? Annabelle said she'd take us."

"Right after breakfast is good with me."

"The train's not for a couple of hours yet."

"Can't hurt to get there early."

"I sure hope we don't run into the boys." Jessie said, as they got up to clear their plates. "I don't suppose Matt said anything about turning up at the train station before he takes off, did he?"

Claudia's plate clattered to the ground from her suddenly boneless fingers. She quickly bent to clean up the mess.

Jessie squatted alongside her to help. "Here, I can get that. Is it your stomach again? Are you feeling faint? Why don't you sit down?"

"I'm fine. Just clumsy, that's all."

"Anyway, maybe we'll get lucky and he'll forget what time we're leaving."

Claudia paused, then resumed mopping up the spill with a napkin.

Jessie spied one of their bunkmates carrying a tray with food. "There's Shirley. Let's ask her. She was busy pumping Jordan for information. Maybe he said something to her." She motioned Shirley over.

"I don't suppose you managed to wheedle out of Jordan what time Matt was taking off today?"

Shirley looked at her watch. "He should be clearing the tower right about now. Jordan was going along to watch. Why?" Shirley nudged Jessie. "Were you hoping for a last send off?"

"Just curious, that's all." When Shirley walked away, Jessie said, "Guess we don't have to worry about Matt anymore."

"That's great."

"Yeah?" Jessie glanced at Claudia to gauge her sincerity.

"Of course. Why would you even ask that?"

"I don't know," Jessie shrugged. "I wasn't sure if you'd want to say goodbye."

"No! Can we not talk about boys anymore?"

Jessie brightened. "Okay by me. Let's go get our gear, say adios, and skedaddle."

The girls all said tearful goodbyes, with promises to write and keep in touch, and Jessie and Claudia were on their way.

Not having slept well the previous night, Jessie tried to nap on the ride. She woke several times to see Claudia staring out the window. She hadn't said much since they left Sweetwater, and Jessie wondered what was going through her mind.

"Are you worried about our assignment?"

"Me? No. Are you?"

"No. How's your stomach?"

"I'm fine, like I told you the other fifty times you asked."

Jessie frowned. It wasn't in Claudia's happy-go-lucky nature to snap. "Sorry if you think I'm a pain."

"It's not that." Claudia rubbed her hands over her eyes. "It-it's just been a long couple of days. Waiting for the decision on our posting, my folks..."

"You being sick. I get it, Claude. I won't bother you anymore." Jessie closed her eyes again.

When next she opened them, it was dark outside. Claudia was still staring out the window. Jessie could see her reflection. Her eyes were swollen, and Jessie thought she saw moisture on her cheeks. "Are you…" Jessie wanted to ask if she was all right, but she cut herself off. There was no point asking a question that seemed only to annoy her lover. Jessie felt very much at sea. She had no idea what to do or how to act.

Claudia crossed her arms over her chest and seemed to pull into herself.

Maybe when they got settled in, Claudia would come around. Jessie sure hoped so. She missed her girl.

When they arrived at the hotel, Claudia got ready for bed first. By the time Jessie took a shower and emerged from the bathroom, Claudia was sound asleep, curled up on her side close to the far edge of the bed.

Jessie watched her sleep for a while. Some of her color had returned, but even in repose she seemed tense. Her eyes flickered under her lids and her forehead was creased with worry lines.

Wanting nothing more than to snuggle up behind Claudia and hold her, Jessie slipped under the covers and wrapped an arm around to pull her close.

Claudia screamed and struggled to get away. She jumped out of the bed and stood next to it, breathing hard, chest heaving, eyes wild.

Jessie was thunderstruck. She lay there looking up at Claudia, wondering what she had done wrong. "Claude?" When Claudia didn't immediately respond, Jessie began to cry. "I-I'm sorry. I only wanted to hold you. It's been so long."

Claudia sat down on the side of the bed and put a tentative hand on Jessie's shoulder. "I must have been having a nightmare. You startled me, that's all. I'm sorry, Jess. You didn't do anything wrong. I'm just jumpy."

Jessie ran her fingers through her hair and fought to get her emotions under control. "I miss my carefree Claude. I miss my lover. My girl. I don't know what to do to make it right, whatever it is. But I want to. I really want to. Make it right, I mean. Tell me what to do, Claude. Please, tell me and I'll do it."

Claudia got back under the covers. "Just hold me tonight, sugar. Can you do that?"

Jessie nodded. "Will you let me?"

"Yes. Yes, I will."

Jessie opened her arms and Claudia lay her head on Jessie's shoulder. A short while later, Jessie heard Claudia's breathing even out in sleep. She closed her eyes and breathed in the smell of her hair, her soap, her essence. This was how she wanted to spend the rest of her life—with Claudia nestled safely in her arms.

Tomorrow, once they found a new home of their own and got settled, everything would fall into place. Jessie was sure of it.

Jessie and Claudia spent the morning wandering around town, getting acquainted with the layout and proximity to the base, shopping for necessities, and looking for a place to live.

On the fourth try, they found a small bungalow for rent on the bus route. It was little more than a shack, with two tiny bedrooms, a kitchen, a bathroom, and a living room, but it would afford them privacy and easy transport to the base. Because it had two bedrooms, even the most suspicious visitor would be appeased.

By evening, they had moved their stuff in and rearranged the furniture to suit their liking.

"Not half bad," Claudia said, wiping the sweat from her brow as she surveyed the living room. "It isn't exactly a palace fit for a queen, but it will do."

"As long as it has you in it, I don't care if it's a shanty."

"Is that so?"

"That's so," Jessie said. Tentatively, she approached Claudia. They hadn't discussed last night's episode, and Jessie still hadn't figured out exactly how to act. "Is it okay to hug you?"

By way of an answer, Claudia opened her arms. She sighed heavily against Jessie's chest. "I'm sorry I've been so…"

"Different?" Jessie supplied.

"Prickly," Claudia said.

"You're forgiven," Jessie murmured into her hair, "as long as I can have my warm, fun-loving, affectionate lover back."

"I promise to try."

131

"Let me know if I have to send out a search party to find her."

"Will do."

"Are you hungry?"

"No. Just tired."

"How tired? You know, this is our last night before we have to report."

"I know."

"It's been forever, Claude." Jessie felt Claudia tense. "If you're still not feeling well or you don't want to…"

"It isn't that…" Claudia became quiet, but rather than interrupt, Jessie decided to wait her out.

"I suppose we should do *something* to celebrate being out from under Hutchins's thumb."

"Don't even mention her name."

"Whose name?" Claudia asked, as she took Jessie by the hand and led her toward the bedroom they decided would be theirs.

In the dim light of the lone lamp, Jessie watched Claudia undress. "Can I help with that?" she asked, as Claudia struggled to reach her bra clasp.

Jessie brushed aside strands of thick, luxurious hair and kissed the side of Claudia's neck. "I love you, Claude. So much." Jessie undid the bra and swept it off Claudia's shoulders. She turned Claudia to face her….and let out a strangled cry. "My God, Claude. You've got bruises everywhere."

Claudia crossed her arms over her chest and looked away. "They're from the accident."

"Still? That was almost two weeks ago." Jessie gently ran her fingers over black and blue splotches that dotted Claudia's arms, shoulders, and collarbones. Claudia shuddered. "Honey, if you're still hurting we don't have to…"

Tears glistened on Claudia's lashes. Jessie caught one on the tip of her finger. Claudia swallowed hard and lifted her chin higher. "I want to. I want to make love with you, sugar. Touch me."

Jessie rained feather-light kisses on each bruise, careful not to use too much pressure. The sight of so many marks marring

Claudia's skin reminded Jessie how close she had come to losing her in the crash. "Is this okay, honey?"

"Come here and kiss me."

The kiss was slow and careful, tender and worshipful. Only their lips and tongues touched, yet Jessie felt sparks all along the length of her body.

Claudia traced Jessie's face, as if memorizing each pore. "I love you, sugar. Don't ever forget that."

"How could I, with you here to remind me constantly?" Jessie smothered Claudia's response with another kiss, this one more insistent, more passionate. It had been almost three weeks since the last time they made love—before the accident, before Hutchins, before Matt Dunphy... She felt, rather than heard, Claudia's gasp, and pulled back. "Did I hurt you?"

"No. M-make love to me, sugar. Please. Make sweet love to me. I want to forget everything in the world but you."

There was something haunting in Claudia's tone, something in her expression, that reached deep into Jessie's soul. Jessie would think about it later, she was sure, but right now, she wanted only to make this night, this moment, the most special Claudia had ever experienced.

They made love for hours, not with abandon, but with reverence. "Welcome home, love. I promise you, no matter where we are in the world, in my arms you will always be home."

"Oh, Jess." Claudia buried her head in the side of Jessie's neck and cried. Even though her voice was muffled, her words were clear. "You mean everything to me. Promise me that nothing can come between us. Promise me I'll always be yours."

"You'll always be my girl, Claude. Now and forever."

They fell asleep that way—Claudia nestled into Jessie's side, Jessie carefully cradling her so as not to cause her pain.

When they woke at first light, Jessie was gratified to see that the shadows had receded from Claudia's eyes, and her color had returned. It wasn't everything, Jessie realized, as she surveyed the numerous bruises covering Claudia's beautiful skin, but it was a good start to their new adventure.

❖❖

The days at the air base literally flew by. Jessie and Claudia were in the air more often than they were on the ground, rarely seeing much of each other until dinnertime.

Jessie was tasked with teaching the inexperienced male pilots how to fly by instruments and taking them up for checkout rides to ensure proficiency on some of the more challenging aircraft.

Claudia would come home at night and tell Jessie funny stories about ferrying VIPs from base to base and occasionally about towing targets for new soldiers who were using live ammunition and whose aim was often questionable. Several times, Claudia's plane accidentally was hit by stray fire. Although Jessie worried about her safety, Claudia always made light of the close calls.

They settled into a comfortable routine, rising at first light, eating a quick breakfast together before heading to the air field, and riding the bus home together at night. Jessie cooked dinner, Claudia washed the dishes, then they would sit together and talk about their day. Often they would make love before falling asleep in each other's arms.

Outside of work, neither Jessie nor Claudia socialized with anyone. They rarely went out or even to the canteen, except for the occasional milkshake or ice cream sundae.

Within a few weeks, Claudia's bruises faded, but not her new-found reserve. When they were alone, Claudia was relaxed and carefree. When they were in public, Jessie noted that Claudia no longer went out of her way to engage others in conversation, and her natural exuberance was missing.

Since it meant fewer boys flirting with her, Jessie didn't know whether to be grateful for Claudia's reticence...or concerned. For the time being, she remained a little of both.

About a month into their assignment, one of the other instructors stopped Jessie as she was walking back into the ready room after a flight. "There's someone here asking for you."

"Is that right?"

"Says she's a friend of yours."

"Who is it?"

"Can't remember her name, but she's waiting over in the canteen for you."

Jessie jogged off in the direction of the canteen, wondering all the while who the mystery person could be. As soon as she walked in, she smiled. There was Shirley, holding court with all the flyboys, drinking a milkshake at the counter.

"Some things never change."

"Jessie!" Shirley stood up and gave Jessie a big hug. "I was hoping I could find you and Claudia. Gosh, it's good to see you."

"What are you doing here?"

"Delivering an AT-10."

"No kidding. How's Janie doing?"

"Haven't you heard? She's engaged."

"Our Janie?"

"Yep. Gonna marry her an instructor at Christmas."

"Wow."

"That reminds me, she sent me with wedding invitations for you and Claudia. She wants all of us girls to be there. Speaking of which, where's Claudia?"

"Off fetching some bigwig from another base, I think. She should be back any minute."

"Good. It'll be great to see her."

"How long are you staying for?"

"The Widowmaker they want me to fly back won't be ready until tomorrow, so I'm stuck here for the night. I was sort of hoping y'all would be able to help me out with a place to sack out."

"Sure," Jessie said. In her mind, she frantically reviewed the state of the bungalow. Were there any obvious signs that she and Claudia were sharing the same bed? "I'll even cook you dinner."

"How very domestic of you. Don't you girls hit the town at night?"

"Nah." Jessie tried to come up with a convincing reason why she and Claudia never went out. "By the end of the day, we're beat. Plus, it saves money to stay home."

"I might have figured you for a homebody but not our girl Claudia. Maybe she was more serious about that boy Matt than I thought."

The sound of his name set Jessie's teeth on edge. She shrugged. It was easier than giving an answer that would invite further questions.

Jessie looked at the clock on the wall. "If you're coming, we'd better head to the bus stop. Claudia will be there any minute."

When they arrived, Claudia already was sitting on the bench. "Shirley?" Claudia jumped up and gave Shirley a warm hug. It was the most animated Jessie had seen her since leaving Sweetwater. "What are doing here?"

"Like I told Jessie, they needed someone to ferry an AT-10 over here. I knew y'all were stationed here, and, since I hadn't heard from either of you, I accepted the assignment so I could check on y'all."

"I'm glad."

"Shirley's looking to bunk with us tonight," Jessie said. "I figured I could give her my room and I could sleep in with you, since it's only for a night."

"I don't want to put you out of your bed, Jessie."

"It's no big deal. I don't mind sharing," Claudia said, quickly. "And wait until you taste Jessie's cooking. She's really good."

"Hey, Shirl, you could come shopping with me and pick out the ingredients while Claudia goes home and gets my room ready for you. Right, Claude?"

"Yep, sounds good to me."

Shirley looked from one of them to the other. "You two are so domesticated it's frightening. Don't y'all have any fun around here? We could hit one of those casinos and make some money."

"More likely lose some money," Claudia said. "They're not in the business of letting you take their profits, you know."

"Yeah, but imagine all the gorgeous flyboys I could meet while I was losing my dough."

Claudia laughed and shook her head. "Some things never change, Shirl."

CHAPTER THIRTEEN

When they arrived home from the store, Claudia was sitting on the sofa, reading a magazine. She looked for all the world as if she'd been there for hours, but Jessie knew better. She could see that "her" room had been readied—her clothes hung on hangers in the door-less closet, and some of her personal things sat on the dresser.

"Why don't you relax with Claudia while I get dinner ready?"

Half an hour later, they were sitting at the table.

I'll be dipped in honey," Shirley said, licking her fingers. "You really can cook."

"I told you she was good." Claudia's voice was full of affection, and Jessie hoped that Shirley didn't notice.

"Have y'all heard the scuttlebutt from Sweetwater?" Shirley asked over coffee and dessert.

"We don't hear much over here," Jessie said.

"What's the news?" Claudia asked.

"Seems like Hutchins went on the war path last week. Accused two women of being in a relationship together. You know," Shirley said, leaning forward conspiratorially, "lesbians." She paused for effect. "The witch kicked those poor girls out of the program without so much as a by-your-leave."

"You're kidding?" Claudia glanced quickly at her, and Jessie knew Claudia was concerned that her expression would give them away.

"Anyone want more coffee?" Jessie took her cup over to the coffee pot so that her back would be to Shirley. She really didn't want any more to drink, but it gave her an excuse to be out of Shirley's line of sight.

"No, thanks. I'm stuffed," Shirley said. "Anyway, rumor has it the girls got caught in a lip lock behind one of the hangars. Can you imagine?"

"Geez. Who saw them?" Claudia asked.

"One of the mechanics heard a noise and went to investigate. Boy, did he get an eyeful!"

"I guess."

"I mean, I never really thought much about it. I imagine there must've been some girls like that while we were there, but I never saw any."

Jessie nearly dropped her coffee cup on the way back to the table. "What's your assignment like?" she asked, desperate to change the topic.

"Not too bad. I don't see much of Janie, since we're both in the air most of the time, shuttling from base to base. Lots of overnights away."

"That must get tiring."

"Actually, I like it. I get to see different parts of the country. How else would I do that?"

"I suppose," Jessie said, glad beyond measure not to have drawn an assignment like that. Being away from Claudia so much would be torture. It was bad enough that they saw so little of each other during the day.

"What are your living arrangements like?" Claudia asked.

"Nothing as sweet as your set up, I can tell you that." Shirley made a show of looking around. "There are five of us WASPs stationed there, so we have one of the barracks to ourselves."

"What's this Jessie said about our Janie getting married?"

"Yeah, can you believe it? I never thought she'd be the first. Frankly," Shirley looked directly at Claudia, "I would've thought you might snag that hunky flyboy of yours long before Janie got her hooks into someone."

"I'll be right back," Claudia said, pushing her chair back.

"What's with her?" Shirley asked, after she'd gone.

Jessie shrugged. "Nothing, as far as I know."

"Well, maybe she's just worried about him being in the line of fire and all that. Maybe she's afraid he won't come back."

Jessie picked up her dish and carried it to the sink. "Could be," she said, trying to keep her voice light. *Come on, Claude, bail me out here.*

"Sorry about that. Must be something wrong with my bladder. I swear, I go to the bathroom three times more often than I used to."

"Maybe you have a bladder infection. You ought to be careful about that," Shirley warned. "I hear that can kill you."

"I don't think having to pee every half hour is fatal." Claudia laughed. "But I'll watch out for it." She sat back down. "So tell us all about Janie's fella."

For the next half hour, Shirley prattled on about the flight instructor who swept Janie off her feet. Then she talked about the wedding preparations, the reaction of Janie's parents, the search for the perfect wedding dress...

Jessie yawned. She looked across the table at Claudia, who looked even more tired than she felt.

"Oh, my goodness. Look at the time." Jessie picked up Shirley's dish and cup. "We've got an early call in the morning."

"Yeah, my bird will be ready at 0650," Shirley said. "I guess I'd better get some shuteye." She stood up. "Can I help you with the dishes?" she asked Claudia, who was at the sink washing the dinner plates.

"Nope. I've got it. You've got dibs on the bathroom."

"That's a first," Shirley said. "I better get in there before y'all change your minds."

Jessie waited until she could hear the water running before saying, "Did you hear what she said about those girls?"

"Of course. I'm not deaf, you know."

"That could've been us."

"But it wasn't, sugar. Not only that, but Shirley, one of the nosiest of our bunch, never suspected a thing."

"Still... You think we're okay here?"

"I'm positive. Heck, we never hardly see each other except at the beginning and the end of the day."

"Yes, but we never socialize, either. Do you think we should make more of an effort to get out?"

The hand holding the sponge paused in mid-air. Claudia leaned heavily against the sink. Without turning around to face Jessie, she said, "Let me see if I've got this right. You, Jessie Keaton, one of the least social people I know, and the woman who never wanted us to meet boys, is suggesting that we deliberately put ourselves in a situation where boys might think we were available to date."

"When you put it that way... I don't know, Claude. I just worry about being found out, that's all."

"Well, stop worrying, sugar. We're fine." Claudia brushed an errant strand of hair out of her face with her arm and set the last dish to dry. "You can have the bathroom next." She walked through the living room and into the bedroom, closing the door behind her.

Jessie remained where she was, looking after Claudia and wondering what just happened.

They bid Shirley goodbye on the tarmac with hugs and promises to be better about keeping in touch, and life returned to normal.

Except that to Jessie it didn't feel the same. Claudia seemed unusually moody; the slightest thing set her off. Not only that, but her internal thermostat was going haywire. She was hot, then she was cold, then she was hot again. Jessie didn't know whether to keep the covers on them or off them. And she was going to the bathroom more often than ever.

"Are you sure you don't need to go to the infirmary and get checked out?" Jessie asked one morning, after Claudia had sweat through the sheets at the same time Jessie was chilly.

"I'm fine. Why?"

"Because you're usually freezing, not hot as an oven, and because you pee every five seconds."

"Do not. Why must you pick apart everything I do?"

Jessie held her hands up in surrender. "I won't even mention that your moods change on a dime. I'm afraid to say anything about anything these days for fear you'll take my head off."

"I'm sorry," Claudia said. "You're right. I don't know what's the matter with me." Claudia pushed her pelvis against Jessie and wrapped her arms around her neck. "Forgive me?" She took Jessie's lower lip in her mouth and sucked on it.

All the blood rushed to Jessie's center. "W-what was I forgiving you for, again?"

"Mmm. Mission accomplished."

"That was tricky."

"I'm like that. Now we'd better get going or we'll be late."

Jessie groaned.

"Don't worry, sugar. There's more where that came from...later."

That was another thing—Claudia was insatiable. Her sex drive had always been strong, but now... Jessie fanned herself. She hoped the day wasn't too taxing; she was going to need her energy for later.

∽ઠ૭∾

They were on their way home after a long day. Claudia, who usually was talkative on the bus ride, was curiously silent. Jessie bumped her with her shoulder.

"You okay?"

"Hmm? Oh, yeah. Fine." Claudia went back to staring out the window.

"You don't seem fine. How was your day?"

"What? Oh, my day? The usual." Claudia twisted her hands in her lap, something she normally didn't do.

"Yeah? You seem kinda nervous."

Claudia turned her head to look at Jessie, then looked away again. "You're imagining things."

Jessie shrugged. It was clear she wasn't getting anywhere this way. "If you say so."

"I say so."

"Okay."

When they got home, Jessie changed her clothes and began the dinner preparations. Claudia disappeared into the bedroom and didn't re-emerge until Jessie called her to the table.

"I'm starving."

"You're always starving lately."

Claudia ignored the comment and heaped more mashed potatoes on her plate.

In another departure from the norm, there was no dinnertime conversation. Jessie searched her mind for a topic that would get Claudia talking, but nothing came to mind. Finally, desperate to hear the sound of her lover's voice, she said, "I think the potatoes might be a little lumpier than normal. What do you think?"

"They taste fine to me." Claudia went back to eating.

"All right. This is too weird. Since when am I the one to start the conversation?" That earned Jessie a shrug, and she watched in awe as Claudia continued to shovel food in her mouth. "Where are you putting all that?"

Finally, Claudia put down her fork and wiped her mouth with a napkin. "I was hungry, and the food was good, as it always is when you cook it." Claudia rose, took her dish to the sink, and began washing the pots and pans.

Jessie had no idea what to think, so she cleared the rest of the table without further comment. "Want me to dry the dishes tonight?"

"I've got it."

Jessie wrapped her arms around Claudia's waist from behind and kissed her on the side of the neck. "I love you, Claude."

The pot Claudia was scrubbing clattered into the sink as she whipped around and devoured Jessie's mouth. Her hands were everywhere at once, unbuttoning Jessie's blouse and pants, unclasping her bra, unbuckling her belt.

Although Claudia's boldness caught her off-guard, Jessie's body responded with a wild abandon. She struggled to relieve Claudia of her clothes. "Bedroom. Now," she panted.

"Right here. Now," Claudia countered. She spun them around and shoved Jessie against the kitchen counter, sucking a nipple into her mouth. Her fingers stroked Jessie until she lost all track of who and where she was. She cried out her climax, and fought to catch her breath, but before she could, Claudia knelt and kissed her center. Jessie moaned, and Claudia ran her tongue the length of Jessie's clit.

"Oh, Claude." There was nothing to do but urge her on, so Jessie cupped the back of Claudia's head and applied subtle pressure.

Claudia responded, ravishing her with a fierceness Jessie didn't know she possessed. Finally, Jessie collapsed to the floor, taking Claudia with her.

They lay in a heap as Jessie recovered. She kissed the top of Claudia's head. "My God, Claude. Where did that come from?"

In answer, Claudia pushed herself up off the ground and offered her hand to Jessie. When Jessie was upright, Claudia tugged her toward the bedroom. Without a word, she pulled Jessie down onto the bed and made love to her again.

"Claude." Jessie guided Claudia up until she was lying on top of her. She saw that Claudia was crying. "Hey. No tears, love. This is no time for tears."

"Make love to me, sugar. Make love to me like you've never made love to me before, and like you might never again."

There was something indefinable in Claudia's voice—something Jessie had never heard before. Was it urgency? Was it intensity? Was it desperation? Did it matter? Not to Jessie. Not at that moment. The only thing she wanted was to give Claudia every ounce of love she felt, just as Claudia had done for her. That she, Jessie Keaton, could be so loved—she never would've believed it possible. So it was with tears in her own eyes that Jessie made love to Claudia. She poured all of her feelings, all the things she wanted to say but couldn't find the words for, into each kiss, each touch, each taste. The night was magic, and Jessie wished it would never end.

When neither one of them could move anymore, they fell asleep tangled in each other. If morning never came, it would be all right with Jessie.

Shortly before dawn, Jessie felt, rather than heard, Claudia get up and go to the bathroom. Several minutes later, when she still hadn't returned to the bed, Jessie sat up.

Claudia was across the room, curled up in a chair, watching the sun peek over the horizon. Her chin was resting on her knees. She looked incredibly sad.

"What's wrong?"

Claudia shook her head, but didn't turn to look at Jessie.

"Come back to bed, love."

Again, Claudia shook her head.

Jessie was perplexed.

"I went to the infirmary."

The words were said so softly Jessie had to strain to understand them. She sat up straighter.

"Why didn't you tell me?"

"I'm telling you now." Claudia's voice was hollow.

"O-okay."

Claudia was quiet for a long time.

"You're scaring me, Claude. What did they say?"

Finally, Claudia made eye contact. "I…" She ran shaky fingers over her belly. "I'm pregnant."

"Wha…" Jessie was certain she'd heard wrong. "What did you say?"

"They ran some tests. Apparently, I'm two months pregnant."

Jessie blinked several times before the words sank in. Every fiber of her being turned to ice. Her whole body tingled and she was sure she would stop breathing any second.

"Aren't you going to say something?"

Jessie got out of bed slowly and went to the bathroom. When she was safely behind the closed door, she slid to the floor and covered her face with her hands. Her mind refused to function, refused to process the information she'd been given. So she sat for a long time, thinking of nothing.

Gradually, reality set in. The scent of their lovemaking penetrated Jessie's nostrils, the sound of Claudia sobbing in the bedroom seeped underneath her skin, the echo of Claudia's words sliced through her heart. Pregnant. Claudia was pregnant. With Matt's baby. There had to be an explanation for it. Claudia—her Claudia—couldn't have wanted this.

Images formed in Jessie's mind—Claudia returning alone from her walk with Matt. She'd looked disheveled and out of sorts. Jessie replayed bits of the conversation. *"Did he do something out there? Did he hurt you?"*

"No."

She said no, more than once, and Jessie had taken her at her word. Jessie didn't know much—well anything—about sex with boys or the odds of getting pregnant by having sex with a boy just once. But she did know Claudia, and there was no question that when Claudia returned to the beach alone, something had changed. She had said she had the flu, but was that really true?

Jessie stood up, splashed water on her face, and exited the bathroom.

Claudia hadn't moved. Her face was haggard. "Jess?"

"Tell me again about that last day in Sweetwater."

"W-why are you asking me this?"

"When you came out of the woods after your...'walk' with Matt, you weren't yourself. You looked shaken, and upset, and horrible."

"I-I told you, I had the flu or a stomach bug."

"Yep. That's what you told me. Was it the truth?" Jessie stared hard at Claudia. Would she even know if her lover was lying? As Claudia continually reminded her, she had a much better poker face than Jessie did.

"Yes." Claudia didn't hesitate, didn't flinch.

"You had the flu, and that's why you were such a mess?"

"I just told you, yes."

"You weren't feeling well, but still you had the desire and the energy to do...*that* with Matt?"

"I didn't feel sick when we went for the walk. It was only afterward."

Jessie tried to detect any hint that Claudia was being disingenuous. There was none. "So Matt didn't do anything you didn't want him to do? That's what you're telling me? I'm assuming that's the only time you..." Jessie couldn't say it, couldn't bring herself to contemplate it. Tears threatened, but she held them at bay. *Please, tell me you didn't want this.*

Claudia closed her eyes and nodded.

Jessie grasped at one last straw. "You aren't protecting Matt, are you? Because you know how I feel about him?"

"No!"

"So you wanted him to..." Jessie sank to the floor in front of the bed. She couldn't even look at Claudia. For a long time, she sat there as tears rolled down her cheeks. "I can't be with you anymore. I can't be around you."

"You don't mean that."

Jessie didn't answer. She finally met Claudia's eyes.

"Jess?"

Jessie shook her head and held up her hand. "The thought of sharing you..." She shuddered. "What was it, Claude? Did you figure you'd just stay with me until Matt came back from the war? Was that it?"

"No, Jess. I would never do that to you." Tears coursed down Claudia's face too, and she began to rock.

"There are a lot of things I never thought you'd do to me. Apparently, I was wrong." It was as if a switch was flipped. Jessie felt dead inside. "So what is it, then, Claude? Because this isn't adding up for me." Claudia squirmed in the chair, but said nothing. "I'll ask it a different way. Have you made plans to marry Matt?"

"What? No!"

"I see. Hopefully he'll make an honest woman out of you before..." Jessie's composure slipped. "...before your baby is born."

"Oh, Jess." Claudia moved toward her haltingly. "It isn't like that. I don't want to marry Matt. I love you, sugar. You're the only one for me."

Jessie held up her hand again. "Don't come any closer." She couldn't stand it if Claudia touched her right now. She jumped up, grabbed a shirt from the closet, and threw it on. She needed a shield. "Maybe you should have thought of that before you..." Jessie made a gesture, then folded her arms protectively over her chest. "Of course you'll marry Matt. You have a baby to think about."

"I don't want to think about it."

"You don't really have a choice now, do you?" Jessie paced in front of the bed. "Have you thought about the consequences? The immediate consequences, I mean."

"Like what?"

"Like, you can't fly while you're pregnant."

"I can't... What are you talking about?" Claudia's voice shook.

"For one thing, four girls washed out at Sweetwater because they got pregnant. It's one of the regulations. You can't fly while you're in that condition. For another, it's not safe for you to fly." Jessie fought hard not to break down. Regardless of what Claudia had done, she couldn't stand the thought of something happening to her. She could miscarry or hemorrhage or something, couldn't she?

Claudia took another halting step forward. "There are only two things I care about in all the world, Jess—you and flying. Nobody needs to know yet. I won't be showing for months. I could keep flying..."

"No." Apart from worrying about Claudia's health, Jessie wouldn't survive if they worked on the same base, knowing that they would never be together again. Even though she didn't run into Claudia often during the day, the idea that their paths could cross, that Jessie would have to see her... It was too much.

"Please, Jess."

Jessie saw the look of desperation in Claudia's face, that face that she cherished more than anything in the world. She couldn't—wouldn't—allow her love for Claudia any room to breathe. Not now. Not ever again. She would have to smother the life out of it, even if it meant destroying her own life in the process.

"If you don't offer your resignation by the end of the day today, I'll go to the officer in charge and get you dismissed with cause."

"Jessie! You can't mean that." Tears streamed down Claudia's face.

"Go home, Claude, or go to wherever Matt is stationed. I-I don't want to see you ever again." Jessie felt her soul shredding, but she pushed forward, needing to finish it. "Please, don't be here when I get back. Don't make this worse than it already is."

"I-I love you, Jess."

"I'm going to be late for work." Jessie closed herself in the bathroom again. She let the shower water run over her, mixing with the tears she no longer could hold back. The soap slipped from her fingers as she tried to control her shaking hands long enough to wash. She tried not to think about the fact that she was washing away the last of their lovemaking. Eventually, she got herself clean and dressed. When she came out of the bathroom, Claudia was nowhere in sight. With a heavy heart, Jessie left the house and walked to the bus stop.

❧❧

Jessie never saw Claudia again. When she got home that night there was a note on the table. It read: "My dearest Jessie. It is my sincere wish not to cause you any more pain and distress than I already have. As you requested, I submitted my resignation. As you read this, I am no longer a WASP." Jessie's eyes misted over, and she was forced to stop reading until she dried her tears. "I made sure I left nothing of myself behind. I'm sure the last thing you want is to be reminded in any way of me. I used some of the money my parents gave me for graduation to pay the rent on ~~our~~ the house for the remainder of the year, so you won't have to worry about that. I know you don't want to hear this, but I love you with all my heart, sugar. Now and always. You ARE the only one for me. Someday, I hope you'll understand and forgive me. Yours for eternity, Claudia"

Jessie sank to the floor and curled up in a ball. She rocked back and forth, wailing and moaning, wishing she could die so she wouldn't have to feel anymore. Eventually, she cried herself to sleep, and dreamt of Claudia.

CHAPTER FOURTEEN

J essie? Are you okay?"

Jessie looked up and blinked. "Claude." She smiled broadly. "I am now that you're here."

"I-I'm sorry, Jessie. It's me, Chelsea, Claudia's great granddaughter."

Jessie's heart jerked. She was embarrassed to realize that she was crying. "Of course you are. Forgive an old woman, I got caught up in memories." Jessie pulled a handkerchief from her pocket and wiped her eyes.

"They're calling your name. Shall I help you up to the stage?"

Jessie looked up at the stage, where her fellow WASPs or their representatives were receiving their medals. How much time had passed? She had no idea. "Thank you, I'll be all right."

She leaned heavily on her cane and rose slowly, making her way up the ramp to shake hands with one of the politicians on stage. Someone else handed Jessie a replica of the Congressional Medal of Honor and thanked her for her service. It was the first time in all these years she could remember someone saying thank you for what she and the others had done for their country. Her eyes welled up again, though this time she managed not to cry.

When the ceremony ended, Jessie spent a few minutes chatting with Shirley, Annabelle, and Rebecca. Unfortunately, Janie didn't live to see this day. Although she sensed that the girls wanted to ask about Claudia, none of them did. It was a subject Jessie had refused to talk about for nearly seventy years, and she suspected they understood the subject remained closed.

Jessie moved away and headed for the exit. She was intercepted before she got halfway across the room.

"Grandma Natalie and I would like to know if you would do us the honor of joining us for lunch."

"Oh. That's very kind of you, but these days I don't have much of an appetite. With all this excitement, I think I just need some rest." With her memories of their time together so vivid, so close to the surface, Jessie was afraid that spending any more time with Claudia's family would be too painful.

"At least let us see you safely back to your room," Natalie said, appearing behind Chelsea. "They've put us all up in the same hotel, so we're going that way anyway."

Jessie could think of no plausible reason to reject that offer, so she agreed.

Safely ensconced in Natalie's rented late-model Mercedes, Jessie sat back for the short ride. "This is a very nice car—must have cost a bundle to rent. You must be doing well for yourself. What is it you do, Natalie?"

"I'm a doctor."

"A doctor?" Jessie's eyebrows rose into her hairline. "That's really something. What kind of doctor?"

"I'm an oncologist."

"Your mother must be very proud." Jessie chewed her lip, unsure whether she truly wanted to know the answer to the question she'd intentionally avoided asking up to this point. "About your mother, Natalie. Why isn't she here, herself? Is Claudia…" In the end, Jessie couldn't bring herself to say the word.

Natalie reached across the console and patted Jessie's hand. "No. Mother is still alive. She's in hospice care."

"Hospice?" Jessie struggled to digest the information. "Claudia's dying?"

"I'm afraid so."

Jessie worked her jaw. She wanted to know how long Claudia had to live, and what was wrong, but she couldn't get the words around the golf-ball-sized lump in her throat and the terrible ache in her heart. She took out her handkerchief with shaking hands and held it to her mouth.

Natalie reached over and rubbed her arm. Chelsea leaned forward from the back seat and patted her shoulder. Jessie simply sobbed and looked out the passenger window. Claudia, her Claudia, was dying.

⊰⊱

Natalie and Chelsea insisted on escorting Jessie to her room, despite her protestations that she was fine. Chelsea swiped the key card Jessie provided and turned on a light. Natalie steadied Jessie on the side opposite from her cane and helped her over to a chair by the window. She opened the curtains to let in some sunlight.

"This really isn't necessary…"

"Here's a glass of water for you." Chelsea held the glass out for Jessie to take.

"Thank you." Jessie smiled at her through a film of fresh tears. She really did so resemble Claudia. "Honestly, there's no need to make such a fuss…"

"Chelsea, stay here with Jessie for a minute, will you?" Natalie asked. To Jessie she said, "There's something I want to give you. It's in our room. I'll only be a minute."

Jessie didn't even have time to object before Natalie was out the door. "Does she always take charge like that, your grandmother?"

Chelsea laughed. "Pretty much."

Jessie shook her head. "She's just like her mother. Speaking of which, where are your mom and dad?"

"Oh. Um, they're spending time with Grandma Claudia while we're here. My mom thought it was important for me to see a part of history."

It was Jessie's turn to laugh. "So, now I'm history, eh? Well, I suppose that's true."

"If it wasn't for you, today's Air Force wouldn't have women pilots, and neither would the commercial airlines. You paved the way. You were the first."

Chelsea's enthusiasm and earnestness warmed Jessie's heart. "Is that so?"

"Sure is…" Chelsea narrowed her eyes. "Are you playing with me?"

Jessie chuckled. "Only a little. I bet you're hell on wheels in school."

"That's what my professors say."

"What are you studying?"

"Mechanical engineering, but I keep telling my parents I want to go into the Air Force. I want to fly just like Grandma Claudia did."

"Whoa, there, young lady. It's not as glamorous as you think, and definitely too dangerous for someone as smart as you."

Chelsea frowned. "That's what Grandma Claudia said."

Jessie took a sip of water to compose herself. "Your great grandma is a very, very wise woman. You should listen to her."

"She says that too."

That startled a laugh out of Jessie. Yep, that was her Claudia all over.

There was a knock at the door and Chelsea jumped up to answer it. She came back with Natalie, who was carrying a box.

"What's this?"

Natalie placed the box on the bed and lifted the lid. She started to take something out, then changed her mind, picked up the box, and brought it to Jessie.

"These are for you." She reached inside, pulled something out, and placed it in Jessie's lap.

Jessie lifted the bundle and turned it over in her hands. It was a packet of letters tied with a ribbon, and each letter had Jessie's name on it. On top was a year: 1943. "I don't understand."

"Mama wrote letters to you. Lots of them. They start from the time she left the WASPs in 1943, and continue right up until a few weeks ago. She never sent them, never tried to contact you. But you were always, always in her thoughts and in her heart."

"Claudia wrote to me?"

"All the time."

Jessie teared up again. "I'm sorry. I feel like a leaky faucet today."

"It's okay." Natalie put a reassuring hand on Jessie's shoulder. "It's an emotional time."

"None of these has an address on it—just my name."

"As I said, I don't think my mother ever intended to send them to you."

Jessie thought about that. "Then why give them to me now? If Claudia didn't want me to have these…" Jessie tried to hand the bundle back to Natalie.

"No. Keep them. Mama hoped you would be here today. She asked me to bring these to you. She was adamant about it."

Jessie closed her eyes and brushed her fingers across the letters, then cradled them against her chest. Claudia's thoughts and dreams were in these, and she wanted to share them with Jessie. She hadn't forgotten her, after all.

She opened her eyes to find Natalie and Chelsea watching her. She placed the bundle back in the box. "Have you read these?" she asked Natalie.

"No. They weren't for my eyes. But I remember many nights sitting at the table, doing my homework while Mama wrote pages and pages to you. No matter how tired she was, she would take the time to write to you before bed."

Natalie motioned Chelsea to head toward the door. "You must be exhausted. We'll leave you alone now. I'm writing down my room number in case you need it. We'll be checking out late tomorrow morning. Please, don't hesitate to call if you need anything. It was an honor and a pleasure to meet you, Jessie." Natalie leaned over, hugged Jessie, and gave her a kiss on the cheek.

Chelsea also gave Jessie a hug.

"I-I'm so glad you were here," Jessie said. "And thank you so much for these." She indicated the letters. Jessie started to rise, but Natalie held up a hand to stop her.

"No. We'll show ourselves out. You take care."

When the door clicked closed, Jessie got up, carried the box to the bed, and set it down.

September 5, 1943

My Dearest Darling Jess,
My hand shakes as I put pen to paper. I cannot seem to stem the tide of tears. I feel so alone. I am taking a train to my parents' house. I

can't say I'm on my way home, because there will only ever be one home for me, and that's with you.

By now you have probably found my note, and you know that I have honored your wishes. I have lost everything that matters to me—you, my standing as a WASP, my future.

I am more frightened than I have ever been in my life. I cannot tell my parents the truth; I can't tell anyone, for the one thing I will never do is put you in jeopardy. I would lose my life first, and I guess in some ways I have.

Perhaps you think I deserve this. Maybe I do. Maybe God is punishing me for loving you so much, but I cannot believe that the kind of love we share is unnatural.

My head is reeling, but the one thing I know for sure is that I love you with all my heart, and I always will.

Claudia

Jessie set the letter aside and looked out the window. Her room offered a spectacular view of the Washington Monument, but she hardly noticed. The date on the letter was September 5th, a day Jessie remembered well.

The floor in the bungalow was hard as a rock. Jessie rolled over onto her back and straightened her legs. It was the middle of the night, and every muscle and joint was sore. She stretched out slowly, working out the kinks. Her eyes were gritty from crying and she felt like she'd swallowed sawdust.

After several minutes, she stood up and gazed around, hoping against hope that she'd dreamt the whole thing. But when she wandered through the rooms, it was as if she'd never been in this place before. All the knickknacks and small touches that Claudia had bought for them were gone. The bungalow no longer looked lived in, it felt sterile and cold.

The medicine chest, usually crammed with Claudia's makeup, perfume, hairbrushes, and lotions, was empty save for toothpaste, Jessie's toothbrush, soap, shampoo, antiperspirant, and a single comb.

Empty hangars hung in the closet where Claudia's dresses and uniforms had been. Dresser drawers held nothing but mothballs and blocks of cedar.

Claudia had changed the sheets and pillowcases. Jessie ran her hands over the bedspread, imagining Claudia's hands smoothing it out. Jessie's clothes, the ones so hastily discarded during their frantic lovemaking, were folded on the chair. Jessie held the clothes up to her face and sniffed. The scent of their lovemaking filled her nostrils and she sank into the chair, balled the clothes up in her fists and crushed them to her chest.

The sound of her agony, the echo of her loss, bounced off the walls and boomeranged back at her. Tears ran down her face and neck to be absorbed by her uniform blouse. They would never make love again. Claudia was gone.

Images of the night before played in Jessie's mind—Claudia's mouth and hands demanding and greedy, Claudia urging Jessie on, taking more and more until Jessie had no more to give, Claudia begging Jessie to make love to her as if she would never make love to her again.

Jessie shot up out of the chair and threw the clothes across the room. Claudia played her. She seduced Jessie, knowing all the while that she was pregnant with Matt's child. Jessie ran to the bathroom and threw up.

Back in the bedroom she sat down on the floor with her back against the bed and wiped her face with a cool washcloth. How could Claudia have betrayed her this way? For two months Claudia had strung her along, let her believe that they had a future together. Would Claudia even have told her about having sex with Matt if she hadn't gotten pregnant?

"Jessie Keaton is nobody's sucker. Not even yours, Claude." Jessie's voice shook with anger. "How could I have been so damn stupid? To think that someone like me could really end up with someone like you... I should have known better."

A shadow crept across the floor and Jessie realized the sun had risen. She stood up, dusted herself off, and readied herself for a new day. If she could just hold onto her anger, she was sure she could make it through her shift without crying.

Jessie picked up the letter again and reread it. *I cannot tell my parents the truth; I can't tell anyone, for the one thing I will never do is put you in jeopardy.* Why in the world would Claudia even have considered telling her parents about their relationship? Of course it would have endangered Jessie, perhaps even ended her career as a WASP, but it would have done more damage, unnecessarily, to Claudia. Despite her protestations to the contrary, she would marry Matt; no one need ever know about her lesbian affair. Yes, Claudia had to tell her parents about leaving the WASPs and the pregnancy. It wasn't as though she could have hidden either of those things forever. But if she married quickly enough, no one ever had to know she had sex before the wedding, and the impending nuptials could have been her reason for leaving the WASPs.

"Wait a minute! Natalie said Claudia never married. I know Claudia told me she didn't want to marry Matt, but that was in the heat of the moment. What else could she have said to me?"

Jessie ran through possibilities in her mind. Maybe she did marry Matt, but he was killed in the war after the honeymoon and before Natalie was born. But why then wouldn't Claudia tell Natalie who her father was? Too painful? Perhaps she married Matt, found out what a jerk he really was, and divorced him before Natalie was born or before she was old enough to remember. She didn't want to tell Natalie who her father was because he was an idiot. Jessie smiled at that scenario. Maybe Claudia's parents found out about the pregnancy and forbade her to marry Matt because he defiled her before the wedding. That seemed doubtful, but nothing else made any sense to Jessie.

Perhaps if she kept reading, the answer would become clear to her.

∽⭑⭒

September 12, 1943

My Dearest Darling Jess,

I'm on a train again, this time to Los Angeles. I feel like a vagabond or a vagrant. My heart is so heavy. It seems I really have lost everything.

I told my parents that I was pregnant and that I had no intention of marrying the father. I wouldn't even tell them who it was...

"Claudia Jean, you most certainly will tell us. And then I will hunt that boy down and make him do right by you."

"Daddy, I don't want to marry this baby's father."

"Sweetheart, why are you talking such nonsense? You made a mistake, but it's not too late to fix it."

"Mama, I don't want to fix this. I'm not in love with the boy, and I have no intention of settling down with him. You don't want me to live my whole life without love, do you?"

"You should have thought of that before you... Well, you know." Mr. Sherwood loomed over Claudia. "Just what do you think you're going to do? How do you think you're going to support this child?"

"I'll find a way. I'll get a job."

"You are so naïve. Do you have any idea what it's like to be an unwed mother? People will stare and point and whisper behind your back."

"I can't do anything about that and it's still no good reason to get married."

"I'm warning you, if you are determined to have this baby out of wedlock, we'll have nothing more to do with you. You'll be cut off without a cent."

"Jonathan!"

"Elizabeth, it's for her own good. I can't have her running about town flaunting her mistakes. It'll be bad for business. She needs to learn to take responsibility for her choices."

"Very well." Claudia stood up. "I guess we're done here." She picked up her bag and carried it to the door. Tears threatened, but she refused to cry in front of her father.

"Take care of yourself, Mama." Claudia's lips trembled. She lifted her chin higher, unwilling to show weakness.

"Baby, please don't go. Jonathan, this is madness. We can't throw our own daughter out into the street, especially not in her condition." Mrs. Sherwood looked from one of them to the other. Claudia didn't budge. Mr. Sherwood waved a hand dismissively and left the room.

"I love you, Mama," Claudia said, hugging her mother tightly.

"I'm sorry, baby. He'll come around."

"I don't think so."

"Wait a second. Wait right here." Mrs. Sherwood ran out of the room and returned a few seconds later. "This is for you." She handed Claudia an envelope. "I've been saving it for a rainy day, but I want you to have it."

"Mama…"

"I insist. Now go before your father finds out."

Anyway, I hear the North American plant in Inglewood, California is looking for assembly-line workers to build AT-6s and P-51 Mustangs. I figure I might have a leg up, seeing as how I know how to fly those birds and we spent all that time hanging around the mechanics back at Sweetwater.

It'll be months before the baby starts to show, so I'm just going to try to forget about it for now (as if I could) and find a way to make a living for myself.

Sorry, seems I got the stationery wet with my tears. I'm trying to keep up a brave front, sugar. I know that's what you would do. I miss you so much there's a hole right in the center of my heart. You're my everything, Jess. Now and always. And I might never see you again and I can never explain.

I tell myself that someday, someday I'll make it right and you'll forgive me. But I think that's just a story I tell myself so that I keep putting one foot in front of the other.

I miss you more than words can say.

Your girl,
Claudia

Jessie fumbled for the box of Kleenex on the nightstand. "Oh my God, Claude. Your parents disowned you?" Jessie tried to put herself in Claudia's shoes—pregnant, all alone with no income and no place to go and…heartsick over losing Jessie?

She told her parents she had no intention of marrying Matt. She only told Jessie that she didn't *want* to marry him. That was not the same as outright saying she wouldn't marry him, and that she didn't love him. Why hadn't she told Jessie that? Everything might have been different if she'd just said she didn't love him.

Jessie tried to recall the conversation that awful early morning when Claudia told her she was pregnant. The news was so shocking, so unexpected. Jessie remembered feeling like she'd been hit with a two by four, then the momentary hope when she'd thought Matt might have defiled Claudia against her will. That was dashed when Claudia flatly denied being forced to have sex with Matt. That was when Jessie went numb, as if there was nothing left inside, and a strange calm descended over her. It was almost what the modern generation would call an out-of-body experience. From a great distance, Jessie had heard herself bully Claudia into resigning.

"Oh, Claude. I wish I'd been stronger back then. I wish I'd been a better person, someone who was more sure of herself and less threatened by the likes of Matt Dunphy. I wish I'd thought I had a real chance to compete for you. Maybe things would've turned out different."

Instead, Jessie had retreated and closed herself off.

Jessie looked down at the faded piece of stationery in her lap. "September 12, 1943. By then I was all the way across the country trying my best to get myself killed."

CHAPTER FIFTEEN

S pending time in the bungalow alone was unbearable. Everywhere Jessie turned, there were reminders of Claudia. If she stood at the sink, she relived their lovemaking on that last night together. If she sat on the sofa, she could see the indentation where Claudia used to sit. And sleeping in the bed they shared was completely out of the question.

Jessie moved into the spare bedroom, but even that was too painful. Claudia's perfume was in the air, her presence haunted every room, and Jessie was beside herself.

"I'd like to request a transfer." Jessie stood at attention in front of Jackie Cochran, who had just flown in to check on her girls.

"Why is that?"

"Ma'am, I heard about Mabel Rawlinson's death at Camp Davis a couple of weeks ago. I know that a lot of the girls are jumpy, and you know I'm one of the best pilots you've got. I think Camp Davis is where I can do the most good right now."

"Is that so?"

"Yes, ma'am."

"This wouldn't have anything to do with Sherwood's resignation, would it, Keaton?"

Jessie schooled her expression to stay neutral. "No, ma'am. I know you're in a bind, and I'm volunteering to help. That's all."

Cochran stared at Jessie for a long time. "Can't say as I believe your reasoning, Keaton, but I sure could use you over there. Wrap up your affairs, get packed, and let's get you a plane. You're going to North Carolina."

Jessie caught the first bus back to the bungalow and packed her things. She found the landlord and negotiated the return of the next two months' rent Claudia had paid him before she departed. All that was left was to clear out.

It should have been easy. After all, the bungalow was just a place she had lain her head for a couple of months. But when Jessie made one last sweep to ensure that she hadn't missed anything, the emotions she'd been holding in check bubbled to the surface. This was the place she and Claudia shared together. The home where they'd shared their dreams, their hopes, their love. It was the last place she'd seen Claudia, and the last place Claudia knew to find her. When she left here, Jessie would be closing the door on a part of her life she had hoped and expected to last forever.

What if Claudia came back? She wouldn't know where to look for Jessie. What if something went wrong and Claudia needed her? This house was the last thing tethering them together.

Jessie sat down at the dining room table. If she closed her eyes, she could hear Claudia's laughter as she recounted snippets of her day. She could see Claudia at the sink doing the dishes. She could feel Claudia's hands kneading the knots in her neck as she sat in this very chair. Walking out the front door meant giving up hope that what was done could be undone.

"Who are you kidding? You were the one who told her you never wanted to see her again. She's never coming back."

Jessie hoisted the duffle bag over her shoulder and hustled outside. There was only one direction to go and that was forward.

Jessie arrived at Camp Davis almost two weeks to the day after the tragic accident that took Mabel Rawlinson's life. There were fifty-two WASPs at Camp Davis, more than at any other base in the country, and every one of them was affected by the loss. Many of them had seen the accident or heard how the canopy on the A-24 Douglas Dauntless failed to release, trapping Mabel inside as the cockpit burned. The wreckage was in a hard-to-reach area off a runway, and removing the charred pieces of metal took time.

The remains of the crash were visible from the air to any plane coming in on that runway—a stark reminder of the dangers they faced every time they went up.

The A-24s the WASPs were flying were war-weary and difficult to keep in flying shape. Yet they were expected to go up every day, multiple times, to tow targets for green soldiers just learning to shoot. A WASP would pilot the plane while an enlisted man would roll out a muslin sleeve on a cable for antiaircraft gunnery practice.

Jessie heard many stories of planes being hit by soldiers with lousy aim. It was one of the reasons she volunteered for this assignment. Without Claudia, she had nothing to live for. If she was killed while doing her patriotic duty to help her country in a time of war, well, at least her life will have had some meaning. She no longer feared death, which set her apart from all of her WASP sisters. She took every dangerous assignment, including dive-bombing toward the guns to simulate a battle, and perilous nighttime flights to train soldiers in spotting planes with searchlights from the ground. The beam could blind the pilot temporarily, leaving her to fly only by instrument. That was fine by Jessie.

Most of the other WASPs avoided her, convinced that she had a death wish and concerned that the rest of them would be expected to exhibit nerves of steel as well. It wasn't that Jessie took chances in the air, for she continued to be an excellent pilot with a reputation for putting safety first. It was that she appeared to have ice water in her veins and to relish flying into harm's way.

Jessie was assigned to one of the barracks on the base set aside for the WASPs. In a way, she was grateful for the din of communal living—it made it harder for her to be alone with her thoughts. She had no desire to make friends and no inclination to chat or take part in any social activities. As a result, she didn't mind in the least that the other girls seemed to give her a wide berth.

At night, she lay in her bed in her small, single room, her mind fixated on Claudia. No matter how angry Jessie was about the betrayal, she could no more stop loving Claudia than she could stop breathing. Every night spent alone was agony. Many nights she cried herself to sleep. She longed to feel Claudia's body against hers, to kiss her lips, to hold her and share the highlights of their days. Jessie often found herself wondering what Claudia would say about something that happened or what funny comment she would make about the way one of the girls wore her hair.

Where was she? Had she gone home to her parents? What had she told them? Was she with Matt? That thought made Jessie nauseous. But Matt was in Germany by now, far away flying bombing runs and trying to kill Nazis.

A couple of weeks after Jessie's arrival, another accident in a Douglas Dauntless killed Betty Taylor Wood. Jackie Cochran, herself, came to investigate the crash. She didn't stay long, and didn't make public her findings. She didn't have to. All the girls on the base were talking about it.

"Jessie? Your name is Jessie, right?" One of the girls Jessie recognized from the flight line was standing in front of her table in the mess, tray in hand. "Can I sit down?"

"It's a free country. Sure." Jessie shoveled another forkful of eggs into her mouth.

"I'm Isabel. Just got here a couple of days ago."

Jessie nodded.

"Did you hear?"

"Hear what?"

"They're saying it was sabotage. Sugar in the gas tank. Can you believe it?"

Jessie made a noncommittal sound.

"I mean, I know some of the guys are really hostile toward us. They resent that they've got to go overseas and we don't."

"Or that we can fly planes better than they can," Jessie said.

"Right. But to deliberately cause someone's death, that's sick."

"Gotta agree with you there."

"Aren't you scared to go up?"

Jessie looked at this young, earnest girl and weighed what to say. "Honestly? No. But that doesn't mean that I don't have a healthy concern for the fitness of the planes we're flying. I do."

Isabel played with her napkin, then gave Jessie a shy look. "The other girls, they say you're crazy. That you must have a death wish or something."

Jessie laughed. She had to give the girl credit for forthrightness. "Maybe they're right."

164

"You don't look insane to me. You look brave and competent and fearless."

"Is that so?"

Isabel nodded.

"Well, Isabel. I'm not someone to be admired, so if I were you, I'd throw my lot in with the other girls."

"They also say you're a real loner. That you're antisocial."

"They're right."

Slowly, hesitantly, Isabel shook her head. "No, they're not. You're wounded and grieving. If they knew anything about human nature, they could see that. It's written all over your face and in the way you carry yourself. I can see that, and I've been here less than a week."

Jessie shoved back her chair. "You're mistaken, and I don't need to be psychoanalyzed by you or anybody else. I've got to get to the flight line." Jessie could feel Isabel's eyes on her back as she walked away. What right did this upstart have to talk to her that way? She didn't know anything about her.

Remind me to play poker with you. Jessie's heart lurched painfully. It was one of the very first things Claudia said to her when they met. Well, Isabel was not Claudia, not by a long shot. Jessie stalked out of the mess and over to the ready room. She needed to get into the air. Ironically, despite the fact that she was being shot at, it was the one place where she felt at peace.

September 25, 1943

My Dearest Darling Jess,

Well, I got hired by North American to work in their Inglewood factory. Mostly, I spend my days tightening bolts and inspecting other people's work to make sure nothing's going to fall apart in the air. It's tedious stuff and I find my mind wandering all the time to you. I wonder what you're doing and if you're staying safe.

I know these planes won't be flown by you, since they're new and in great shape, and all we ever got to fly were the worn-out wrecks that came back from overseas. Still, every time I tighten a bolt or check a seam, I do so with loving hands on the off chance one of them ends up with you in the cockpit.

I'm living in a room in a rundown boarding house, but it's right down the street from the factory, so I'm saving money on transportation. So, the other day I was carrying groceries up the stairs and juggling my keys at the same time. I got to the top of the landing and the bag broke. You can imagine the mess that made. There I was, on my hands and knees, and I saw a pair of shoes in front of me. It was a lovely old gentleman who offered to help me. It put a smile on my face for the first time in forever and made me feel just a little less alone.

Jess, I worry about you constantly. Are you eating right? Are you getting any sleep? Are you remembering to drink lots of water out there in the desert? Have you made any friends? Are you being careful in the sky?

I wish more than anything I could change things—that we could go back to the way we were. I miss you so much it hurts deep inside, and I love you more than anything in the whole wide universe. But I know all the wishing in the world won't win me your forgiveness or change the reality of my pregnancy. I won't write about that here, because I know you don't want to hear about it.

Sigh. Here I go crying again. I wonder if I'll ever stop.

Your girl, now and always,
Claudia

Jessie folded the letter carefully and replaced it in the envelope. She rubbed her eyes and glanced at her watch. It was two o'clock. Time to take her next round of pills. God, she hated being old and infirm. She thought about Claudia, lying in a bed somewhere, waiting to die. Jessie was grateful that at least Claudia had family by her side, a loving daughter who had given her a grandchild and a beautiful great granddaughter. Jessie had no one.

Just as she reached the bathroom to get herself a glass of water and her medicine, there was a knock at the door.

"Who is it?" Jessie asked, looking through the peephole.

"Room service, ma'am."

"I didn't order any room service."

"No, ma'am. It was ordered for you by…" Jessie could see the young man consult a piece of paper on the tray. "…Natalie and Chelsea."

166

"Of all the…" Jessie opened the door to permit the bellboy entry.

"Where would you like this, ma'am?" He looked around. "Perhaps on the table over there?"

"That's fine." Jessie followed him over toward the window. "What is it, anyway?"

"Scrambled eggs, fruit, and bacon, ma'am. There's a note." The bellboy reached into his pocket and pulled out an envelope addressed to Jessie.

"Very well. Thank you," she said, fishing in her pocket for her wallet to give him a tip.

"Thank you, ma'am. Enjoy the rest of your stay. I'll just see myself out."

When he was gone, Jessie sat down at the table and removed the cover that was keeping the food warm. She placed the napkin in her lap and opened the envelope.

"We know you said you didn't have much of an appetite, but you really should eat something. I spoke to Mama on the phone and told her we saw you. When I said you turned down our invitation to lunch, she insisted I order this for you—said it was your favorite. When I reminded her that it was mid-afternoon, she said that wouldn't matter to you.

I've learned over a lifetime never to argue with my mother. So this is for you.

Enjoy, Natalie & Chelsea."

Jessie blinked several times and reread the note. Claudia remembered. How was that possible? It had been sixty-seven years since the last time they'd eaten together, and Claudia remembered Jessie's fondness for breakfast foods. She'd always made fun of Jessie because she would eat scrambled eggs and bacon for dinner. She would insist that Jessie have some fruit with her meal to balance things out.

Jessie picked up the fork, but her hand was shaking so badly she had to put it back down. It was unfathomable that Claudia still could be thinking about her all these years later, that she wouldn't have forgotten, that even on her deathbed, she would worry about Jessie's well-being.

"Okay, Claude, I'll eat a little, but only because you asked me to." Jessie picked up the fork again and tasted the eggs.

It was only after she finished eating that Jessie realized she'd never taken her medicine. She made her way to the bathroom and swallowed the pills with water. Then she returned to the bed and retrieved another letter.

Christmas, 1943

My Dearest Darling Jessie,

Merry Christmas, darling. I see the wreaths on the doors, the families picking out Christmas trees together, the decorations in store windows, and hear the caroling, and all I can think about is how much I wish I was spending the holiday with you. I window shop in the stores and daydream about what I would have bought you. I won't tell you here, because if I ever get the chance to spend the holiday with you, I don't want to spoil the surprise.

It is a lonely, desolate time for me. I miss my parents, I miss the joy of the season, and most of all, sugar, I miss you. What are you doing for the holidays? Have you found someone you're sweet on? The thought makes me a little crazy, I admit, but I do so wish happiness for you. It's not fair to want you to be miserable just because I am.

I know I said I wouldn't talk about the pregnancy to you. Alas dear Jess, I have no one else. Please forgive me, but I need to pour my heart out somewhere, and since you're my one and only, you're elected. I'm starting to show. My belly gets bigger every day, and it's harder and harder to hide the fact that I'm with child. I'm desperately afraid that if my bosses find out, I'll lose my job. I've been trying to save money for when the baby comes, and I've managed to hold onto most of the money my mother gave me the last time I saw her (when my father disowned me). But I know I will need that money to live on once the baby is born until I can work again, and in the meantime, I keep having to let my clothes out. Pretty soon, I'm going to have to buy new, looser fitting clothes.

Not only that, but I have to figure out where I'm going to have the baby. I can't stay here—the landlord will kick me out for sure. Oh, Jess. I'm so frightened. I don't know what I'm going to do or how I'm going to manage all by myself.

I wish more than anything I could have your strong shoulder to lean on, your arms around me as I sleep, and your voice in my ear telling me everything is going to be all right, even if it's a lie.

Anyway, enough of the depressing stuff. I love you with all my heart and soul and hope you are safe and well.

Your girl,
Claudia

Jessie returned the letter to its envelope and wrapped up the stack for 1943 with the ribbon. Poor, poor Claudia. Pregnant and all alone, with no one to rely on and no place to go. It must have been awful.

Jessie hadn't had much of a Christmas, herself, as she recalled. The girls in the barracks got a little tree and decorated it, and there was a turkey dinner in the middle of the day, but Jessie hadn't felt very festive, so she mostly stayed in her room. It seems that they were both miserable, after all.

CHAPTER SIXTEEN

S he hadn't meant to nod off, but when Jessie glanced at the clock she realized she'd been asleep for nearly two hours. She still held the packet of letters marked 1943 in her hands. It was almost four o'clock in the afternoon.

She pulled the box toward her. "Damn, Claude, there must be hundreds of letters in here." Everything was neatly, methodically filed by date, month, and year. "I can't read them all in a day, love, though believe me, I want to." She ran her fingers lovingly over the envelopes. "For now, I hope you'll forgive me if I settle for the Readers' Digest version."

By Jessie's calculation, the baby would have been born in April, 1944.

April 13, 1944

My Dearest Darling Jessie,

The baby is kicking harder than ever. I can't find a comfortable position to sleep in, so I lie awake at night and think of baby names. So far, I've narrowed it down to Peter, Jasper, Richard, or Nathan if it's a boy. If it's a girl, I've thought about naming her Jessie, but I doubt you'd approve, and I know that if I did name her that, I'd only miss you more every time I called her name. Believe me, I don't need any more reminders of how much I wish you were here with me. Sigh. If the baby's a girl, the possibilities are Sara, Michelle, Sandra, or Natalie.

Mrs. Rourke, the nice Irish lady who took me in when I got kicked out of my last place for being single and pregnant, says it's probably a boy based on how hard it kicks. I'm not convinced...

"I've got eight wee ones, dear. I'm pretty sure I should know by now what it'll be, and I'm telling you, it's a boy."

"Maybe, but I sure hope it's a girl."

"And why would that be?"

"I don't have any experience with boys. I wouldn't know the first thing about raising one."

"Hah! No experience with boys, she says, standing there nine months pregnant. I should think you've had *some* experience, now haven't you?"

Claudia's face reddened.

"Aw, it's all right, child. I didn't mean nothing by it. Just making a bit of a joke is all."

Claudia turned away so that Mrs. Rourke wouldn't see the tears in her eyes. "I'll just go finish sewing that dress for you. Should be done by tomorrow."

"That's a good girl. Don't tax yourself too much, now."

"I won't."

Claudia retreated to her room, sat on the edge of the bed, and cried. She cried for things she couldn't change, she cried over being reduced to sewing, mopping, washing, and doing odd jobs in exchange for food and lodging, and most of all, she cried for the life she could have had—the life she wanted—with Jessie.

"Sugar, I'd give anything in the world to be back in Vegas with you, flying planes and making sweet love. God, Jess. I didn't think it was possible to miss one person so much. I'm so lost without you."

She pulled a box out of the closet, rummaged inside, and took out a needle and thread. She found the pattern and the pieces of material she had cut and sat down to hand sew the dress. "What I wouldn't give to be able to afford one of those fancy Singer sewing machines." As she found herself doing often these days, Claudia stared out the window and daydreamed.

"Ohmigod." She doubled over and held her belly. "That was the worst one yet." Then she looked down and saw the puddle underneath her. "Mrs. Rourke! Mrs. Rourke, please, help me!" Claudia started to stand and sat back down. Her heart hammered in her chest. "Mrs. Rourke! Something's wrong. Please, help me!"

When she didn't hear anything, Claudia pushed herself up and looked down from her second story window. Mrs. Rourke was in the garden, planting flowers. Claudia screamed as another pain ripped through her. She knelt with her hands on the windowsill until she could catch her breath. After awhile, she was able to open the window and lean out. "Mrs. Rourke! Please, come quick. Something's wrong."

Mrs. Rourke looked up and shaded her eyes. "What's that, dear?"

"Help! I'm…" Claudia bent double again with a strangled cry.

"Oh, goodness. On my way, dear. Stay right there."

Claudia's eyes were wild and her breathing was irregular. Beads of sweat broke out on her forehead.

"There, there, dear," Mrs. Rourke said, bursting into the room. "What's— Oh. Oh, goodness. Okay. Okay. Don't panic, dear."

"I'm so scared. Wha…What's going on?"

"Your water broke."

"What does that m-mean?" Another pain sliced through her, and Claudia grabbed the windowsill.

"It means your baby is coming."

"N-now?"

"From the looks of it, right now. All right. Let's get you lying down." Mrs. Rourke guided Claudia into a prone position on the bed. She leaned out the window. "Jerry! Jerry, run across the street and get Doc for me. Hurry now!"

"It w-wasn't supposed to happen like this."

"Babies have their own schedule, that's for sure. This one's obviously in a real hurry to get here."

"W-what am I going to do?"

Mrs. Rourke smothered a chuckle. "Do, dear? Why, you're going to have this baby, that's what."

"Right h-here?"

"Unless I miss my guess, there's no time to move you anywhere else."

"I got him, Ma. I got him." Jerry stood in the doorway, panting and staring.

"Jerry Rourke! Don't stand there. This isn't a place for you. Make yourself useful and get some clean towels. And put some water on to boil."

"Yes, Ma." He continued to stand there, gawking at Claudia, who was writhing in pain on the bed.

Claudia turned her head, glared at him, and yelled, "Get your perverted self out of my room. Now."

Mrs. Rourke chuckled again as Jerry sprinted out of the room. The sound of his footsteps on the stairs echoed through the house. "Guess you told him."

"S-sorry Mrs. Rourke."

"Don't be, child. He deserved that. Darn teenaged boys."

"Emily?"

"Up here, Doc. Second door on the right, second floor." Mrs. Rourke took Claudia's hand and squeezed. "See, dear? Nothing to worry about. The cavalry's on the way."

An elderly gentleman walked into the room and strode across the floor. He wore a stethoscope around his neck and carried a leather satchel. "What have we here?"

Claudia looked up into kindly, gentle eyes. "It hurts so much."

"Okay. Let's have a peek." He turned to Mrs. Rourke. "How long has she been like this?"

"Her water broke about fifteen minutes ago. But…"

Claudia took in the expression on Mrs. Rourke's face. It was a cross between perplexity and concern. She grabbed the doctor's arm. "Am I going to be okay?" Panic was making it difficult to breathe.

"Like I said, let me examine you, then we'll know more." He held the stethoscope to her chest in several places, then placed it on her belly. "Mmm-hmm. Ah-hah." He felt her belly. "I'm going to need you to bend your knees and raise your legs."

Claudia screamed as yet another pain tore through her. She couldn't stand it anymore. "Please. Help me."

"That's exactly what we're going to do, young lady. Bend your knees and raise your legs." He returned the stethoscope to its perch and opened his bag. "Emily, we're going to have to do this here. Her contractions are too close together. There isn't enough time to move her."

"Are you going to be able to put her out?"

"No. Not here."

"I was afraid of that," Mrs. Rourke said. "At least I got to be unconscious for all of mine. What do you need me to do?"

"We'll need a couple of clean bed sheets and towels, hot water, a bowl, and a basin. Once we've got all that in place, I'll tell you the rest."

Claudia looked from one of them to the other. "I'm going to have my baby here?"

"No choice, I'm afraid. You're too far along to get you to a hospital."

"But—"

"Don't worry, dear. Doc, here is the best. He's delivered all eight of mine. You'll be just fine." Mrs. Rourke scurried out of the room.

"Is this your first?" Doc asked, as he prepared his instruments.

"My only," Claudia ground out as another contraction took her breath away.

"Every woman says that when she's in the throes of labor. When you see this beautiful baby and hold it in your arms, you'll forget all about the pain. I'm willing to bet a pretty thing like you will have an entire baseball team by the time you're done."

Tears leaked out of Claudia's eyes. The last thing she wanted was to think about ever having to go through this trauma again. She hadn't meant to go through it in the first place.

Mrs. Rourke bustled back in with two clean sheets and some towels. "Here we go."

"Emily, can you help Claudia remove her undergarments and cover her with the sheet?"

"Certainly."

"I'll be right outside. Just let me know when you're ready."

"Okay, dear, I'm going to need you to help me. When I say, lift your backside off the bed. I'm going to pull your dress up over your hips and take off your underpants."

Claudia nodded. Sweat was pouring off her face, dribbling down her neck and between her breasts.

"Okay. Now."

Claudia pushed down with her feet and struggled to lift herself off the bed long enough to allow Mrs. Rourke to peel her panties off. As she lowered herself, another contraction hit, and she screamed.

"Just breathe, dear. Breathe. Short, quick breaths. That's it."

"May I come back in?"

"Yes, Doc. She's decent."

Claudia grabbed Mrs. Rourke's arm. "Don't go. Please. I'm so scared."

"I'm not going anywhere, dear. I'll be right here with you. Doc needs some hot water, but I'll come right back. Don't you worry about a thing." She patted Claudia on the shoulder.

"Okay, Claudia. Your contractions are less than five minutes apart. I'm going to need to take a look."

As Doc lifted the bottom of the sheet to check Claudia's cervix, she closed her eyes tightly. Yes, he was a doctor, but he was a man first.

"I need you to try to relax a little. I know this is stressful, but the more I can see, the better I can help you. Take a deep breath for me, will you?"

Claudia did, and let it out slowly. Just as the doctor stepped back, Claudia had another contraction. "Is... Is it going to be okay? I mean, am I going to be okay?"

"I sure hope so. I haven't lost a patient all week."

Claudia gasped.

"I'm kidding." He gazed at her kindly. "Levity is always a good thing. Especially when you're frightened."

"Have... Ugggggh!" Claudia took shallow breaths until the contraction passed. "Have you ever delivered a baby in someone's home before?"

"A few times. It's not ideal, but I know what I'm doing, I promise."

Claudia nodded.

"I'm back, dear. See? I told you I wouldn't be gone long." Mrs. Rourke placed a trivet and a cauldron of boiling water on the dresser. She hustled back out the door and returned another minute later with a bowl of cold water and a washcloth.

Doc busied himself sterilizing his instruments in the boiling water, while Mrs. Rourke mopped Claudia's face and neck with a cool washcloth. "There, is that better?"

"Yes. Thanks."

"The contractions are coming faster. We're just about ready," Doc said. "Claudia, when I tell you to, I want you to push. Can you do that?"

Claudia closed her eyes and set her teeth.

"If it helps you, dear, think about someplace you'd rather be," Mrs. Rourke whispered in her ear. "I imagine that might be anyplace but here."

Claudia smiled thinly. She only wanted to be one place, and that was with Jessie. So she would hold onto that.

"Okay, Claudia. Push."

Claudia did. And did, and did. After an hour, she felt something shift. "Doctor?"

"The baby is coming. That's it. One more time, Claudia. I can see the head."

The pain seared Claudia's insides. She felt as though she would break in two.

"Push!"

"Arrrrgh!" Claudia closed her eyes and thought of only one thing. "Jessie!!" Claudia crushed Mrs. Rourke's hand in a vice grip.

"Push harder."

Tears flowed into Claudia's hair. "Jessie," she said, more quietly.

"I've got it. That's it. Stop pushing."

"Jessie," Claudia wept quietly.

"It's a girl," Doc said. "It's a healthy baby girl." The baby let out a cry. "Get me the other clean sheet and a clean towel, please, Emily." He cleaned the baby and placed it in the sheet before cutting the umbilical cord.

Mrs. Rourke wiped Claudia's face again. "You did it, dear. You did it. Well done. And you got what you hoped for after all— it's a girl."

"How do you feel?" Doc asked.

Claudia tried to catch her breath. "L-like a buzz saw cut me in half."

Doc and Mrs. Rourke laughed. "Very good. Would you like to meet your daughter?"

Claudia nodded and held out her arms. Doc placed the little bundle on her chest, and Claudia wrapped her arms around her daughter for the first time. She gazed down at the tiny fingers and toes, the cap of red hair, and the angelic face. "My daughter." She looked up first at Mrs. Rourke, and then at the doctor. "My daughter," she said, with wonder.

"She's beautiful, dear. Is her name Jessie?"

"What?" Claudia's eyes opened wide.

"You kept calling Jessie. Is that what you've named her?"

"No." Claudia said quickly. She closed her eyes as tears fell again. "Her name is Natalie. Natalie Amanda Turner."

"Natalie Amanda Turner," Mrs. Rourke repeated. "I like it. It has a nice ring. I bet she'll be a star."

Claudia closed her eyes. She was so very tired.

"We'll let you get some rest now, dear. Little Natalie and I will be right here when you wake up."

We have a daughter, Jess. A beautiful, angelic little girl. I'll always consider her yours and mine. Always, because that's how I would want it. If anything ever happens to me, our Natalie will know to go to you, wherever you might be, for you will always be our home.

I'm exhausted, darling, and I must get some rest while our baby sleeps, so I'll sign off for now.

I love you always.

Your girl,
Claudia

Jessie put down the letter and wiped a tear from her cheek. "Oh, Claude. I'm so sorry I wasn't there. So sorry for so many things." She blew her nose. "Natalie Amanda Turner. Turner?" Jessie re-read the last few paragraphs of the letter. Matt's last name was Dunphy. Who was Turner? Perhaps Claudia explained in a subsequent letter.

Jessie opened the next envelope and scanned the contents. There it was, in the third paragraph.

It was a spur of the moment decision, changing my last name and Natalie's. Her birth seemed like the perfect time to make a fresh start. By burying Sherwood, I would no longer have to worry about bringing shame on my family. I had other reasons too, but I won't bore you with them here. My only regret is that if you ever try to find me (oh, and my dear, dear Jessie, I hope you will), you won't be able to trace me. Still, I think it's better this way, so please forgive me.

It all made sense to Jessie now. She frowned. It was no wonder she hadn't been able to locate Claudia all those years ago when she had searched...

"Why are you looking for this woman, again?"

"None of your business. I'm paying you to find her, not to ask me questions." Jessie glared at the private detective. "Will you help me or not?"

He shrugged. "Your money's as good as anyone's I guess."

He searched for two weeks before calling Jessie to tell her he'd hit a dead end.

"What do you mean, you've come up empty? I'm not paying you for empty."

"Listen, I tracked down her parents. They weren't any too happy to see me, I can tell you that. They haven't seen her in years. After that, the trail goes cold. There's no record of a Claudia Sherwood anywhere."

"What about Claudia Dunphy?"

"Tried that too. Even went to backass Sweetwater, Texas. Found a grave marker for a Mr. and Mrs. Dunphy. Townsfolk say the woman was in her late eighties and died a few years back. The husband died in World War I."

"That must be Matt's parents."

"Well, whatever it is, there's no record of any other Dunphy in that burgh."

"Was there a grave marker there for a Matt or Matthew Dunphy?"

"Nope. Like I said. Dead end."

"Thanks for nothing," Jessie said. She put her fist to her forehead and pushed, trying to forestall the headache that was starting behind her eyes.

"It's not my fault, doll. I did what you asked. I'm not a miracle worker, you know."

"Apparently." Jessie hung up. There it was, she really never would see her Claudia again. "Well, it was a long shot, anyway. I guess I wasn't meant to find you, Claude." She put her head in her hands and cried. "I just... I just wanted to know that you were okay. That you were happy and had a good life. That's all."

Jessie poured herself a drink as the loneliness closed in around her like a shroud. It was always there, lurking, no matter whether she was alone or in a crowd. There only ever had been one person who pushed back the shadows, and it seemed that Jessie was destined never to see her again. She swirled the liquid in her glass and stared out the window at the night, but saw only her own reflection in the glass—a sad, pathetic figure. She closed the shade to shut out the image.

CHAPTER SEVENTEEN

Let's see…" Jessie thumbed through 1944 until she came to December. She held Claudia's Christmas letter up to her nose and sniffed. She imagined she could still smell the sweet perfume on the pages. Or maybe it was more than her imagination.

She wondered if Claudia had been able to go back to work at the Inglewood plant after Natalie's birth. If so, it was possible that she did have a hand in a plane that Jessie flew…

"Keaton, I've got an assignment for you."

"Yeah? I'm listening."

"I figure you might be tired of towing targets."

"It's all right."

"Yeah? Then maybe you don't want to know that they're tinkering with the damn P-51 again over in Inglewood—trying to fix the balance and visibility issues. We've been given one to test fly."

Jessie raised her eyebrows. The arrival of a P-51 at Camp Davis was big news.

"Are you game?"

The P-51 Mustang, with a maximum air speed of 440 mph and a range of six hours flight time. Jessie had flown an earlier version with a lesser engine, but this…this was something else. "Why me?"

"Call it an early Christmas present. You in or not?"

"I'm in." Jessie jogged off to get ready.

In the air, the P-51 was magnificent. With nothing but blue skies and a few broken clouds at 30,000 feet, Jessie was in a world of her own. This was the way she liked it—this was what she lived for.

"God, Claude, you'd love it up here. This isn't like anything we were flying." Jessie clicked her jaw shut. Normally, being in the air was the only place where Claudia's absence didn't haunt her. But it was such a picture perfect day. All Jessie wanted to do was to share the experience with the woman she still loved more than she cared to admit. She wished that they could have had this moment together to remember for an eternity.

Jessie banked the plane steeply to the right. It responded like a dream. She corrected and banked the other way. "There's no use wishing and dreaming for things that will never be. Get the job done and get your head out of the clouds."

When she'd finished testing maneuverability, function, visibility, and speed, Jessie radioed the tower that she was ready to bring the P-51 back down.

"Roger. You're cleared for landing. By the way, there's a big meeting about to get underway. All of the WASPs have been asked to muster. Better hustle or you'll miss it."

"Roger. Over and out."

Jessie made her descent and brought the bird in for a smooth landing. She wondered what was going on. In June, Congress had defeated a measure that would have militarized the WASP. In October, Jessie heard rumors that the WASPs were being disbanded, but she hadn't put much stock in them.

By the time she arrived, the meeting was just underway. She stood in the back of the room.

Isabel spotted her and came to stand by her side. "Glad you could make it."

"All right. Settle down, everyone." A hush fell over the room. "I'm sure you've been hearing chatter about the fate of this program. I'm here to tell you it's true."

The crowd started to buzz. "Hang on, hang on. I've got my orders. As of 20 December 1944, the WASP program will be disbanded. On that date, all of you will be expected to pack up and be on your way. That's all. You're dismissed."

"Just like that? That's tomorrow!" Isabel turned to Jessie. "No, 'thanks for your service,' or 'we really appreciate everything you did, you were a great help to the war effort'?"

Jessie stood stock still, staring straight ahead. So this was it. She'd studiously avoided thinking about life after the WASPs. Where was she supposed to go? Was she supposed to go home and pick up where she left off, as if her whole life hadn't been transformed by joining the WASPs and meeting Claudia? She headed toward the exit.

"Jessie?" Isabel caught up to her.

"What do you want from me?"

"Don't you have anything to say?"

"Think about the way we've been treated all the way along, kid. What did you expect? A twenty-one-gun salute? We go out the way we came in, without fanfare or support."

"And that's okay with you?"

Jessie shrugged. "I didn't get in it for the attention. I love to fly. It's what I do. It's what defines me. Period. I got a chance to do what I love and to support my country at the same time. That's why I'm here. Why are you here?"

Isabel chewed her lip. "I love to fly too. And I wanted to make a difference."

"Let me guess—you need someone else to tell you, you made a difference, right?"

"Well, it would be nice."

"Listen, out in the world, you'll be waiting a long time for folks to recognize you. Be strong enough to trust your own judgment. Do you think you made a difference?"

Isabel straightened up to her full height. "I know I did."

"There you go. You don't need anything else."

"Are you always so sure of yourself?"

"Me?" Jessie thought of Claudia, and how she had made Jessie feel like an awkward bumbling, babbling fool. "Not always." Jessie picked up her pace and left Isabel behind.

She went back to the barracks and packed up her things. A lot of the girls were milling about, talking about their plans for the future. Some of them were looking forward to getting married and settling down. Others wanted to go back to school. A few were thinking about traveling around the country together.

Jessie let all the conversation wash over her. She knew she should be concentrating on her immediate future, on where she would lay her head tomorrow night, but all she could do was wonder where Claudia was. The baby would be eight months old now. Was it a boy or a girl? Was Claudia healthy? Were they living with her parents? Maybe if she and Matt were married, Claudia would have returned to Sweetwater to live with Mrs. Dunphy until Matt came home from the war.

Jessie stretched out on the bed with her hands under her head and her legs crossed at the ankle. This was a regular exercise of hers—to torture herself with thoughts of Claudia and her life. This time, though, was different. Always when Jessie daydreamed, she fantasized about Claudia coming for her, using her connection to the WASPs to find out where Jessie was stationed. She pictured Claudia pleading with her for another chance to be together, to raise the child as a couple, to live out the rest of their days as a family.

After today, any likelihood, no matter how remote, of Claudia being able to locate Jessie decreased to virtually nothing. It wasn't that Jessie believed that Claudia would come back, it was that the possibility existed. "Not anymore," Jessie muttered. "You're on your own, Keaton."

Not knowing what else to do with herself, Jessie decided she should probably head back to Indian Lake. At the very least, she needed to check on the cabin and make sure it was still habitable. Since she had very little cash, living for free made sense...at least until she could save some money. Presumably her plane remained in the hangar in Lake Placid where she'd left it. If she could get the old truck running, she could take a ride over and see if she could drum up some business carrying passengers around New England.

In the early morning hours, Jessie hoisted her duffle bag and slipped out before any of the other girls stirred. There was no one she needed to say goodbye to. She would leave the WASPs as she came in—alone and friendless.

"Well, Claude," Jessie said, taking a sip of water and unfolding the letter from Christmas 1944, "going home was about the worst thing I could've done." She shook her head. "I have no idea what I was thinking. I had way too much time on my hands and nothing better to do than spend my days and nights fixated on you. Even I knew it wasn't good for me, although I didn't much care at the time. I was in a bad way. I sure hope you fared better than me."

Christmas 1944

My Dearest Darling Jessie,

Another Christmas without you. It's unbearable. Our little Natalie is a very sweet baby. She doesn't cry or fuss much, and she mostly sleeps through the night. Still, I had no idea how tiring being a mother would be. I'm exhausted most of the time. Between taking care of the baby and taking in sewing jobs, I have very little time to myself.

What time I do have, darling, I spend thinking about you. Oh, how I wish I could be with you. I look up in the sky and imagine I see you flying overhead.

I don't get much news here, but one of the girls who works in the Inglewood factory has kept in touch. She stopped by the other day to see the baby. A friend of hers is in the WASPs, stationed at Santa Monica. She told me the most horrible news. She says the WASPs have been disbanded. I couldn't believe my ears.

Of course, the first thing I thought was, "Poor Jessie." Where are you, sugar? Are you still in Las Vegas? Will you stay there and find work? I'm desperate for word of you, but I don't want to violate your privacy. You made it very clear you never want to see me again, and, as much as that rips my heart out, I will honor your wishes.

Sometimes I almost convince myself that you only said that in the heat of the moment, and that if I showed up one day, you'd throw your arms around me and take me back. Then I tell myself I'm only being silly and selfish, that you don't want anything to do with me. On those days I cry often.

Well, enough of the maudlin.

Mrs. Rourke has been very good to me and Natalie. She watches after her sometimes to give me a little break, and she drums up sewing business for me with her friends. She tells them someday I'll be a great fashion designer. As if.

I've almost saved up enough money to buy that Singer sewing machine I've been eyeing. That ought to make the jobs go much quicker, not to mention save my fingers and eyesight.

Oh, Jess. I do want to know you're safe and that you've got someplace to go. Will you go back to upstate New York? I hope not. That place is too small and isolated for you. You need to be around people, darling. You spend too much time apart.

Listen to me, still fussing after you as if I could have a say. Well, the baby just woke up, so I have to go.

I love you with all my heart and soul. Merry Christmas, Jess.

Your girl,
Claudia

✒✒

Jessie grabbed her cane and hobbled to the bathroom. She dabbed at her eyes and splashed water on her face. The years had been kinder to her than they should have been, she thought. The face that stared back at her was almost free of wrinkles and age spots. Her eyes remained clear and alert. The cap of gray hair was thick and not too unruly.

"You got off lucky, that's for sure." Jessie shook her head. She'd spent so much of her life defying the odds—taking unnecessary risks, daring God to take her. There was nothing He could do that would be worse than leaving her to live without her Claudia.

There was so much she wanted to forget, so much she chose not to examine too closely. Were it not for Claudia's letters, Jessie gladly would have left the past alone altogether. But this was Claudia—her Claudia—and for her, Jessie would walk through fire still, or revisit a life of which she was not proud.

Jessie considered the ten years after the WASPs were disbanded the lost decade. Apart from resurrecting her flying taxi service, she saw no one socially, made no friends, rarely went into town except to pick up groceries, and became so reclusive that she missed the McCarthy hearings and the Communist witch hunt altogether. It was uncanny that, even from so far away, Claudia knew what was good for Jessie. "You were so right, Claude. I never should have stayed alone for so long. I forgot what it was like to be in society."

It might have gone on that way forever, had it not been for a chance encounter with a woman whose car broke down on the side of the road when Jessie was on her way to the Lake Placid air field. It was August, 1954.

"Thank you for stopping."

"What's the problem?"

"I'm not sure. It just stalled and won't start again."

Jessie assessed the woman. She wore an expensive-looking dress and more jewelry than Jessie could ever remember seeing on one woman in one place. "You're not from around here."

"No. New York City. My husband came up here to buy a piece of property. I hate listening to men talk business, so I thought I'd see a little of the countryside."

"Doesn't look like you'll be seeing much of anything until your car gets fixed." The woman pouted, and it reminded Jessie of Claudia. It amazed her how much that could still hurt.

"What am I going to do?"

Jessie sighed. "Get in."

"I'm sorry?"

"Get in my truck. I'll give you a ride into town, and we'll get Charlie, the mechanic at the garage, to come take a look at your car."

"That's awfully nice of you..."

"Jessie."

"Jessie. I'm Regina."

That already was more information than Jessie wanted to know. She had an uneasy feeling, the kind of gut reaction that told her Regina was trouble. She was pretty, obviously rich, and had the kind of smile that no doubt made men melt. While it didn't have quite the same effect on Jessie, she felt a tingling sensation in parts of her body she had long since pronounced dead.

Jessie pulled back onto the road.

"So, Jessie." She could feel Regina watching her. "What is it you do for a living?"

"I'm a pilot."

"A pilot? How fascinating."

"Not really."

"Well, it is to me."

Jessie counted. The silence lasted all of twenty-two seconds. "What kind of pilot?"

"A good one."

Regina laughed. "And modest too. That's not what I meant."

"I know."

"The strong, silent type, eh? I like that."

Now Jessie knew she was in trouble. "I fly an air taxi. People hire me who want to sightsee or want to get from here to there and don't want to drive."

"That's much better. Thank you. For a second, I thought I was going to have to torture the information out of you."

"Funny, you don't strike me as the violent type."

"Guess you never know about people, do you?"

"Guess not. We're here." Jessie pulled into the gas station. She came around and opened the door for Regina and helped her out.

"Ooh. Such a gentlewoman. Why, thank you."

Jessie walked toward the garage without answering. "Hey Charlie. Look lively. Got a fancy woman here who needs your help."

"Hey, Jessie." Charlie wiped his greasy hands on a rag and followed her out. "What's the problem?"

"Her car broke down about eight miles down the road. Looks like it overheated."

Charlie frowned. "I can go take a look, but it'll be a little while. Gotta fix old Paul's car first. You know how he is. Grumpy old cuss."

"Yeah, I know."

"Hello," Charlie said, as he got a look at Regina. "Isn't everyday a dame like that waltzes into my garage."

"Easy, Romeo. She didn't walk in, she came in my truck. And she has a rich husband."

Charlie sighed. "All the good ones are taken." He walked over to Regina and doffed his cap. "Hello, ma'am. Jessie here tells me your car needs some work."

"Yes, can you help me?"

"Yep. I sure can. But it will probably be a couple hours before I can get away from here."

"Oh. Guess I'll have to find something to do for a while, huh?" Jessie noted that Regina hardly looked crestfallen. "Maybe Jessie would be kind enough to keep me company?" She batted her eyelashes.

"I have work to do," Jessie muttered.

"I understand. I certainly wouldn't want you to lose any business on account of me. How about if I pay you to show me the sights?"

Jessie frowned. Regina was definitely trouble. Then again, she could use the money, and she didn't have any flights booked this morning. "All right. Let's go."

Regina clapped her hands in delight.

"Sorry, Charlie." Jessie winked at him. "I'll drop her back off around lunchtime."

"Wish I was the one showing her the sights." He chucked Jessie on the shoulder. "Have fun."

Jessie strapped Regina in, ran an instrument check, and asked the tower for clearance to take off. When they were airborne, she turned to Regina. "What do you want to see?" Regina was staring at her in that same disconcerting way. Jessie tried hard not to squirm under the scrutiny.

"Show me someplace private. Someplace you don't take anyone else."

Jessie swallowed hard as the tingling started again. As Claudia would surely attest, Jessie wasn't always swift on the uptake, but she would've had to be dead not to recognize the suggestion in the tone and timbre of Regina's voice. It had been eleven years since Claudia left. In all that time, Jessie hadn't so much as looked at another woman.

"Won't your husband be missing you?"

"Chad?" Regina threw her head back and laughed. "The only thing he ever misses is his money. He doesn't care what I do, as long as I'm discreet." Regina reached over and ran a long, painted fingernail along the length of Jessie's thigh.

Moisture pooled between Jessie's legs, and she tried to ignore the thrum of desire that pulsed through her. She knew this was a bad idea, knew she should turn the plane around and take Regina back to the garage to wait for Charlie to fix her car. But that's not what her body wanted, and Claudia was never coming back. She blew out an explosive breath. "Hang on."

Jessie flew them to Burlington, Vermont, and parked the plane. Just down the street from the airport was a quaint little inn where she sometimes stayed overnight when she was too tired to fly home. She told Regina to stay out of sight while she went to the reservation desk.

"Hey, Charlotte."

"Early in the day for you, Jessie, isn't it?"

"Yeah. I didn't sleep well last night, and I've got a few hours before I need to be back. I thought I'd get a room and catch some shuteye for a bit. Doesn't pay to fly tired."

"Sure. I don't want you having an accident on my conscience. Room twelve is free. It's all yours."

"Thanks, Charlotte." Jessie took the key and walked away. When Charlotte turned her back to talk to someone in the office, Jessie hustled outside.

"Ready, sugar?" Regina asked.

Jessie backed up as if she'd been shot. Her breath stalled in her chest. "What did you say?"

"I said—"

"Never mind. Don't ever call me that again." Jessie rubbed her hand over her heart. "*Ever!*"

"Okay," Regina said, holding up her hands. "I promise. I didn't mean anything by it."

Jessie thought about running and never looking back. Then she glanced at Regina again. It was clear she had no idea what she'd done wrong. *It's not her fault.* Eleven years later, Jessie missed Claudia as much as she had when she left. *Regina is not Claudia. Eleven years is a long time. After today, you'll never see this woman again.* Jessie convinced herself that she could do this. "Room twelve, down the hall and to the left. You take the key and go first. I'll follow you in a minute or two."

Maybe if she shut her eyes tightly enough, she could imagine it was Claudia she was making love to. Or maybe, for just a few minutes, she could lose herself and forget. Either way, it was time to move on. Jessie counted to one hundred and walked down the hall.

CHAPTER EIGHTEEN

Yeah, Claude. I knew I shouldn't have done that. Oh, that woman was more than attractive enough, and it was obvious I wasn't the first girl she'd ever lured into a tryst. But, even after eleven years, I wasn't ready to take that step with anyone except you."

Afterward, Jessie remembered, she'd cried for days. "It felt like I betrayed you, Claude. Like I turned my back on what we had. What I did with Regina in that room had nothing to do with love and everything to do with scratching an itch, not to mention the fact that she used me. I was so ashamed."

Jessie watched the sun as it dipped below the horizon outside her hotel room window. Over the years there'd been too many women. None of them filled the empty spot in the center of Jessie's heart. "All this time, sweetheart, it's only ever been you."

What did Natalie say? Didn't she say her mother never even had been on a date? Was that just a child's perception? If Matt really never came back into the picture, was it possible that there had been no one else in Claudia's life? Had she remained faithful to Jessie all these years?

Jessie fingered the packets of letters. Did she really want to know? She answered her own question by reluctantly reaching back into the box. She might not want to know, but she desperately needed to know.

August 10, 1945

My Dearest Darling Jess,

The war is over! A B-29 dropped the atomic bomb on a Japanese city. Can you believe it? I don't suppose you got to fly one of them.

I'm so torn. Naturally, I'm ecstatic that we've won and that our troops will be coming home. On the other hand, I'm jumpy as a cat. I know it's silly to worry. After all, Matt doesn't even know I was pregnant, doesn't know that I've got a new last name, and has no idea where to find me. Still, I have nightmares that he might try, and I awake drenched in sweat.

I suppose I could do some snooping to try to find out where he is, but I don't want to set off any alarm bells. Who knows? Maybe he died in combat or maybe he's found some other girl by now. I hope so.

I give myself pep talks. I remind myself, dear Jess, that you and I are the only ones who know that Matt is Natalie's father. That's a secret I will take to the grave, and I can't imagine you're anxious to blab that, either.

Oh, dear. Speaking of Natalie, she's just awoken from her nap and is looking for her mama. I wish you could see her, love. She's a got a gorgeous mop of curly hair, blue-blue eyes, and the cutest dimple on her cheek. If you could pick her up and hold her, darling, I know you'd fall instantly and irrevocably in love with her, as I have. Children are so innocent.

That's all for now. Wherever you are, sugar, know that I love and miss you more than ever.

Your girl,
Claudia

"Well," Jessie put the letter aside and searched for another from a different year, "I guess that puts one question mark to rest. You really didn't have any intention of marrying Matt." All these years later, it still niggled Jessie. The Claudia she knew wasn't likely to make a casual decision to have sex with anyone. So, if she wasn't interested in Matt as husband material, why had she agreed to let him bed her?

September 5, 1950

My Dearest Darling Jess,

I don't know who cried harder at taking our darling Natalie to school for the very first time today. I think it was probably equally traumatic for both of us.

She wore a beautiful yellow dress that I made for her with my own hands—that is, the Singer and I made it for her. It's amazing how much faster I can get outfits done now that I don't have to sew them by hand. I laugh at myself sometimes when I think that I've got three loves in my life—you, Natalie, and my sewing machine.

I went over to see Mrs. Rourke after I dropped Natalie off. It's so nice that I was able to get us our own place within walking distance. Natalie so loves her "Rookie," as she calls Mrs. Rourke. When she was younger, she couldn't pronounce Rourke, so Rookie was as close as she could come. It's endearing, really. And Mrs. Rourke loves Natalie right back, as if she were her own. Sometimes, she'll watch Natalie for me so I can have some time to myself. Not that I'm doing anything with that time, but it is nice to know I don't have to be on "mom watch" every second.

Mrs. Rourke keeps trying to get me to go out more and socialize.

"A lovely young woman such as yourself, all alone in the world without a man to support you and that adorable child. It's not right, I tell you."

"I'm fine, Mrs. Rourke. Natalie and the sewing keeps me plenty busy, and I can always come over and talk to you."

"It's not the same, and you know it. You're barely scraping by. You need a good, strong man in your life. Someone to love you and provide for you the way my Arthur does me."

"Change the topic, please."

Mrs. Rourke glared at Claudia. "All right. It's time for you to spread your wings."

"Mrs. Rou—"

"Ah, ah. Let me finish. You're the best seamstress I've ever seen. It's a waste for you to sit at home creating beautiful clothing for people who can't pay you what your work is worth."

"Thank you for the compliment, Mrs. Rourke, but I hardly think—"

"Good Lord in Heaven, girl. Are you ever going to let me finish a thought?" Mrs. Rourke gave Claudia "that" look, the one that made even her older children stop dead in their tracks.

"Sorry, ma'am."

"As well you should be. I've made some inquiries on your behalf. Showed some of your work to a friend of mine who has some connections in Hollywood."

"You…" Claudia opened her mouth and closed it again.

"That's right. Don't look so shocked." Mrs. Rourke puffed herself up. "I've got friends in important places."

Claudia shouldn't have been surprised. Mrs. Rourke was a social butterfly who seemed to know everyone's business. "I didn't mean to imply that you wouldn't know people, it just surprises me that you would spend time talking about me."

"Well, of course, dear. I love you as if you were my own. I want to make sure you have the life you should, that's all. Anyway, my friend loved your work. She showed it to her friend, who is working over at one of the big studios."

"No kidding?"

"No kidding. And that's not all."

"It's not?" Claudia couldn't believe it. Someone in the movies had seen one of her dresses. Or maybe it was a suit?

"Nope. You have an appointment tomorrow morning to see the head costume designer at Twentieth Century Fox."

"T-tomorrow?"

"That's right." Mrs. Rourke looked very satisfied with herself.

"But what would I wear? What will I say? Should I take samples with me?"

"Calm down, dear. I'll help you pick out an outfit. You'll tell them how much experience you have and that you've been designing clothes from scratch for a regular clientele for years. Then you'll show them some of your designs and some of your craftsmanship and they'll hire you on the spot."

"But my designs are nothing more than pencil drawings on pieces of scrap paper."

Mrs. Rourke patted her hand. "That'll be fine, I'm sure. They just need to see what you're capable of. Now come on, let's go over to your place and pick out something smashing for you to wear."

Well, Jess, darling. You won't believe it. I got the job! Me, designing costumes for big movie stars. Can you imagine? You know how much I love the pictures. The first movie I'll be working on is a film coming out in the next year or so, called *Monkey Business*. Wait until you hear who's in the cast! It stars Cary Grant, Ginger Rogers, Charles Coburn, and Marilyn Monroe. Oh, sugar. Me, designing dresses for Ginger Rogers and Marilyn Monroe. And maybe a suit for Cary Grant. He's so elegant!

It's a little nerve-wracking. Not only that, but I'm going to have to hustle in order to drop Natalie off at school on time, get to the studio, and be back at school to pick her up.

I am so tired, and tomorrow is my first day at work, so I'll sign off now. How I wish you were here to share my days and nights, darling.

Your girl,
Claudia

Jessie whistled in appreciation. "A costume designer? That must've been the perfect job for you, Claude, and I bet you were great at it." Jessie recalled their shopping excursion in Palm Springs and how Claudia had looked in that gown. She sure had a sense for fashion…

September 6, 1950

My Dearest Darling Jess,

I'm sitting here with my feet up. Boy, do they ache! I spent most of the day measuring, cutting, and running from place to place. My goodness, who knew it would be so exhausting?

Alas, there were no star sightings. I got stuck fitting over sixty extras for a single scene. It was insane. And these actors. They think they're God's gift to women. Three of them asked me on dates (of course, I said no, darling), and another patted my behind. Rest assured, I gave him a piece of my mind.

In the end, I survived the day, but I'm not so sure this is the right place for me. I'll give it a little more time before I make up my mind but don't let anyone tell you this is a glamorous life.

Speaking of glamorous, our little girl is turning into the belle of the ball. After only two days in school, she already has an invitation to play at a classmate's house. I'm inclined to accept, since I do so want Natalie to socialize and make friends. As I know you know, being an only child isn't easy. So tomorrow, she'll go over to Frieda's house to play with her dolls. Oh, to be a little girl again, with no obligations or worries.

Still, I wouldn't trade my life for anything. If I did, then I never would have met you. No matter what else is true, darling, that will always, always, be the highlight of my life. I try not to think about how long it's been since last I saw you, kissed you, held you. When I do, the longing is nearly unbearable. See? Here I go.

I love you, sugar, with every fiber of my being. When I lie in my bed at night, I imagine that you are holding me in your arms, and I go to sleep with a smile on my face. And so it will be tonight.

All my love, your girl,
Claudia

Jessie closed her eyes and squeezed the bridge of her nose. Sometimes, that would help stave off a headache. She was having more and more of those these days.

She easily could picture Claudia sitting at the dining room table in her stockings with her feet on a chair, drinking a tall glass of lemonade. The tip of her tongue would brush her upper lip as she concentrated on putting the words on the paper. Or Claudia lying in bed…

It had been sixty-seven years since the last time Jessie saw Claudia, the last time she held her, the last time they made love. The longing was almost as acute today as it had been all those years ago. What she wouldn't give to hold her Claude one more time…

⋙⋘

April 13, 1960

My Dearest Darling Jess,

Today, as you know, is our sweet Natalie's sixteenth birthday. I'm laughing at myself because it would be impossible for you to know when her birthday is, since I haven't sent any of these letters. Still, sometimes it feels so much like you're here with us I forget that I'm really only writing so that I can feel close to you. Pretty pathetic, huh?

Here I am, thirty-eight years old, and I pine for you today as much as I did when we were youngsters back in Sweetwater. You are, and will always be, my one and only, darling. My friends have never understood why I always turn down requests for dates. They all have husbands (and, in one case I'm pretty sure, a girlfriend). They can't know what it feels like to be consumed by love for someone I can only have in my dreams.

What about you, sugar? Is there someone special in your life? The very thought of it makes my knees turn to rubber and my heart pound out of my chest in rebellion. I harbor no illusions that I'm your one and only after so much time, especially since you probably believe I married Matt.

Sorry, I got the paper wet again. Sometimes I just can't help myself. Where was I? Oh, I started by talking about Natalie. I'll go back to that, since that's a safe topic.

Sweet sixteen. She's a wonder, Jess. I really think you'd like her a lot. Of course, you'd love her because she's our daughter. But more than that, she's an outstanding person. You'd be so proud. She's at the very top of her class—smart as a whip. And she's a good girl. She doesn't get into trouble like so many other kids her age. Oh, she goes out to the drive-in every now and again with her friends. But she spends more time preparing for her debate team matches and doing chemistry experiments that I can't begin to understand.

For her sixteenth birthday, she wanted me to take her up flying. Can you imagine? Says she wants to be a pilot like you and me. She recites back to me the stories I told her as a small child of our adventures in the sky at Avenger Field. I've tried to tell her that in real life it's not romantic to have your engines cut out midflight, but she ignores me.

"If it was good enough for you and Jessie, it's good enough for me."

"Things were different back then."

"Right. The planes are safer nowadays."

"You're maddening, child, and you're wearing me out."

"Then we can go?"

"I didn't say that. Jess and I, we had a lot of hours as experienced pilots before we ever got to Sweetwater. And still, it was a dangerous business. Women lost their lives."

"But not you. You crash-landed twice and hardly suffered a scratch."

"I was very lucky."

"You were very good. And from what you've always told me, Jessie was even better."

"She was, but if Jessie was here right now she'd lock you in your room and forbid you to come out until you gave up on this silly notion."

"It wasn't silly for you two. So is it only silly because I'm the one who wants to do it?"

"Of course not."

"You fly every day."

"That's work."

"So am I supposed to worry every time you go up?"

"No, Natalie. I'm an experienced pilot."

"You've never been afraid to let me fly with you before."

"That's because I'm the one at the controls."

"You always say the Cessna 172 is a good, safe, sturdy plane."

"It is."

"Then it should be perfect for you to teach me on it."

"You are incorrigible and relentless, you know that? Why can't you be like normal girls your age and want me to take you to a rock 'n roll concert or something?"

"Elvis is a dream. If you were going to take me to one of his concerts, I might consider it…"

"And pigs can fly if you think I can get us a ticket to that."

"You have all these connections. You fly these big Hollywood stars and rock 'n roll geniuses from gig to gig and home again. Surely you could lean on one of the—"

"Absolutely not, young lady. How many times have I told you that's not permitted? I'm nothing more than a chauffeur in the air."

"So you keep telling me. I never get to meet anyone famous. You make costumes for them, you fly them around, and everything, and I never get to even shake their hands." Natalie crossed her arms and pouted.

"You are so underprivileged, child. Poor baby. I'm such an awful mother. Natalie, honey, have I ever missed your bedtime? Ever?"

"No."

"Do you have any idea what it takes for me to be home in time to make you dinner most nights? Or to kiss you goodnight before bed? Or to help you with your homework? Or to drive you and your friends to the drive-in or the hamburger joint?"

"I know. I'm sorry, Mama. I always tell you, you work too hard." Natalie gave her mother a hug. "Now, will you give me that flying lesson?"

As you might have guessed, sugar, I can't deny our girl anything. So, this afternoon I took her up in the Cessna 172. Teaching her to fly brought so many memories of Sweetwater and Vegas flooding back. I didn't think I could handle it emotionally, but I managed not to cry until I got her safely down and I was alone. It should have been you taking her up, not me. She's special, Jess, and darn it all, she has an uncanny aptitude for flying. As I said, you'd be proud of her.

I miss you so much it hurts, darling.

Your girl,
Claudia

So Claudia had gone back to flying, after all. And not just any flying, either. She was pilot to the stars. "Good for you, Claude. They were in excellent hands."

Jessie re-read the first few paragraphs of the letter.

What about you, sugar? Is there someone special in your life?

Jessie sadly shook her head. By April 1960, she was living in a small apartment in lower Manhattan...

"Come back to bed, tiger." The naked woman lay sprawled across Jessie's bed, half tangled in the sheets.

"It's time for you to go home."

"But I just got here a little while ago."

Jessie paraded naked back in from the kitchen, scooped up the woman's clothes, and thrust them at her. "Get out."

The woman pouted and batted her eyelashes.

"Doesn't work with me. Put on your clothes or I'll send you out the door 'as is'."

"You wouldn't."

"Do you really want to test me?" Jessie had a hangover to beat the band, and all she wanted to do was change the sheets, take a shower, and go to sleep. "I'm going to count to three..."

"Okay, okay already. Sheesh." The woman sat up, making no effort to hide her glorious body. "Are you sure, tiger? I could go one more round for you." She made a point of looking Jessie up and down.

Jessie folded her arms menacingly over her chest. "One."

The woman stood up slowly and hunted for her lace panties. "I get the point." In the middle of getting dressed, she paused. "Why'd you bring me here, anyway?"

Jessie shrugged. "You said you wanted to know what it was like to have intercourse with a woman. You practically begged me for it. I was just fulfilling your fantasy."

"Pretty sure of yourself, aren't you?" The woman narrowed her eyes. "What makes you think that satisfied my itch?"

Jessie laughed harshly. "It might have been the three orgasms you had, or the screams for more, or your nails on my back urging me on..." Jessie examined her non-existent cuticles. "Or it might have been you telling me it was never this good with your husband."

The woman had the grace to blush. She hurriedly put on the rest of her clothes. "Are you even going to tell me your name? Don't you even want to know mine?"

"No." Jessie escorted the woman to the door.

"I don't suppose there's any chance for an encore another time?"

"No." Jessie opened the door.

"Here's your hat, where's your hurry." The woman sighed. "Well, it was nice while it lasted, tiger." She patted Jessie on the cheek and disappeared down the stairs.

When she was gone, Jessie closed and bolted the door, then leaned heavily against it. Every time this happened, she promised herself it would be the last time. What was wrong with her anyway?

She shoved away from the door and strode over to the bed, where she gathered the sheets and threw them in the laundry basket.

In the shower, Jessie let the scalding hot water wash away her shame. She leaned her forearm against the tiles and rested her head on it. The tears flowed freely, as they always did after sex.

Thoughts of Claudia, tightly locked away during these interludes, flooded to the surface, bringing Jessie to her knees.

"Oh, Claude, I'm so glad you can't see me now, can't see what I've become."

Most of the women Jessie took to bed were married to wealthy and powerful men. They considered her something exotic and forbidden, and that added to their excitement. She never approached them—they always seemed to find her. In truth, she considered herself little more than a conduit to satisfy these women's curiosity and to relieve their boredom.

It wasn't about love. Jessie was careful to avoid any possibility of bedding someone with whom she might be tempted to have more than one night or afternoon of pleasure. Love was an emotion that was reserved solely and exclusively for Claudia. There was no room in her heart for anyone else.

Alone in the shower, Jessie allowed herself to mourn all that she had lost. She stood up again and leaned her forehead against the cool tiles. Her fingers found her nipples, then her belly, then her center. She called up a treasured memory of making love with Claudia, and let her imagination take over. It was Claudia pinching her nipples, Claudia running her hand downward, Claudia's mouth on her clit, Claudia's fingers inside her.

Jessie gasped and shuddered. These were the only times she let her guard down—the only times she allowed the real Jessie to emerge, still quiet, shy, and unsure of herself.

As the ghost of Claudia brought her to orgasm, Jessie affirmed, "Now and always, my love. It's only ever been you, as it will always be."

CHAPTER NINETEEN

The moon was rising outside the hotel window, and Jessie was starting to tire. So many years remained between her and Claudia, and the day was slipping away too quickly. For reasons she didn't fully understand, she was determined to bring herself current on Claudia's life before she left Washington. Natalie hadn't said she needed the letters back, but Jessie figured she should have them for posterity. She thought about that.

If Natalie read the letters, then she would know that Claudia and Jessie were lovers. Jessie considered. In this day and age, that wasn't such a big deal, was it? But back then... And how would Natalie feel, knowing her mother was a lesbian?

In the conversation at the ceremony, Natalie alluded to the fact that she knew Claudia was in love with Jessie. But that was different than having written proof, wasn't it?

Jessie glanced at the bedside clock. She was wasting valuable time debating with herself. She should keep reading and decide what to do about the letters when she was done.

November 22, 1963

My Dearest Darling Jess,

I'm crying as I write this. Our beloved president is dead. What is this world coming to? Everyone wandered around the set in a state of disbelief as word spread. Eventually, we were all sent home.

In order to distract myself from this dreadful news, I'll tell you that I received a letter today from our brilliant daughter, Natalie. She is having a grand time at Stanford University, learning lots and making

more friends than she knows what to do with. Tuition is expensive—
$1,000! But, if it helps her to have a better life than I had, I'll gladly take
a third or fourth job to make it happen for her.

I've forbidden her from becoming a pilot, so now she's set her sights
on medicine. Our little girl wants to be a doctor, Jess. I never would've
envisioned that such a thing was possible for a woman. A nurse, yes,
but a doctor? I'm so proud, my buttons are going to burst.

Are you watching Walter Cronkite report on the television, wherever
you are? I wish you were here to hold me, sugar, and tell me everything
will be all right. Poor Jackie looks positively beside herself. Who can
blame her?

I love you, now and always.

Your girl,
Claudia

Jessie folded the letter. Who didn't remember where they were
when President Kennedy was shot? It was mid-afternoon in New
York, and Jessie was sitting in her favorite chair watching *As the
World Turns*. The soap opera was a guilty pleasure. When Walter
Cronkite broke into the program with the news that Kennedy had
been shot and then again a little later confirming his death, Jessie
cried.

Thinking about it even so many years later still made her eyes
well up. "No time for that now, old sod. Get on with it."

June 21, 1969

My Dearest Darling Jess,

Dr. Natalie Amanda Turner. It has a lovely ring to it, don't you
agree? Natalie blushes every time I introduce her as my daughter, the
doctor. She constantly reminds me that she still has residencies to do,
but as I say to her, "Your diploma says you're a doctor of medicine. Who
am I to argue with that?"

Eventually she relents, if only to shut me up. I am visiting her right
now. She wanted me to meet her new boyfriend, so I just finished
having dinner with them. He seems like a nice enough boy, though I'm
not sure any boy would be good enough for our daughter in my eyes. I
know, I know, I'm biased. In any event, I continue to marvel at how the
tumultuous times haven't seemed to faze Natalie a bit. Perhaps it's

204

because she always has her head in a book, but with all the hullabaloo at Berkeley and on other campuses, I should think she'd be more affected. Not that I'm complaining, mind you.

How about you, my love? Are you in the thick of things or sitting out the strife tucked away in the mountains somewhere? All this talk of "free love" and protesting against the war. Can you imagine if our generation had done this? I can't. Maybe I'm just getting old.

I'll tell you this, darling. I'm not too old to remember making sweet love to you and I wish more than anything that I could do that again. I miss you still.

Your faithful girl,
Claudia

The summer of 1969. It was one of those periods that defined Jessie's life, and she had no trouble at all recalling what was going on for her. Sitting out the strife? "Not exactly, Claude. If you only knew…"

"Hey good-looking. What's the action tonight?" A tall, leggy blonde leaned against the bar and gave Jessie the once over.

"It's summer in Greenwich Village, it's hot and humid, and the cops are out hunting for fays. Nothing new to report."

"Same old, same old. Got a light?"

Jessie reached into the pocket of her new jeans. She didn't smoke, but she always carried a lighter to accommodate the ladies. "Here you go."

"I know I've seen you in here before."

Jessie shrugged. "Probably. I hang out here once in a while."

"Yeah?" The woman blew out a stream of smoke. Why is that?"

Jessie looked down at herself and back up, her eyebrows arched. "Where else would you expect to find someone like me?"

"You mean a strong, handsome butch?" A red fingernail traveled the length of Jessie's vest.

"Whatever you say."

"I say I wouldn't mind seeing the rest of what you're hiding under there."

Jessie pushed the woman's hand away. "Not tonight."

The woman pouted and gave Jessie a smoldering glance. "Can I get a rain check?"

"Maybe."

Before the woman could respond, the front double doors opened and police burst in.

"Shit," Jessie said. "Here we go again."

The house lights were turned on and everyone was told to line up. Jessie prepared for what she knew would follow—a female officer would escort her to the bathroom so that she could prove she was wearing at least three articles of women's clothing.

Yet, as Jessie looked around her, something seemed different tonight. Men refused to produce their identification and others refused to have their clothing checked. The police seemed antsy, and Jessie smelled trouble brewing.

"All right, that's it. The lot of you are coming downtown."

An officer pulled Jessie's hands roughly and slapped handcuffs on her.

"These are too tight. They're cutting off my circulation."

"Yeah, what are you gonna do about it?" He intentionally brushed against her breasts.

Jessie wanted to spit in his eye. Instead, she glared daggers at him. He dragged her by the handcuffs out to the waiting paddy wagon.

"The hell with this," Jessie muttered. She had no desire to spend the rest of the night in a jail cell. As soon as he turned his back after putting her in the paddy wagon, she escaped. He came after her again. Again she eluded him. The next time, she felt his billy club crack her on the head. Her vision went hazy as he threw her back in the wagon.

"Come on, come with me." Someone helped Jessie up and led her out of the wagon and into the middle of a gathering crowd. "Let's get you out of here."

Jessie tasted blood in her mouth. Her head was bleeding and her vision was less than stellar. "I don't live too far from here. Just a little ways down Christopher Street."

"Okay. Show me where."

Jessie blinked and tried to clear her vision. "Another block on the left." She tried to make out the features of her savior in the dim light from the streetlamp. He looked vaguely familiar, like she had seen him somewhere before. "Who are you?"

"I'm Jason, although my friends call me Lila." He smiled at Jessie and winked. "I've seen you at the bar a couple of times. I remember because you seem a little old for that crowd. No offense."

"None taken. You're probably right, but I like to watch the dancing, and it's close to my place, so..." Jessie tried to orient herself. "Okay. Three brownstones down on the left."

"Got it. You have a key?"

"Sure." Jessie tried in vain to put her hand in her pocket. The handcuffs she still wore prevented her from being able to reach.

"You want me to get that?"

Jessie sighed. "Doesn't seem like I have much of a choice."

"I'll be gentle. I promise."

"I bet you say that to all the boys."

Lila laughed delightedly and clapped his hands. "I like you..."

"I'm Jessie."

"...Jessie." He fished in Jessie's pocket and pulled out her apartment key.

"Third floor, second door to the right."

"Of course, a sturdy butch like you would never live on the first floor. That would be too convenient. You need to show your virility."

"You look like you're in pretty good shape to me. Stop your complaining." Jessie bumped him in the shoulder.

They climbed the stairs to the third floor, and Lila let them into Jessie's apartment. He looked around and whistled. "Nice pad."

"Thanks."

"You're so neat."

"What were you expecting?" Jessie motioned him toward the kitchen.

"I don't know. I've never been in a butch's place before."

"There's a handcuff key in the cookie jar on the counter."

Lila's eyebrows shot up.

"I like to be prepared." Jessie tried for nonchalance. The key had been given to her by one of her trysts—a female cop—in case she ever got in trouble.

"I'll say, sugar," Lila said, as she worked the key in the lock.

Jessie's body tensed, and she sat down heavily.

"Did I hurt you?"

"N-no." Jessie bit her lip and blinked back the tears that sprang instantly to her eyes. Lila was watching her, so Jessie looked away.

"Oh, honey. What is it?" Lila finished removing the handcuffs and stroked Jessie's shoulder.

"Nothing."

"That doesn't seem like nothing to me." He pulled out a chair and sat down, knee to knee with her. In his eyes was deep, genuine compassion. When she didn't say anything, Lila said, "I tell you what. I'll go get you some bandages and fix up your head, and you compose yourself. You can tell me all about it after I make us some coffee. Which way is the medicine cabinet?" Jessie pointed. "Okay. Back in a jiff."

When Lila finished patching up Jessie's head and cleaning up the blood, he brewed a pot of coffee and handed Jessie a cup.

She hadn't had any intention of telling this stranger anything. But it was close to the anniversary of that day at Sweetwater Lake—the day that changed the course of her life and cost her Claudia, so her emotions were closer to the surface than normal. The trauma of nearly being taken to jail to suffer whatever fate awaited her there also weighed heavily on Jessie.

And so, for the first time ever, she unburdened herself and told another human being about losing the one great love of her life. As she finished, she leaned forward and looked Lila in the eye. "I've been stuck in this sort of limbo ever since. I love Claude with all my heart. I can't change that. There isn't room for anyone else in there. But I know she isn't coming back. So I fill my life with empty, meaningless interludes."

"What did I say that set you down this path?"

"Claudia's pet name for me was 'sugar.' I can't hear it without thinking of her and remembering."

"Of course you can't." Lila put his hand on her knee. "I'm sorry."

"You didn't know."

"Still, I don't like to cause anyone pain, however unintentionally."

"You're a sensitive soul, Lila, and a good man."

"Thanks. Lord knows I've seen enough cruelty to last a lifetime." His eyes took on a faraway look. It was a look Jessie had come to recognize in recent years.

"You a vet?"

Lila nodded. "You can't imagine what it was like over there. The things I've seen."

"You're right, I can't." Jessie paused. "Want to talk about it?"

"Not right now, thanks." Lila got up and walked around, examining the keepsakes on Jessie's shelves. He picked up a picture and ran his fingers over it. "The P-51 Mustang. Now that's a sweet plane."

Jessie got up and joined him. "You know planes?"

"Fly them. That's part of what I was doing over there…flying missions." He put the framed snapshot back on the shelf. "I want to hear all about—what did you say they were called?"

"The WASPs."

"I want to hear all about everything tomorrow morning over breakfast." Lila batted his eyelashes at her. "Can you cook?"

"Can I cook? I make the meanest omelet this side of the Mississippi."

"I'll be back at…" He made a show of looking at his watch. "…at ten o'clock."

Jessie groaned. "That's only six hours from now."

"Hey. You owe me. I got you a 'get out of jail free' card tonight."

"I suppose."

"Good. See you at ten." Lila swept out the front door.

It was the beginning of a beautiful friendship—the first and only friendship Jessie ever had, apart from Claudia. Jessie put shaking fingers to her lips. She missed Lila. Over the years, they shared their deepest feelings. They became each other's touchstones. Jessie spoke of Claudia to him, and he shared the horrors of Vietnam and his subsequent nightmares with her. He passed away from AIDS in 1987. Jessie spoke at his funeral.

"What would you think of all this fuss today, Lila? Me, meeting Claudia's daughter and finding out that Claudia never did marry or take another lover. It's something, isn't it? All those years, I was so sure she was unreachable."

Jessie stood up and stretched. She was stiff from sitting for so long. A look at the clock told her it was time for her next round of medications. She thought about ordering room service again, but she really wasn't hungry. Besides, eating would only make her sleepier, and she had no intention of going to bed until she was done reading.

∽৯⇔

December 22, 1969

My Dearest Darling Jess,

Merry early Christmas to us, sugar. We're grandparents! Natalie gave birth this morning to a beautiful, healthy baby girl—Lisa Jane Barnes. Our son-in-law Josh is over the moon. Personally, I think forty-seven is too young to be called grandma, don't you, darling?

Natalie's experience was so much different than my own. I was with her during labor, and Josh was pacing outside. Natalie knew what to expect, and she gave birth at the hospital where she is doing her residency. It was all very civilized—nothing at all like my frantic, homespun experience.

Josh and I are getting along much better now that he's not so afraid of me anymore. I guess he figures I'm over being angry that they didn't tell me Natalie was pregnant when I was here in June, even though they already knew...

"I'm sorry, Mama. I thought you'd be so ashamed of me. I mean, you think I'm this perfect child, and here I am, pregnant and unmarried."

Claudia laughed. "Do you really think I'm in a position to judge you or that I would, sweetheart? If so, then I haven't done a very good job of raising you."

"You did a great job. You're the best mom in the whole world." Natalie enveloped Claudia in a hug.

"I don't know about that, but I do know how much I love you and that I would love you no matter what. Except maybe if you became an axe-murderer. We might have to talk about that."

"Mama!"

"Are you planning to marry Joshua?"

"He prefers to be called Josh. And yes. That's the other reason I came home. I wanted to invite you to the wedding. Can you come?"

"I don't know." Claudia's eyes twinkled. "When is it? I have a very busy social schedule. I'll have to see if I can squeeze you in."

"Very funny. We've set the date for July sixteenth."

"July sixteenth? That's next week!"

Natalie bit her lip. "I know. But we wanted to get married before the baby starts to show. You know. I don't want people staring, thinking awful things about me, and talking behind my back."

That was something Claudia understood better than almost anybody. "Okay. Just tell me where to be, and I'll try to find something to wear by then."

"Um, one more thing." Natalie looked nervous.

"What is it, baby girl?"

"Will you make my wedding dress?"

"Will I..." Claudia's eyes misted over. "You want me to make your dress?"

"You're the most amazing designer ever, and I want to have something of you in the ceremony. All these years, it's just been the two of us. This is one last thing we can do together, you and me."

Tears rolled down Claudia's cheeks. Her little girl was all grown up. "I'd love to make it. Of course, you haven't exactly given me much notice here."

Natalie threw her arms around her mother's neck. "I know you can do it, Mama! Can we go pick out material?"

"Right now?"

"Yes!"

Claudia thought she'd never seen Natalie look so radiant. "Let's go, then. Time's a-wasting."

Anyway, sugar. Natalie and the baby will be in the hospital for a few days, so I'll be cooking for Josh. I'm not as good a cook as you, of course, but I can make the basics.

Lord, I wish you were here with me to celebrate. I miss you so much, darling. Never more than on special occasions like this one. And Christmas being so close compounds the ache.

I love you with all my heart, sugar.

Your girl,
Claudia

"Well, Claude," Jessie said, as she put the letter back in the envelope, "looks like Natalie didn't always have her nose in the books, eh?"

CHAPTER TWENTY

Jessie closed her eyes and tried to imagine what it would've been like if she had chosen to fight for Claudia and their future together. Claudia's letters made clear that they'd have raised Natalie together, as a family, something Jessie had never considered.

Over the years, Jessie calculated the age of the child. When she saw kids of a comparable age, she wondered if Claudia's daughter or son were like this boy or girl. But Jessie never envisioned herself as part of the picture.

"Who are you kidding, Keaton?" The fact that the baby belonged to Matt, the very act of its creation, made Jessie sick to her stomach. It was only after so many years had passed and now, with the knowledge that, for whatever reason, Matt had never been a presence in Natalie's life, that Jessie could even entertain the notion of being part of a family.

Having kids was never a desire for Jessie. She didn't think she had either the patience or the temperament for it. But if it had been Claudia's child—*their* child—that was another matter.

Viewing Natalie as a person, rather than as Matt's seed, made a significant difference. Apart from his genetic contribution, Natalie purely was a product of Claudia's mothering, which was reason enough for Jessie to love her.

And now for Claudia there was a grandchild in the mix. Jessie could imagine her doting on little baby Lisa. She wanted to read all about it, but time was not her friend. She drummed her fingers on the packet for 1970. She should leave these years for later. "Just one peek, then I'll move on."

September 5, 1970

My Dearest Darling Jess,

I'm so nervous. It's been almost thirty years since I sat in a classroom. Am I crazy? These college kids are so young. They have their whole lives in front of them. I'm just an aging grandmother with nothing better to do with her life.

Being alone in the house has become unbearable. Natalie doesn't write or call me the way she used to. She doesn't need me—she has Josh, her career, and their baby. As you can tell, I'm feeling low.

I rattle around in this place with too much time to think about us, to mourn for what should have been. My body still remembers the feel of your fingers and your mouth, and my mind reminds me that memories are all I'll ever have.

I'm not going back to school so much to forget, love, for you know I can never do that, nor do I want to. I'm going back to school so that I can occupy my mind and so that I can have a future to look forward to. I'm planning to go to law school after I finish my undergraduate degree. I know, after all these years. Surely, I must be nuts. But if I keep on the way I am... Well, darling, suffice it to say I can't keep on the way I am.

I've thought about trying to contact you. Oh, sugar, I've thought about it so many times. But, by now I'm sure you've found someone who makes you happy, someone who won't disappoint or hurt you. So I'll leave well enough alone.

I'd better get some sleep. Class starts at eight o'clock tomorrow morning.

Please know, wherever you are, how much I love and miss you. You are my life, still.

Your faithful girl,
Claudia

Jessie dropped the letter in her lap and wiped a tear from her cheek. "Oh, Claude. I was sure you'd forgotten all about me. We were both so wrong. So wrong about so many things. And now you're dying. Oh, God."

She bowed her head and let the tears flow. After a while, she got up, splashed more water on her face, and hobbled around the room to get her circulation going again. If she were younger, she would've been doing pushups and jumping jacks. "You wish, Keaton." She rolled her shoulders and sat down again with the box. It was time to finish this exquisite torture. To have Claudia so near on the pages, and yet so far away. It was agonizing.

Jessie sorted through the packets. By 1977, Claudia would have graduated from law school.

July 6, 1977

My Dearest Darling Jess,

Today was my first day at the law firm—a rookie lawyer at the age of fifty-four. All the other freshman lawyers are in their twenties. I feel like a dinosaur.

Natalie says she's proud of me. Isn't it supposed to be the other way around? She, Josh, and little Lisa came to my graduation, which was lovely. I can already tell that Lisa is going to be tall, like her dad. At seven, she's almost eye-to-eye with me now! Boy, is she a pistol. Where Natalie was sweet and quiet at that age, Lisa is outspoken and fearless. I can only imagine what kind of teenager she's going to be. But our Natalie is a great mother, and Josh is a good father. If anyone can handle this handful, it will be them.

But I digress. Back to my first day on the job. As I told you when I was offered the position, this firm specializes in Hollywood contracts—the kind of deals made between actors and studios, what happens when someone breaks a contract and stuff like that. I know it sounds fascinating and maybe it will be eventually, but for today it was pretty dull. I sat at my desk and read reams and reams of paperwork in order to get caught up on the cases to which I'll be assigned.

Truly, I'm lucky to have landed this job. Not many firms would hire someone as old as I am. My years of experience working on studio lots and with actors, directors, and production folks are what got me in the door. I guess the partners figure I understand the system and I know some of the players, so I'll be an asset. I sure hope so.

I really want to be good at this, Jess. Heck, I really want to be good at anything. These days, apart from being "Grandma," I feel pretty useless.

Well, I don't want to depress you further. I miss you, love. Sometimes I torture myself by vowing to show up on your doorstep, wherever you are, and beg you to take me back. I think, maybe now I can explain and you'll forgive me and we can start over. Then reality

215

sinks in and I know that cannot be. I still cry often. Did you know that I have an old photo of us? I can't remember who took it, but I've had it forever. I keep it on my bedside table, now that I'm the only one in the house, and I kiss you every night. Still pathetic after all these years.

I love you, sugar. Now and always.

Your girl,
Claudia

Jessie frowned. She'd never envisioned that her bubbly, effervescent Claudia could sound so down. "I hate that you struggled, sweetheart."

What would Jessie have done if Claudia had shown up on her doorstep unannounced? "I would have made love to you until neither one of us could move." Jessie laughed at herself. Here she was, an old woman, still thinking about making love to her sweetheart. Was that a good thing or just sad? She dug back into the pile.

December 24, 1987

My Dearest Darling Jess,

It's another Christmas Eve, my 44th without you. Natalie and Josh are away on vacation skiing in the Alps. Like all teenagers, Lisa didn't want anything to do with her parents and certainly not her fuddy-duddy old grandmother, so she's off somewhere with friends celebrating her eighteenth birthday doing God-only-knows what. At least Natalie got her to agree to go to college in the fall. Believe me, with Lisa, that's a major accomplishment.

So, here I sit, alone again with my memories. I've been watching old movies—*It's a Wonderful Life* with Jimmy Stewart is one of my favorites. *Casablanca* will be coming on next. Every time I see that movie I think about our date. Humphrey Bogart, Ingrid Bergman and ice cream afterward. Nothing has ever been so sweet.

Oh, sugar. What I wouldn't give to go back to those wonderful, heady days when we were first falling in love. If only...

Merry Christmas, darling. I love you, Jess. Now and always.

Your girl,
Claudia

"I love you too, sweetheart," Jessie whispered, her lips trembling. "I always have, and I always will, even after death takes us. God, how I wish now that you knew that. I can't stand the thought of you dying without knowing that you were always loved. I never stopped. And Lila would kill me if he were alive today."

"Jess?" Lila's voice was scratchy and weak.

"I'm here, sweetheart. What can I get you?"

Lila fumbled for Jessie's hand. "I don't have much time left."

"Don't say that," Jessie's voice cracked and tears filled her eyes.

With tremendous effort, Lila pushed himself up in the bed. "We both know it's true, so let me finish." Jessie opened her mouth to say something, then shut it again. "That's better." He coughed, and his body was wracked with spasms. Jessie held him until they passed.

"You need to conserve your energy."

"For what?" He tried to laugh. "You need to listen, and I need to talk." He labored to suck in a deep breath. "I don't have much time left, but you do."

Jessie held Lila a little tighter. The idea of spending the rest of her life without him there to talk to, to fly with, to enjoy the theater and movies… It didn't bear thinking.

"I need you to do something for me."

"Anything."

"I need you to go find Claudia and tell her how you feel." Jessie stiffened. "Sugar… Yes, I called you that on purpose, what are you going to do, beat me up?" Lila coughed again. "If you've learned nothing else from me, it should be that life is too short to have regrets. Life is too short to live without love. Jess"—he held her face in his hands and made eye contact—"you've known the kind of love in your lifetime that I only ever dreamed of. Please, promise me you won't waste the opportunity to tell her how much you love her."

"You're such a drama queen."

"I'm not kidding, Jess. Please, promise me. I won't die in peace until you do, and I so want to die in peace." He leaned heavily against her shoulder. She laid him back down gently, guiding his head onto the pillow.

"I tried to find her…"

"That was thirty years ago. This is now. Try again. Try harder. Try until you find her. Promise me." Lila panted, trying to catch his breath. His hand tangled in Jessie's shirt. "Promise me."

There was a desperation in his eyes Jessie had never seen before. She worked hard to keep her composure. He so hated when she lost it, said it was unseemly for a big butch like her.

"I… I promise you."

"You promise me, what?"

"I promise you that I will try to find Claudia and tell her how much I love her. Okay?"

Lila smiled a beatific smile. His grip on Jessie's shirt relaxed, his eyes fluttered, and he stopped breathing.

"Lila? Lila? No! You can't just leave me. No! Lila! No!" Jessie put her head on his chest and cried. "Don't leave me. Please. Don't leave me."

Jessie shook her head. Losing Lila before his fortieth birthday sent her into a tailspin. She didn't leave her apartment for weeks. She missed committee meetings for ACT UP—the new militant AIDS action group Lila had insisted they join. She called in sick to her day job at the New York state senate minority leader's lower Manhattan office.

Worst of all, Jessie didn't make much of an effort to keep her promise.

"I wanted to work up the nerve, Lila. I did. Since the WASPs had been granted military benefits in 1977, I tried to follow the paper trail to see if maybe there was some official record of where she was. But they wouldn't tell me anything. I know you're probably disappointed that I didn't try harder. I just couldn't do it."

Even with Claudia on her deathbed, Jessie wondered if she had it in her to face her lover. What would she tell her about what her life had been like? Natalie hadn't said what Claudia's illness was,…maybe she suffered from dementia and was only lucid some of the time. Maybe she wouldn't even know who Jessie was. Jessie couldn't bear that.

She thought about calling Natalie's room to ask her, then she looked at the clock—it was after one o'clock in the morning! She'd been reading Claudia's letters for more than eleven hours, and she still was twenty-three years away from the present day.

Time was slipping through her fingers, so Jessie picked up the last letter in the bottom packet.

≪≫

February 19, 2010

My Dearest Darling Jess,

I am dying. There, I've said the words aloud. The doctors tell me I've got less than six months, but I'm betting I've got less than three. I don't want to tell Natalie, because I don't want her to make a fuss. She's still so busy with her medical practice and flying around the country to give lectures. She's very important in the field of oncology, you know.

Also, today is my great granddaughter Chelsea's eighteenth birthday. Who thought I'd live to see that? I do feel blessed. She's a good girl—got a far better head on her shoulders than her mother did at that age. She's more like Natalie than Lisa, thank God. At any rate, I don't want to spoil Chelsea's birthday celebrations.

I'm afraid, darling, that this will be my last letter to you. They're moving me today to a hospice center. I'd much rather die at home, but that would mean someone would have to stay with me around the clock, and I don't want to inconvenience anyone. So I haven't said anything about it. Still, I'm proud that I've managed to live all by myself for so long.

I've made only one promise to myself all these years—it's what has kept me going, even when I didn't think I wanted to live anymore. I swore to myself that before I died I would tell you the truth about what happened on that day at Sweetwater Lake. I can't die and not have you know, and I'm as confident as I can be that there will not be any reprisals or repercussions.

I did not want to go on that walk with Matt and I told him so. He ignored me and, with a tight grip on my arm, continued to lead us deeper and deeper into the woods until I couldn't hear anyone's voices anymore. I was so frightened. I demanded that he unhand me and that we return to the group.

He wouldn't let me go. He was babbling about how it was his last day, and I should give him a proper sendoff. I told him I had no interest in what he was suggesting.

Dear Jess, he said horrible, horrible things. And then he...he forced himself on me. I screamed, I fought, I clawed, I pleaded. Nothing worked. He was so much bigger and stronger than me... I couldn't stop him, though God knows I tried.

Jessie dropped the letter. It fluttered to the floor. She didn't notice. She threaded her fingers through her hair and pulled. She rocked back and forth and closed her eyes tightly as hot tears leaked out onto her face. She couldn't erase the image from her mind. It was far worse than anything she had conjured when she was convinced it was consensual.

The idea of a frightened Claudia being hurt, violated in the worst way... It made Jessie want to wring Matt's neck. She wondered idly, if, at her advanced age, she was physically capable of it. If so, she would hunt him down with her last breath...if he was still alive.

"Why, Claude? Why didn't you tell me? I would've taken care of that punk. He never would've bothered you again. Heck, he never would've bothered anybody again because he wouldn't have had the equipment for it."

Why did Claudia lie? Not once, but several times. She lied twice when she came out of the woods that day, and she lied again repeatedly on the morning she said she was pregnant.

"Why, Claude?" Jessie rose slowly and made her way to the window. The flashing lights of the Washington Monument blinked back at her as she gazed out over the Mall. "We could have had the life we wanted. I would have raised Natalie as my own. All you had to do was tell me the truth. Why, Claude? Why?"

Jessie wiped angrily at her tears. She was angry about a life snatched away from her—from both of them—that should have been theirs. What had possessed Claudia to let all that slip away?

Jessie stooped over and reclaimed the letter from the floor. She didn't want to read anymore, but she knew she had to. It was Claudia's dying promise to herself. Jessie already had let Lila down, she couldn't let Claudia down too.

Oh, Jess, darling, how I've wished all this time that I could have told you the truth back then. But I couldn't risk it—couldn't risk that his threats might be real. I hinted at it the day I told you about the baby, do you remember? I left you a note. I closed it by saying I knew you didn't want to hear it, but that I loved you with all my heart, then and always. I said you were the only one for me and that I hoped someday you would understand and forgive me.

That was as close as I felt I could come to telling you the truth without putting you in danger. You see, sugar, he threatened to do the same thing to you and then kill you if I ever told. I would never put you in jeopardy. I couldn't. To imagine him doing to you what he did to me... I couldn't bear it.

So I let you send me away. I let you believe something that was as far from the truth as it could be, in order to keep you safe. And I've kept the awful secret for sixty-seven years, because I never knew if he was telling the truth and if he could find you. It was a chance I wasn't willing to take. There were other reasons too, but I don't want to dwell on all that.

When I changed my name and Natalie's, it was to keep Matt from finding us. I was so scared that he would come looking for me when he got out of the service. I realize that by changing my name, I made it nearly impossible for you to find me, but I felt as though I didn't have much choice. That is one of my biggest regrets. Deep down inside, I always hoped that somehow you'd figure it out and come rescue me. Or that you'd forgive what you thought I'd done and fight for me.

It isn't your fault that that didn't happen, lover, so please don't beat yourself up about it. It was the unrealistic whim of a silly woman who had lost everything that mattered to her—the only thing that mattered to her—you.

Now you know the truth, darling, and it's too late.

I'm putting this and all my letters to you in a box and giving them to Natalie for you. I understand we WASPs will be receiving the Congressional Medal of Honor next month. I don't know how they managed to track me down, but they found me and sent me the notification. Obviously, I won't be able to be there, but I'm hoping you will. I'm sending Natalie in my stead, and giving her instructions to find you and give these to you.

God speed, my one and only love. I am, as I have always been, yours for eternity. I love you, Jess. Find me in Heaven.

Your girl,
Claudia

Jessie blew her nose again. She wouldn't let it happen. She simply wouldn't allow it. Claudia could not die without knowing that Jessie's love for her burned as strongly as it did six decades ago.

She picked up the piece of paper on which Natalie wrote her room number, gathered up her cane, and headed for the door.

CHAPTER TWENTY-ONE

J essie knocked again. When that got no response, she
rapped her cane against the door.

"Just a minute," came a voice from inside. After several
seconds, the voice, now much closer to the door, asked, "Who is
it?"

"It's Jessie."

"Jessie?" She heard the chain come undone and then the bolt
slide back as the door flew open. On the other side stood Natalie,
hair disheveled and eyes wild. "Are you all right? Do you feel all
right?" Natalie reached out and put her fingers on Jessie's wrist to
take her pulse.

Jessie pulled back. "Am... Am I too late?" She hadn't expected
to get emotional. Not yet.

"Do you want to come in?"

"No. At least not right now. Am I too late? Your mother—am I
too late?" Much to her chagrin, tears started to flow down Jessie's
face.

"Come in for a minute. Please." Natalie pulled Jessie inside
and turned on the light. Chelsea remained dead to the world.
"What's this about?"

"Am I too late to tell... Am I too late to see your mother?
Would she know me? Where is she? How do I get there?"

"Slow down, Jessie. Here, have a seat." Natalie tried to steer
her to a nearby chair.

"No. Please, I need to know..."

"Okay. I spoke to my daughter just before bedtime. Mama is
resting comfortably. There's been no change. She has periods of
consciousness, but she tires easily and drifts off."

"Is her mind…"

"Blessedly, Mama has all her faculties. She's sharp as a whip, although the pain medications occasionally make her spacey."

"Where is she?"

"She's at a hospice facility near her home in southern California."

"Please give me the address. I'll make arrangements." Jessie would leave now if she could find a way.

"That won't be necessary."

"I need to see her." Panic rose up. Would Natalie try to stop her from seeing her beloved Claudia?

"I understand. I'll take you there, myself. Tomorrow, or should I say…later this morning, if you like."

Jessie was fully focused on the task at hand. "But I'll need a plane reservation…"

Natalie chuckled. "Consider yourself reserved."

Jessie's eyes narrowed. "I don't need you to pay for me."

Natalie put a hand on her arm. "You're misunderstanding me. I flew us here. On my own private jet. I'll take you back with us, if that suits you."

"I thought your mother said she didn't let you become a pilot."

"She never let me become a professional, commercial pilot. I've had my license since I was sixteen. Mama taught me herself."

"And you've got your own private jet? Not a prop plane, but a jet?"

"That's right. It's handy for getting from obligation to obligation."

"I guess you must make pretty good money, then. Jets aren't cheap."

Natalie laughed again. "I do quite well, thank you. Now, it would be my honor to take you to my mother's side. I can't think of any gift I could give her that could be greater than that."

"You're not humoring an old lady?"

"Absolutely not. I never humor old ladies at three o'clock in the morning."

"Oh." For the first time since she'd picked up Claudia's last letter to read, Jessie became aware of the time. She blushed. "I'm so sorry. I didn't—"

"Please, don't worry about it. I'm used to being awakened in the middle of the night when I'm on call." Natalie's eyes twinkled. "Wheels up at 1300. Does that work for you?"

"Just tell me where to be."

"I'll have Chelsea come to your room at 1100 and help you with your bags. In the meantime, I suggest you try to get some rest."

Jessie turned to go. At the door, she stopped to face Natalie. "Thank you." The tears began to flow again. "Thank you so much."

Natalie pulled Jessie into a hug. "It's my pleasure. Will you be able to make it back to your room all right? Do you need me to go with you?"

"Goodness no. I'll be fine."

"Okay, then. I'll see you soon."

Jessie headed back toward the elevators. Within twenty-four hours, she would see her beloved Claudia again.

"Would you do me the great honor of being my co-pilot, Jessie?"

Jessie surveyed the plush interior of the jet. "A Gulfstream G450? You own a Gulfstream G450?"

Natalie smiled. "I see you've kept up on your aircraft."

"Ceiling of 45,000 feet, average speed 528 mph. They didn't build them like this back in the war." Jessie ran her hand lovingly over the controls.

"Have you flown one of these?"

Jessie raised both eyebrows. "I'm not even allowed to drive a car anymore. You think they'd let me at the controls of a honey like this?"

Natalie laughed. "I'd be willing to bet my life and Chelsea's that you could take us all the way across the country solo."

"That'd be a foolish bet on an old woman like me." Jessie continued to examine the cockpit. "Take a look at these displays. Incredible. They do everything but brush your teeth for you."

"Are you saying you don't need any skill to fly one?"

"No, no. I'm just jealous we didn't have anything like this back then."

Natalie glanced at her watch. "We've got to get going. Will you help me finish checking her out, Jessie? And take the co-pilot's chair?"

"I'd be honored." Jessie read off the checklist to Natalie, and before long they were buckled in and cleared for takeoff.

Jessie watched as Natalie taxied onto the live runway and lifted the plane into the air. "Very smooth. Your mother was right—she said that even at sixteen you had an uncanny aptitude for flying."

"Mama said that?"

"Mmm-hmm. She was very proud of you, you know."

Natalie checked in with the tower as they climbed to altitude, then she set the auto-pilot. "And I have always been very proud of her. She's a great mom." Natalie's voice broke. "The best."

Jessie reached over and covered Natalie's hand with her own.

Natalie smiled in gratitude. "You know, from the time I can remember, she drummed one thing into my head. She'd say, 'If anything ever happens to me, you find Jessie Keaton. Jessie will take care of you. Who are you going to find?' And I would have to repeat your name until Mama was satisfied that I knew it by heart."

Jessie's heart tripped. "Really?"

"Honest to God." Natalie crossed her fingers over her heart. "I knew who you were from the time I could talk. Heck, I wouldn't be surprised if I said your name before I said 'Mama'."

"But Claudia didn't have my address."

"No. And, as far as I know, she never tried to find it. When I questioned her about it, since I thought it would be practical if I actually knew where to find you if I needed to, she would say that I was a smart girl, I'd figure it out when the time came."

"You must have been curious. Did you try to find me, yourself?"

Natalie feigned indignation. "And go against my mother's wishes?" She shook her head. "No, I wouldn't do that. I have to tell you, though, for the longest time when I was small and before I understood that children were supposed to have a mommy and a daddy, I thought you were my other parent."

Jessie, who'd been taking a sip of water, choked.

"Are you okay?"

Jessie blotted the water on her shirtfront. "Fine." Jessie glanced toward the back of the plane. Chelsea was stretched out and appeared to be sleeping. "Is that all she does?"

Natalie shrugged. "She's a teenager. It's what they do when they're not texting, tweeting, Facebooking, or playing video games."

"Is she going to college?"

"Yes. She says she wants to major in Women's Studies."

"Women's... What the heck is that?"

"Darned if I know. More importantly, I have no idea what such a degree qualifies one for." Natalie checked their heading to confirm that they were on course. "I'm a little worried about her. She's very close to Mama, and she's taking all of this pretty hard."

Jessie pursed her lips. Chelsea wasn't the only one having trouble with the idea of Claudia dying. "Wha— Jessie cleared her throat. "What's the matter with Claude?"

Natalie's eyes teared up. "Breast cancer."

Jessie closed her eyes. "How long has she had it?"

"She was diagnosed last month. It's her second bout." Natalie's hands shook. "Here I am, one of the top oncologists in the world, and I can't even save my own mother."

Jessie took Natalie's hand. "Your mother and I, we've lived long lives. Eventually, your body just gives out. You're not God, dear. Sometimes," Jessie paused and gathered herself, "sometimes it's just your time. I'm sure there wasn't anything you could do to change the outcome. You mustn't blame yourself."

Natalie chewed her lip and watched out the windshield. "Pardon me for asking something so personal, Jessie, but how long have you got?"

Jessie pulled her hand back as if she'd been struck. "I'm sorry?"

"Chelsea saw your medications when she went to get you a glass of water yesterday. They're similar to the medications Mama's taking. She memorized them and told me about it."

Jessie blew out an explosive breath and turned her head away to gaze at a passing cloud. Up here, in the air for one last time— she just wanted to enjoy it without thinking about the gathering shadows. She was quiet for a long time.

"I'm sorry. I didn't mean to be so blunt." The regret in Natalie's tone gave Jessie a pang.

"No. You're fine. It's just that I haven't told anybody I was sick. There wasn't anybody to tell." Jessie fiddled with her watch. It was embarrassing, to be so alone in the world.

"Oh, Jessie. Maybe you didn't know it, but you've always been family to me...to all of us. You're not alone. You don't have to be." Natalie stroked Jessie's arm. "I don't want you to be."

Jessie fished in her pocket for a Kleenex and blew her nose. "That's very sweet, but I'm fine."

"I'm sure you are, but I meant what I said."

Jessie nodded. She was well aware that she hadn't answered Natalie's question about a timeframe. She had no intention of doing so. It was time to change the subject.

"Something's been bothering me."

"Yes?"

"I know your mother changed her last name to Turner, but the military didn't know that. How is it that they were able to find her and send her an invitation to the ceremony?"

"They didn't find her. I found them."

"I don't understand."

"Well, I knew Mama was a WASP. I saw a newspaper article about Congress passing the bill honoring all of you with the Gold Medal, and I called Mama's congressperson. They asked for proof, since they didn't have the name Turner on file. So I went through an old trunk Mama had stored in the attic with all her keepsakes in it and found all of her papers, her uniform, and pictures of your graduating class. I also found her birth certificate listing her as Claudia Sherwood and her original social security card."

"That explains one mystery."

Natalie checked their location. They were changing from one airport tower's responsibility to another, so she checked in and confirmed their location and heading.

Jessie's eyelids were getting heavy. She hadn't slept at all last night, thinking about everything she'd read in Claudia's letters, all the memories that dredged up for her, and what today would bring. Natalie's hand on her shoulder made her jump.

"Why don't you get some sleep for a while? We've got a couple of hours to go yet. There's a nice, comfortable berth back there where you could stretch out."

"No. I'm all right. I don't want to leave you alone up here on such a long flight."

"Why, Jessie, are you going to take me up on my offer to fly this jet, after all?"

Jessie smiled. "The very first time we flew together, I was at the controls and your mother keyed the radio. She asked me if I knew how to land that bird. I think I told her she'd have to wait and see for herself."

"Mama always said you were the best pilot she'd ever seen or flown with."

"Your mother was a little bit biased."

"Maybe, but I never knew her to exaggerate." Natalie stretched her arms over her head. "Please, Jessie. Get some rest. It's going to be a long day."

Jessie's energy was flagging, and she did want to be at her best when she saw her Claudia... "I will, on one condition."

"Okay, what's that?"

"If you need to be relieved for a minute or two to stretch your legs or use the restroom, you'll wake me."

"I tell you what. I'll go now, if you'll take the controls for a minute, then I won't have to disturb you later."

"Fair enough."

"Okay then, Captain. You've got the plane."

Jessie sat up straighter and surveyed the control panel in front of her. The fourteen-inch LCD displays were crystal clear, and everything was digital. She checked outside the windshield. The sky was a brilliant blue with only an occasional puffy cloud to provide contrast.

The last time she'd flown a plane was twenty-three years ago. Lila had wanted to take one last ride in the sky before he died. He'd begged Jessie to agree, and they'd hired a male nurse to ride along to keep Lila comfortable. The day was a lot like this one, and the flight was glorious.

After Lila's death, Jessie couldn't bring herself to get back in a cockpit. Between memories of the WASPs and Claudia, and memories of weekends spent flying with Lila, it was all too much for her. And now, here she was, eighty-eight years old and on her one last ride in the sky. She wondered if Natalie intentionally engineered the moment to give her this opportunity in the pilot's chair. Did it really matter?

Watching the radar, the altimeter, the air speed, checking the navigational points. It brought back a lifetime of memories. Going up as a young girl for the very first time, her first solo flight, the freedom she experienced while in the air. It was the only place Jessie felt she could escape her father's disapproving glare. It was her refuge and her one true home.

Then there was her time with the WASPs. Those magical months with Claudia. And afterward, flying was the only thing that kept Jessie sane. She lost that for a while when she moved to New York, but Lila helped her find her way back to the sky.

Perhaps it was poetic and just that her last flight should be with Claudia's daughter. Jessie shook her head. Of all the things she envisioned happening in her life—this wouldn't ever have made the list. Lila would have loved the delicious irony of it.

"Enjoying yourself?" Natalie sat back down.

"Well, I didn't bring us down accidentally, so I'd say it was a good turn, wouldn't you?"

"Careful, or I'll make you land her."

Jessie held up her hands. "And here I thought you'd want Chelsea to have a long, full life."

Natalie looked at Jessie long enough to make her squirm. "I like you. I like you a lot. I can see why Mama was so in love with you."

Jessie shifted uncomfortably in her seat.

"I've done it again—stuck my foot in my mouth. For what it's worth, Mama never said it in so many words. It was in her face, in her eyes whenever she spoke of you, in the fact that she would never go to bed without writing to you first. It was obvious from the fact that a beautiful woman like her would never even consider going on a date, despite attracting numerous would-be suitors of both sexes..."

Jessie's stomach twisted at the notion of other women pursuing her girl. She knew that was patently unfair, considering her own history, but jealousy wasn't about logic, was it?

"And it might have been that picture of the two of you she kept by her bedside. I think she always believed I didn't know about it. But I caught her kissing it once. The next day, when she wasn't home, I went in her drawer and took out the photo. Her lipstick was on your lips. Even as naïve as I was, I understood what that meant."

Jessie kept her eyes straight ahead. It wasn't that she was embarrassed by her sexuality, it was that Claudia obviously had chosen not to address the issue. "What does your mother say?"

"Like I said, she never addressed it directly."

"Then I think we ought to honor your mother's sensibilities."

"Fair enough. I'm sorry if I offended you, Jessie. That wasn't my intent."

"You didn't." Jessie unbuckled her harness. "I really am quite tired. I think I'll take advantage of that nap offer, if you don't mind."

"Go right ahead, I'll wake you before we land."

Jessie headed for one of the berths in the aft galley. She was bone-tired and unused to being buffeted by so many emotions. For now, she wanted to shut down and dream of her reunion with her beloved Claudia.

CHAPTER TWENTY-TWO

The scenery flew by as Jessie watched out the passenger window of the car. She ran nervous fingers through her hair and wished that she had taken the time to look in a mirror before they'd left Bob Hope Airport in Burbank.

"You look great," Chelsea offered from the back seat. "You're going to blow Grandma Claudia away."

Jessie dropped her hand into her lap. Was she really that obvious? "How far away is this place?"

"Not far," Natalie said, as she moved into the left-hand turn lane. "We'll be there in about five minutes."

Jessie's stomach did a somersault. The idea of being this close to her Claudia, after all these years, was so much to absorb. "Shouldn't we call ahead?"

"Why?"

Jessie rubbed her moist palms on her pant legs. "T-to tell your mother she's about to have company."

"There are regular visiting hours. Mama knows that one or more of us will be there almost every day sometime during the afternoon. She'll be expecting us."

"But not me," Jessie said, quietly.

Natalie glanced over at her before returning her eyes to the road. "Surely you're not worried that Mama won't want to see you."

"It's not that, it's just..." What, exactly, was it? It was hard to put it into words. "What if she's not up to seeing me?" That wasn't really it, but it was something tangible she could say.

"There's only one way to find out," Natalie said, as she pulled into a parking space and cut the engine.

Omigod. Claudia's inside this place. Just through those doors. Jessie wasn't at all sure that her legs would hold her. She sat perfectly still and tried to get her breathing under control. Now that the moment was here... *This is no time to get cold feet, Keaton.* She fumbled with the door handle. She was mortified to see that her hands were shaking.

"Here, let me get that for you," Chelsea said, jumping out of the back and opening Jessie's door from the outside.

"Thank you," Jessie muttered. "I'm not as infirm as I appear, I assure you." Jessie felt the blush creep up her neck. Never had she felt more inept.

"I know." Chelsea offered Jessie her arm to help her stand up. She smiled kindly as she handed Jessie her cane. "For what it's worth, I think it's adorable that you're nervous about seeing Grandma Claudia."

"I am not—"

"Whatever you say," Chelsea said, winking.

Natalie, Chelsea, and Jessie made their way together through the front doors. "Mama is down this hallway and around the corner."

Jessie nodded dumbly. She spied a little gift shop to her left. Flowers. She should bring her girl flowers. "Would you mind terribly if we made a small detour?" She indicated the shop with her cane.

"How cool! You want to bring her flowers." Chelsea practically bounced out of her shoes. "That's the sweetest thing."

Jessie looked around. "It's no big deal..."

"Uh-huh." Chelsea's grin reminded Jessie so much of Claudia.

"Anyway," she mumbled, as she made her way into the shop. There were so many colors and so many kinds of flowers. Jessie looked at the different arrangements. There were too many from which to choose. Then she saw the single red rose with the baby's breath in a crystal vase tucked away behind some daisies. If she stretched, she could probably reach it.

"You want that?" Chelsea asked her.

Jessie frowned. Just how closely was this kid watching her? "Yes, please."

234

"Excellent choice." Chelsea leaned around Jessie and snatched the vase off the shelf. "Grandma Claudia will love it." She carried the vase to the checkout counter and waited while Jessie paid.

"All set?" Natalie asked, as she closed her cell phone. "I just checked in with Lisa. She was here this morning. She says Mama's having a pretty good day."

The three women walked in silence. When they reached the fourth door down in the next corridor, Natalie brought them to a halt. "Here we are."

Jessie's heart hammered in her chest. "W-why don't you both go in first, so that Claudia isn't caught totally off guard."

"I told you—"

Jessie straightened up to her full height. "I know what you told me, but I'd really rather know that your mother is aware that I'm here and that she wants to see me, before I go waltzing in there."

"Okay," Natalie said.

"Here you go, Jessie." Chelsea handed Jessie the vase as she entered Claudia's room with Natalie.

Jessie took a deep breath and leaned against the wall just outside the room.

"Hi, Mama." Natalie's voice carried into the hallway.

"Hi, Grandma Claudia."

"Two of my favorite women." There was no mistaking it. Claudia's voice was hoarse but strong and clearly recognizable. Jessie smiled. Her Claude.

"How are you feeling?"

"Like I could take your Gulfstream out and do loops."

Jessie nearly laughed out loud. Yep, that was definitely her girl.

"That's good, Mama, because I have a surprise for you."

"You're giving me the keys to the plane?"

Natalie's laughter carried out to Jessie. "I love you, Mama, you know that?"

"I do. And it's a good thing, since I invested so much money in you."

"Very funny."

"Grandma Claudia, you have a visitor."

Jessie could tell by the tone of Chelsea's voice that she was bouncing again.

"I have two. I may be old, but I can still see, sweetheart."

"No. You have *another* visitor."

"What are you talking about?"

"Mama, Jessie is here."

There was a long pause.

"What did you say?"

"Jessie is here, Grandma Claudia. She's right outside the door. She came all the way from Washington with us to see you."

Another pause.

"Mama, are you all right?"

Jessie pushed off the wall as alarm spread through her. Her pulse hammered in her ears.

"Jessie? *My* Jessie is here? Here, as in, in the building?" Jessie released the breath she'd been holding. Claudia was okay, after all.

Chelsea laughed. "She's just outside that door."

"Oh. Oh, goodness. You're serious?" The excitement in Claudia's voice warmed Jessie to the core.

"Absolutely. She's here, Mama, and she wants very much to see you."

"You found my Jessie."

"Oh, don't cry, Grandma Claudia. We found your Jessie. She's awesome."

"You found my Jessie. After all this time."

"Here, Mama. Here's a Kleenex."

Jessie heard Claudia blow her nose.

"You want me to tell her to come in, Grandma Claudia?"

"What? Right now? With me looking such a fright? Heavens no."

"Whoa, Mama. Lie back down."

"Help me. Oh, dear. I've got to get dressed. Natalie, get me that green dress, you know the one. And I need makeup. I've got to put my face on. Where's my hairbrush?"

Jessie ran a hand over her face. Claudia wanted to look good for her. For her. It was too much to hope for.

Jessie could hear a lot of activity in the room, and she imagined Natalie and Chelsea helping Claudia prepare for a moment sixty-seven years in the making. She wanted to tell Claudia not to bother with all that, not to expend her precious energy on trivial matters, but she understood that Claudia likely was as nervous as she was.

As the sound of footsteps approached from inside the room, Jessie moved away from the door and tried to act nonchalant.

"Hey, Jessie. Sorry for the delay. Grandma Claudia's ready for you now." Chelsea took stock of Jessie standing a few steps down the hallway from the door. "You weren't standing all this time, were you? Are you okay?"

"Thank you, Chelsea. I'm fine."

"Grandma Claudia wanted to look her best for you," Chelsea whispered conspiratorially in Jessie's ear. "She's pretty as a picture."

"She was always pretty as a picture," Jessie whispered back and patted Chelsea on the cheek.

"Go get 'em, tiger." Chelsea stood back and beamed.

"Stop looking at me like that." Jessie's admonition only made Chelsea grin bigger. Impulsively, she stepped forward, straightened Jessie's collar, and gave her a fierce hug.

Flustered, Jessie dropped her cane.

"Oops. My bad, Jessie. I'll get it." She did, handing it back to Jessie with a wink.

Jessie squared her shoulders and started forward. After two steps, she stopped.

"What's the matter?"

"Take this," Jessie said, handing Chelsea her cane.

"But, Jessie."

Jessie held up a hand and shook her head. She would not let Claudia see her looking infirm or weak. She wanted to be that twenty-year-old gallant butch that Claudia remembered. One deep breath, and she strode forward, praying that she wouldn't fall flat on her face.

She lifted her chin up as she came around the doorframe. And froze. There was her Claudia, sitting up in a recliner, looking breathtakingly beautiful.

No one spoke. It was as if time stopped. Slowly, Jessie smiled through her tears. "Hello, Claude."

"Hi there, sugar. Fancy meeting you here." Claudia held out her hand. "What took you so long?"

"We'll just give you two some privacy."

"But Grandma, this is just the coolest thing ever. I want to—"

"Come on, Chelsea. We're going."

Jessie barely noticed as Natalie slipped out the door, taking Chelsea with her and closing the door behind her.

"You look even more beautiful than I remember, Claude."

"You're still not a good liar, sugar, and I could still clean your clock at poker."

Jessie laughed. "I have no doubt, and I'd gladly let you." Carefully, she closed the distance between them and handed Claudia the flower. "I mean it. You look as pretty as I remember. Prettier."

"Thank you for this." Claudia sniffed the flower and placed it on a nearby table. "And you look positively swarthy. My heroic girl."

Jessie took the hand Claudia offered and gently kissed it. The tears swimming in Claudia's eyes matched her own.

"Claude."

"Jessie."

They spoke at the same time.

"You go first," Jessie said.

"No, you."

"Okay, then. Claude..." Jessie's voice shook, and she paused to compose herself. "Claude, I need you to know that I never stopped loving you. Never." Jessie bowed her head as her tears overflowed. "I love you as much today as I did sixty-seven years ago. No one but you ever had my heart."

"Oh, Jess. Do you know how long I've waited to hear you say that?"

Jessie nodded. "As long as I've waited to say it, sweetheart." She put her hand to Claudia's cheek. "My beautiful, magical Claude."

"Kiss me, sugar. Kiss me like you used to."

"What if someone comes in?"

Claudia chuckled. "At this point in our lives, do you really care?"

"I was only concerned about your honor."

"To heck with that, Jess. Kiss me, already."

Jessie leaned down and cupped the back of Claudia's neck. When their lips met, everything that had happened in Jessie's life in the intervening years disappeared. There was only Claudia, melting underneath her, taking and yielding all at the same time.

"I love you, Jess. With all my heart and soul. I never thought I'd get the chance to say that to you again in person, but I'm so glad I did."

"I love you, Claudia Sherwood. For eternity and beyond." Jessie leaned away from Claudia in order to bring her face into better focus. "That reminds me. Where did Turner come from?"

Claudia laughed, which brought on a coughing fit. Jessie scrambled to the nearby table and picked up a glass of water for her.

When she was able, Claudia said, "Lana Turner, of course. You remember my penchant for the movies."

Jessie nodded knowingly. "Figures. I don't know why that didn't occur to me."

"It was the first thing that popped into my head, though don't ask me why I was thinking of a glamorous movie star when I was so busy feeling decidedly unglamorous."

For the first time, Jessie noticed that, underneath the makeup, Claudia looked exhausted. "We ought to get you into bed, love."

Claudia winked. "I've waited a long time for you to make me that offer again, sugar."

"I'm serious. This is a lot to take in—a lot of excitement for both of us—and I can see that you're tired."

Claudia's lips formed a thin line. Quietly, she said, "I'll have plenty of time to rest soon enough. I don't want to waste a second that I could be spending with you."

"I didn't say I was going anywhere, did I?" Jessie offered Claudia her hands. "I promise, I won't leave your side." Carefully, lovingly, she pulled Claudia upright and steered her into her arms. Claudia fit neatly underneath her chin as Jessie stroked her back. She breathed in and caught a whiff of Claudia's perfume. It was the same scent she'd worn all those years ago. Jessie smiled into her hair.

"I want to stay like this forever, sugar."

"Me too." After a few minutes, Jessie said, "I've got a confession to make."

"I'm listening," Claudia said against her chest.

"My legs aren't as strong as they used to be. I think I might need to sit down."

"Of course. Help me to the bed, darling."

Jessie guided them over to the bed, where she used her remaining strength to lower Claudia slowly onto the mattress. Jessie sat down with her and rested. "Can I help you get undressed?"

"I thought you'd never ask. My nightie is in the closet. Get it for me?"

When Jessie returned, Claudia was struggling to unzip her dress.

"Here. Let me do that."

Claudia hesitated with her hand on the zipper.

"What is it, love?"

Claudia's lower lip trembled. "You should know before you do this that I don't have the body I used to."

Jessie leaned forward and kissed Claudia's mouth. "You're beautiful." She finished undoing the zipper and nudged Claudia to lift up so she could help her out of the dress.

"Wait, sugar." Claudia sounded panicked.

"What is it?" Jessie paused with her hand on the clasp of Claudia's bra.

Claudia tried to catch her breath. "I need to rest for a minute. And I need to tell you something."

"I'm listening." Jessie lowered her hand and brushed her fingers across Claudia's bare back. She was as slender as ever, maybe more so.

"I…" Claudia swallowed audibly.

"It's okay. Whatever it is, it's okay."

"They took my left breast, Jess. I'm deformed." Claudia leaned into Jessie. Her shoulders shook.

"Oh, honey. They prolonged your life so that we could be together again. You're still you, every bit of you. Nothing else matters." Cautiously, Jessie reached up and unhooked Claudia's bra, sweeping the straps off her shoulders, off one arm, and then off the other. There was an angry red scar where Claudia's beautiful left breast had been.

Claudia tried to fold her arms over her chest, but Jessie stopped her. "Don't." She ducked her head and gently kissed where

Claudia's nipple used to be, then brushed her lips the length of the scar. When she finished, she met Claudia's fearful gaze. "I love you, Claude. You're every inch a beautiful, desirable woman. I'm going to have to beat off the competition with a stick."

"As if," Claudia said, her voice choked with emotion.

Jessie lowered the nightie over Claudia's head and settled it over her body. Then she pulled down the covers, lifted Claudia's legs, and tucked her in.

Claudia's eyes started to close, and with obvious effort, she strained to open them again.

"Don't fight it. You need the sleep."

"I need you more." Claudia's speech started to slur.

"I already told you, I'm not going anywhere."

Weakly, Claudia patted the bed next to her. "Lie down with me, sugar. Hold me. Please?"

Jessie knew she would never deny Claudia anything, ever again. She sat down on the side of the bed and took off her shoes, then slid under the covers and pulled Claudia into her arms. The bed was not really big enough for both of them, but they would make do. She stroked Claudia's hair as she heard Claudia's labored breathing even out.

When she was satisfied that Claudia was sleeping peacefully, Jessie closed her own eyes and surrendered to slumber.

CHAPTER TWENTY-THREE

In her dream, Jessie was holding Claudia as she slept, their hearts beating in synchrony. It was such a wonderful feeling, she never wanted to wake up. Then she caught a hint of Claudia's perfume in the air and her eyes flew open for confirmation.

Claudia was nestled with her head on Jessie's shoulder, her breathing somewhat labored but regular. Jessie stroked her hair and kissed her softly on the forehead. "I love you, Claude," she whispered, not wanting to wake her. Jessie flinched as the door to the room slowly opened, but she did not move or relinquish her hold on Claudia.

Natalie peeked her head in, then entered quietly and approached the bed. If she was surprised at or upset by the tableau before her, she gave no indication of it. "How long has she been asleep?" she whispered.

"How long ago did you leave us alone?"

"About three hours. I took Chelsea home and came back."

"Then she's probably been asleep about two-and-a-half hours. She was exhausted, although she never would have admitted it."

"Sounds about right. How are you holding up?"

"I'm fine."

"Do you need me to get your meds for you?"

"Not just yet." Jessie didn't want to be reminded about her own frailties. "I didn't... I don't want Claude to know."

"Know what?" Claudia said, weakly. Her eyes remained closed.

"Nothing, love. Go back to sleep."

Claudia snuggled closer. "Are you really here, Jess? Or am I hallucinating?"

"I'm really here. Go back to sleep, sweetheart." Jessie rubbed Claudia's shoulder gently and kissed the top of her head. Claudia settled down and her body relaxed back into sleep.

When Jessie looked back up, Natalie was smiling broadly. There were tears in her eyes. "I haven't seen her sleep this peacefully since she's been here." She turned around to compose herself. When she faced Jessie again, she said, "Thank you. Thank you for coming back with us and putting that smile on Mama's face. Thank you for loving her."

"Your mother was always easy to love. I can't remember a time when I didn't love her."

Natalie was quiet, and Jessie could see there was something on her mind. She was afraid she might know what it was.

"It's none of my business why you and Mama ever parted ways..."

"You're right." Jessie hoped her response made it clear the topic was off-limits.

"Let me finish, please." Natalie began to pace. "I mean, the times were different then, and I'm sure it must have been so hard for you both. Obviously, you had your reasons and Mama had hers. I... I just wish for both of you it could've been different. It's so clear how much in love you two are, even after all this time. Mama has been so alone and lonely all these years." Natalie's voice broke. "Anyway..."

Jessie nodded around the lump in her throat. If she spent too much time thinking about how different their lives could have been... Well, it just didn't bear too much thinking. So she decided to change the topic. "I have a huge favor to ask of you."

"Anything."

"You haven't heard it yet. You might want to wait."

"I'm listening."

"It's not for me, so much as it is for your mother."

Natalie nodded.

"She didn't want to tell you, because she didn't want to be a burden or to make your life difficult."

Natalie moved closer to the bed. "What is it?"

"I'm sure you did what you thought was best for Claudia."

"Please, just tell me what it is. I'm feeling awful and I don't even know why yet."

"Your mother really wants to be home. She wants to die in her own bed, surrounded by her own things. She wants her dignity and privacy." Natalie blinked several times, but said nothing, so Jessie continued. "It's not that there's anything wrong with this place, and I'm sure the care is more than adequate. But it's not the same."

"Why didn't she tell me?" Natalie's voice was filled with self-reproach.

"As I said, she didn't want to trouble you. She understood that being at home meant she would have to have around-the-clock care."

"Oh, Mama." Natalie swallowed a sob and put shaking fingers to her lips. "If she'd just told me." Natalie's eyes pleaded with Jessie for understanding. "I only wanted her to have the best care possible. If anything happens here, there's a doctor on call and wonderfully caring nurses. I... I..."

"Natalie," Jessie waited for Natalie to look at her, "your mother knows you only want what's best for her. She never thought otherwise. Neither do I, for what it's worth, and she'll probably kill me for saying anything."

Natalie frowned.

"Listen, I'm here now, and I'm not going anywhere. I could take care of her—"

"Jessie, I know you mean well, but you're not in any condition to take care of Mama. You have no idea what she requires. She has to be lifted, her bedpan changed, she needs sponge baths and medications." Natalie ran her hands through her hair and resumed pacing. "Okay."

Jessie simply raised an eyebrow and watched as Natalie worked through whatever she obviously was debating in her head.

"Okay." Natalie stopped pacing and turned to face Jessie. "Mama always put me first. She sacrificed so much for me and never asked for anything in return. She never let me help her financially or pay her back for medical school, despite the fact that I know she needed the money. The greatest gift I could give her is time alone with you."

Natalie nodded to herself. Jessie wondered if she even remembered there was anyone else in the room.

"So here's what I'm going to do. I'm going to arrange for a private nurse to stay in the house. She'll be upstairs, and you and Mama will be downstairs in Mama's room, so you'll have as much privacy as possible. I'll interview the nurse myself to make sure she understands and has no problem with your relationship."

Jessie tried not to fidget. To hear Claudia's daughter talk about them like this was disconcerting and not a little uncomfortable.

Natalie finally looked Jessie in the eye. "Does that sound acceptable to you?"

"It's fine with me, if it's okay with your mother."

"Jessie, do you have any…help at home?"

"If you're asking me if I'm capable of being on my own, the answer is, I've always taken care of myself, and I don't intend to stop now."

"Understood. I don't want to infringe on your independence. I just want to be clear in my own head on what the nurse's responsibilities will be."

"I'd like to be responsible for as much of your mother's care as I can be."

"I understand that. I'll be back shortly." Natalie swept out the door.

After she left, Jessie lay her head back on the pillow. The pounding in her head was excruciating, but she wasn't about to let Natalie or anyone else know that. When she closed her eyes, she saw spots. She breathed in through her nose and let the air out slowly through pursed lips.

Claudia stirred briefly and Jessie brushed her fingers across her cool cheek. "We're going home soon, love. You and me, together."

⊰⊱

"We're going to my house?"

"That's right, love."

"But how? Why?"

"Don't you worry your pretty little head about it. Just lie back and enjoy the ride."

Nurses' aides wheeled Claudia down the hall to a waiting ambulance. Jessie hobbled alongside. She finally had to give in and use her cane.

Natalie already was at the house, readying Claudia's room and familiarizing the private nurse she'd hired with the layout and Claudia's requirements. Jessie marveled that Natalie had been able to arrange everything in a matter of hours. She imagined, though, that Natalie was used to being efficient and in charge. She smiled. Natalie certainly was her mother's daughter.

The drive to Claudia's house was uneventful. Jessie rode in the back of the ambulance with her and held her hand. When they reached their destination, the ambulance driver helped Jessie down the steps. Then he and another young man lowered Claudia's gurney from the back and wheeled her inside.

Jessie paused to survey the exterior of the house. It was bright and cheery, surrounded by beautiful flowerbeds leading up to a cozy wraparound porch. It was quintessential Claudia. She smiled a bittersweet smile. The two of them would have been very happy here.

Natalie appeared in the doorway. "Coming, Jessie?"

Jessie used the porch railing and hoisted herself up the steps. She paused to rest at the top.

"Are you feeling all right? You look tired."

"I'm fine, thank you. It's just been a long day." She looked to the west and the sunset.

"I'm sorry. I should have realized. Let me show you to Mama's room. I've already moved your suitcase in there."

Jessie walked into the vestibule of a lovely, quaint home. Hardwood floors were covered with patterned rugs. The furniture was lived-in but not worn out. Everything was neat as a pin. The artwork was tasteful. Claudia had come a long way since their tiny makeshift rental home in Las Vegas. "Is this the house you grew up in?" she asked Natalie.

"For as long as I can remember. Mama still keeps my room upstairs. Chelsea used to get a kick out of it when she stayed here as a small girl. Of course, the place has been updated some over the years."

"It's very nice."

"Mama picked it because it was close to work for her and she could get home in time to meet me at the school bus." Natalie smiled. "I can't remember more than a handful of times that she missed getting me off that bus."

They arrived at the threshold to Claudia's room. Her personal space. Jessie peeked in from the doorway and took it all in. It was spacious. The walls were a warm, pale blue, adorned with Monet prints. The floors were a rich honey oak. Two dressers and two night tables offered ample drawer space and an inviting queen-size bed sat in the middle of the room.

Claudia was already in the bed, covered up to her chin by a fluffy, colorful comforter. She looked so small and frail. Jessie blinked away tears.

"Fancy meeting you here," Claudia said. Her voice was weak but clear.

"Welcome home, sweetheart." Jessie closed the distance and took Claudia's hand.

"I know you had something to do with this, sugar. Thank you." Claudia looked at her daughter, standing at the foot of the bed. "And thank you, my sweet Natalie. Two of the best presents I could have wished for, all in one day. You brought my Jessie to me, and you brought me home. I love you."

"I love you too, Mama. So much." Natalie cleared her throat and looked away.

"I promise to take excellent care of her, Natalie."

"I know you will, Jessie." Natalie pulled Jessie into a gentle hug. "I'm so glad you're here."

"Me too. Thank you for making this possible."

"Um, I'm going to go get Cecily. She's the nurse. I want you both to meet her before I go." Natalie disappeared down the hallway.

When Jessie looked back at Claudia, she was staring at her. "What is it, Claude?"

"First, I can't believe you're really here, in my home, with me. I can't tell you the number of times I dreamed of this. Second, you look positively worn out, and I'm worried about you."

"You're worried about me? Don't be silly."

"You're still a bad liar, sugar. There's something you're not telling me."

248

Before Jessie had to answer, Natalie returned and Jessie breathed a huge sigh of relief.

"Mama, Jessie, this is Cecily."

"Hello, there. It's great to meet both of you."

Jessie shook Cecily's hand. She had to admire Natalie's resourcefulness and thoughtfulness. If Cecily wasn't a lesbian, then Jessie's last name wasn't Keaton.

"I'm going to give you this bell. If you need anything, all you have to do is ring it. Otherwise, I won't bother you except at medication or meal times, or when it's time to check blood pressures, respirations, and the like. Does that suit you?"

"That will be fine, dear," Claudia said from the bed. "Thank you. Don't I recognize you from the center?"

Cecily smiled. "Very good. Yes, I work there part-time as a nurse. The rest of the time I take private assignments like this one."

"I wanted someone you'd be familiar with and someone who was familiar with your routine and your needs, Mama."

"You always take such good care of me. Thank you."

"Jessie, can I help you settle in? Put away your things?" Natalie asked.

Jessie's head hurt so badly she barely could see straight. "If you could just show me to the bathroom so I could put my toiletries away, that would be wonderful."

"I'll do it," Cecily said to Natalie. "That way you can spend a few minutes with your mother."

Jessie unzipped her bag and removed her toilet kit. She handed it to Cecily. She was surprised when Cecily put her hand under her elbow and forearm to support her.

"I've got you," Cecily whispered. "Don't worry, your girl can't see this from her vantage point."

Jessie started to protest but subsided. Surely, it would be worse if she fell on her face. "Thank you."

The bathroom was part of the master suite, and Jessie admired its layout. There was a walk-in shower and a separate tub, twin sinks and medicine cabinets. Plenty of room for two people.

"Is it time for your medicine, Jessie?" Jessie looked sharply at Cecily. "Natalie told me." She rushed on, "Please don't be mad at her. I'm a trained nurse. I need to know how to help. I understand that you want and value your independence. That was made quite clear to me. You needn't worry. But I'm a professional, and I can spot when someone's in trouble. Right now, you look like you've about reached your limit. So please, let me help. I promise not to let anyone else see. It'll be our little secret."

Jessie studied Cecily's eyes. She seemed earnest and not the least bit patronizing. "Deal. Whatever I tell you about my condition, you keep to yourself, right?"

"Absolutely."

Jessie frowned. "What about the day nurse, surely you can't stay here full-time without a break?"

"She's going to have to know something, Jessie. Tomorrow's my day off from the center. I'll stay as long as I can, but sooner or later, I'm going to need relief."

"I can take care of myself during the day. Been taking care of myself all my life."

"Okay. I tell you what. We'll cross that bridge when we get to it."

"Fair enough."

Cecily efficiently unpacked Jessie's things. She examined the bottles of pills, familiarizing herself with the dosage, then hid them in the spare medicine cabinet so they wouldn't be in plain sight. "I see you've got some powerful meds for migraine relief. But you don't suffer from migraines, do you?"

"No," Jessie admitted.

"How long?"

"Hard to say. They do a CAT scan every few weeks. It's inoperable."

"Which centers?"

"Mostly affects walking and balance and occasionally my vision."

"Feels like a blinding headache?"

"Yeah."

"Having one of those now?"

"Yeah."

"When's the last time you took something for it?"

"Last night."

"I'll get you some water."

"Wait." Jessie put a hand on her arm. "I don't want to be out of it. I want to be sharp for every second I have left with her."

Cecily nodded. "I understand. How about half a pill? Just enough to take the edge off but not enough to make you too drowsy?"

"Okay."

"And then you need to get ready for bed. You both need some rest. I'm guessing you wouldn't mind snuggling up with that beautiful girl in there, right?"

Cecily's eyes twinkled, which helped to lessen Jessie's discomfort. Today's generation was so open, so matter-of-fact about things that in Jessie's day barely would have been spoken of in whispers.

As if reading her mind, Cecily said, "I'm sorry. Have I made you too uncomfortable? I just want you and Claudia to know that I get it, and you're cool with me."

"I appreciate that. It's an age thing. To be able to experience the kind of openness and acceptance your generation enjoys...well, it just boggles the mind."

"We've still got a long way to go, but we've come a long way from the dark ages."

"We'd better get back in there." Jessie accepted the glass of water and the half pill from Cecily.

"Do you need help getting ready for sack time?"

"No, I can handle it. Just need to get my clothes."

Together, they walked back into the bedroom. Cecily let go of Jessie's elbow when they got close enough so that either Natalie or Claudia could see the support being offered. Claudia was asleep, Natalie sitting in a chair by her bedside.

"Everything okay?"

"Yes, thanks. I'm just going to get ready for bed."

"Do you need anything to eat? It's been a long time since you had something."

"No. I just need to lie down for a little while. Maybe after that."

"Okay. Well, I need to get home and see my husband. I'll call first thing in the morning to see how you're doing and likely stop over on my way home from work tomorrow night. Mama's had about as much excitement for one day as she can stand, I think.

251

She'll probably sleep for at least a few hours now. You could probably use at least that much rest, yourself."

Jessie nodded. She couldn't remember the last time she'd put in a day that was either as emotionally charged or as physically active as today had been. Surprising herself, she stepped forward and initiated a hug with Natalie. "Thank you, again, for being so welcoming and for bringing your mother home. I wish... I wish I'd gotten a chance to know you much sooner."

"Me too, Jessie. It's nice to have the whole family home now, though."

Jessie let go and stepped away. "Until tomorrow, then."

"Until tomorrow," Natalie agreed, motioning Cecily to see her out.

"I'll be upstairs if you need me, Jessie." Cecily called over her shoulder.

When they were gone, Jessie stood by the side of the bed watching Claudia sleep, in the bed her lover always had dreamed of sharing. She thought she should pinch herself, but if it was a dream, she didn't ever want to wake up.

CHAPTER TWENTY-FOUR

Jessie was awakened by a debilitating, skull-rattling flash of pain. Keeping her eyes closed to protect them from the light, she took in and let out several shallow breaths.

"What is it, sugar?" Claudia's hand caressed the side of Jessie's face.

Jessie cracked her eyes open slowly. "It's nothing. Why are you awake?"

"Don't try to change the topic, Jess. Please," she put her hand over Jessie's heart, "don't shut me out."

"Never." Jessie blinked, trying to bring Claudia's face into focus. "Are you okay?"

"I hurt like a son-of-a-gun."

Jessie struggled to sit up. She reached out and grabbed the bell from the night table.

"What are you doing?"

"Getting Cecily so she can give you your meds."

"I don't want my meds."

"You just finished saying you were in pain."

"I did. But the pills make me sleepy, and I don't want to waste time sleeping that I could spend awake with you."

"I bet Cecily could find a way to help you out that wouldn't put you to sleep." Jessie rang the bell before Claudia could talk her out of it. She couldn't stand the idea of Claudia being in pain.

Cecily knocked and entered. "What can I do for you? It's about time for your meds, Claudia, and I could check your vitals so that I don't have to bother you again."

"Claudia's in a lot of pain, but she doesn't want to take anything that will make her too tired. Got any suggestions?"

Cecily affixed the blood pressure cuff to Claudia's arm and took her readings, then held her wrist and took her pulse. "It's eleven fifteen now. You don't want to sleep through the night?" Cecily asked Claudia.

"Life's too short and precious to spend it with my eyes closed all the time."

"Gotcha. How about if I give you a little something to eat to absorb the medication? Then I'll give you a half dose instead of a full one. That way you can keep your wits about you, and it will dull the pain a little."

"I hate to see you hurting, love," Jessie said.

Claudia let out a long-suffering sigh. "I just know it's going to knock me out."

"Not for too long, though," Cecily promised. "While I'm in the bathroom, I'll get you a bedpan. You about ready for that?"

Jessie felt Claudia tense beside her. "I tell you what. I'm going to get up and use the facilities. You two negotiate whatever you need to do while I'm gone." Jessie understood only too well; she would've felt the same way. As much as she wanted to be the one to care for her lover, in this instance, it was better to trust it to Cecily and give Claudia her dignity. Jessie sat up slowly and threw her legs over the side of the bed.

"I'll just go with you to get Claudia's things." Cecily winked and put her arm around Jessie, making it look for all the world like she just was being friendly.

Jessie knew better but appreciated that Cecily was taking most of the load. Her legs felt like rubber and her brain was banging around in her skull.

When they reached the bathroom, Cecily said, "You take another half a pill too, Jessie. You won't be any good to her if you can't see straight."

"I really don't want—"

"I promise you, I'll dose both of you so that your meds wear off at about the same time. It'll only be for two or three hours max."

"Okay," Jessie agreed reluctantly, knowing that she would never be able to go back to sleep with her head feeling the way it did. "But I want a guarantee that I'll only sleep as long as Claudia does."

Cecily laughed. "I'm no chemist, and I'm not a miracle-worker, but I'm as sure as I can be. Just depends how your bodies process the chemicals." Cecily retrieved the bedpan from under the sink and the meds from the cabinets. "I'll take care of your girl and come back. That way you should be ready to go back to bed and it'll look natural for us to return together." Cecily put Jessie's pill on the counter with a glass of water.

"You're sneaky." Jessie smiled. "I like that."

⊰⊱

Jessie climbed back in bed after Cecily left. "Better, love?"

"Not yet," Claudia answered. "Jess?"

"Hmm?"

"Before you lie back down all the way. Can I..." Claudia blushed, something Jessie never had seen her do before.

"What is it?"

"I want something, but I'm embarrassed to ask."

"Anything, Claude. Anything you want is yours." Jessie touched her forehead to Claudia's.

"You might want to hear what I'm proposing, first."

"You want to go skinny dipping by the moonlight?"

That surprised a laugh out of Claudia. "Close." She ran her fingers along Jessie's jaw, sending a shiver through her. "It's been so long... I want to lie naked with you for just a little while. I want to feel your body against me." She rushed on, "I know it's foolish for a woman my age and in my condition—"

"Yes." Jessie's voice trembled. "Yes, a hundred times yes, love." Jessie scooted down and grabbed the hem of Claudia's nightgown. "Can you help me at all?"

"What do you need?"

"Can you lift your bottom a little?"

"For you? I could move the world."

It was a struggle, but Jessie managed to get them both naked. She laid the clothes within easy arm's reach. When she turned back, Claudia was staring at her. "I-I'm sorry, Claude. I know I'm not that sleek, toned twenty-year-old anymore—"

"You're perfect, sugar, just the way you are." Claudia's voice was raspy. She beckoned Jessie with her finger. "Come kiss me."

The kiss was slow, tender, reverent, and far more powerful than any Jessie could remember in her lifetime. Their bodies slid together. Jessie felt Claudia's hesitation when their chests touched, and she only pulled her lover closer. "You're beautiful, Claude, as you say, just the way you are."

"Bet you say that to all the girls," Claudia said, her words becoming slurred and slow.

"There's only ever been one girl who had my heart, and she's right here in my arms." Jessie felt her eyelids grow heavy. She tucked Claudia tightly against her and got them comfortable. "Sweet dreams, love. I'll see you there."

"See you there." Claudia repeated, as her breathing evened out into sleep.

The sound of Claudia's uneven breaths awakened Jessie. She lifted her head and watched Claudia's chest rise and fall. It seemed as if she was struggling for air. Jessie felt panic rise up inside her. Then Claudia's eyes opened.

"Are you okay, sugar?"

"Me? I'm fine. Are you okay?"

"I'm still here, and that's something."

"Yes, it is."

"What time is it?"

Jessie glanced at the large digital clock on the bedside table. "Three twenty-five in the morning."

"Time is slipping away."

"Don't say that." Jessie stroked Claudia's cheek.

"It's the truth." Claudia shrugged. "So I have another special request."

"I'm all ears, love."

"I want to sit out on the porch swing with you and look at the stars one last time."

Of all the things Jessie imagined Claudia might ask for, that wasn't it. "Okay." She thought about trying to carry Claudia outside. She was too afraid she'd drop her. "Let me get us dressed again, and I'll ask Cecily to help me get you to the swing."

"That would be lovely."

৵৹৵

The porch swing was remarkably comfortable, and Jessie rocked them gently as Claudia leaned into her welcoming embrace.

"Aren't they gorgeous, sugar?" Claudia asked, looking up at the stars. "Just like I remember when we were flying, only they were a lot closer then."

"When's the last time you flew?"

"Natalie took me up last year so I could admire the new plane. Boy, imagine if we'd had something like that back in the war."

"It sure is a honey."

"Did she let you fly it?"

"She threatened to make me land it just to prove all your boasting about me was deserved."

Claudia chuckled. "I bet you'd have brought her in smooth as silk."

"You overestimate my abilities these days. I did, however, fly it on autopilot for a couple of minutes while she stretched her legs. Didn't crash it or take us off-course, so I suppose that's something."

They were quiet for several minutes as they enjoyed the light breeze and the sounds of nighttime. It was Jessie who broke the silence. "She's a great girl, Claude. Natalie, I mean. You did a fantastic job with her."

Claudia reached up and kissed Jessie's chin. "Yeah, she's pretty special, isn't she? I'd like to take all the credit for that, but really, it's just who she is."

"You're too modest. I-I'm glad I got a little chance to know her."

"I'm glad too, sugar. I always hoped you'd get to meet her in my lifetime."

"Sorry it took me so long." Jessie shifted uncomfortably. She knew it would be hard, but there were things that needed to be said, conversations that needed to occur while there still was time. "Claude?"

"Mmm-hmm."

"I'm sorry for everything. I shouldn't have believed you that day when you came out of the woods, and I certainly shouldn't have believed you that morning in Vegas." There, she'd said it.

"You had no reason to doubt me, sugar. You have nothing to apologize for. I don't know how I would have felt in your place."

"I should have known you would never two-time me and especially not with a piece of trash like Matt. If I'd had more self-confidence and believed I deserved you…"

"It was my fault, Jess," Claudia said so quietly Jessie had to strain to hear her. "It was all my fault."

"What? What was your fault?"

"All of it."

"Don't you dare take responsibility for what that monster did to you." Jessie's body shook with rage.

"I was so sure…" Claudia's voice cracked and she took a second to compose herself. "I was so sure I could handle him. So sure he was a harmless blowhard. So sure appearing to date a boy would throw off suspicion and he would never come between us. It was my pride and arrogance that led to what happened."

Jessie struggled to sit up a little straighter and pulled Claudia with her. She turned so that they were face-to-face. She needed Claudia to see what was in her eyes and what was in her heart. "You listen to me. I know you didn't go on that walk willingly. I know you fought hard. I know you tried to stop him and couldn't. I know he hurt you physically, and I can't imagine what he did to you emotionally. I know if I could, I would hunt him down even now and strangle him with my bare hands—after I finished cutting off his genitals. So don't you, even for a second, sit there and believe any of it was your doing."

"But, Jess—"

"No, Claude. Matt did what he did and took what he took, not because of anything you did or didn't do. It really had very little to do with you. He was a nasty, hateful, hate-filled, mean, arrogant, entitled SOB who preyed on an innocent girl." Jessie's eyes opened wider, as everything clicked into place for her. "In the end, he accomplished exactly what he set out to do—he took you away from me. That was always his goal, don't you see?"

Claudia nodded slowly. "I suppose you're right. If I'd been less traumatized, frightened, and frantic, I might have understood that. But alas, we can't go back and undo what was done so long ago, can we?"

"God, I wish we could, Claude. I've missed you so much."

"Surely, you haven't been alone all this time?"

Jessie's ears burned with shame. "I wish I could say I'd been as nobly celibate as you, but you were always the stronger one. I've done many things I'm not proud of."

"Don't be ashamed to have found love, sugar. I always wished that for you. It's another reason why I didn't try to find you. Knowing how you felt when we parted, I was convinced that you would forget about me and move on, find someone you could love, and live happily ever after. I didn't want to be selfish and interfere with that."

"Love?" Jessie laughed harshly. "Who said anything about love? You are the only person I've ever loved, sweetheart. I had sex with other women to punish myself—to remind myself that I wasn't good enough for anything more than a passing fling. I let them use me, and I used them. I never allowed myself to get emotionally involved with any of them. Heck, I never even had sex with the same woman twice."

"Oh, Jess." Claudia closed her eyes. "That must have felt so empty."

"That was the point. I was empty. The only woman who filled my heart had chosen another path—so I believed, anyway." Jessie shook her head. "Did you really not try to find me because you didn't want to disrupt my life?"

"That was part of it. It was complicated, sugar."

"I'm listening."

"The things Matt did to me that day." Claudia swallowed hard. "The things he said he would do to you if I told. I was terrified for you. I couldn't—wouldn't—allow him to destroy you. I knew you, sugar—you wouldn't have been able to live with the idea that a boy, especially one like Matt, could overpower you. But he could have. He was savage." Unconsciously, Claudia fisted her hand in Jessie's nightshirt. "And I knew that if I told you the truth, you would have gone after him. He would have enjoyed breaking you and believe me, he would have. So you see"—Claudia looked up at Jessie, tears spilling onto her cheeks—"he won either way. This way, at least I knew you were physically and emotionally safe from his brand of torture."

Jessie captured one of Claudia's tears on her fingertip. "And all those years afterward? You could've come to me. Surely his threat didn't carry all that weight so many years later?"

"My fear of him and what he was capable of never lessened, sugar. The memory of what he did, how his face looked, what his voice sounded like...that never faded. Many nights I woke screaming in the middle of the night, sweat pouring off me, picturing him looming over you."

"I'm so sorry, Claude."

"Me too. And then there was Natalie's safety to consider. You and I were the only ones who knew who her father was. If I went to you and he somehow found out, he would be able to figure out that Natalie was his, and I could have lost her to that monster. God only knows what he would have done."

"Logically speaking, the chances that he would have carried out his threats after returning from the war were slim. You know that, right?"

Claudia shook her head. "Not to me they weren't."

"I suppose that kind of terror isn't logically based, is it?"

"No." Claudia sighed heavily and rested her head again on Jessie's shoulder. Jessie could see that she was tiring.

"Do you want to go back inside, love?"

"In a minute. I don't want all that ugliness to be the last thing we think about out here on this beautiful night, when there are so many stars in the sky."

"Okay." Jessie searched her brain for a pleasant topic. "So you let Natalie get her pilot's license, after all. And you flew big muckety-mucks all over the place. Good for you, Claude."

Claudia smiled. "Like you, flying was in my blood. I couldn't just walk away altogether." She hugged Jessie tighter. "Did you go back to flying when you got home?"

"For a short spell right after the WASPs. But then I moved to New York City and I gave it up for a long while."

"Then you found it again?"

260

"I did." Jessie smiled at the memory. "I met a gay boy who called himself Lila. He rescued me from being arrested one night outside a gay bar in Greenwich Village."

"Jessie!"

"Well, I did find my share of trouble…or, more accurately, it found me." Jessie stroked Claudia's hair. "Anyway, Lila was much younger. He'd been a pilot in the Vietnam War. He convinced me to fly with him. So on weekends we'd go up."

"Sounds like fun."

"Oh, I wish you could have met him, Claude. You would have been fast friends."

"He sounds special."

Jessie turned wistful. "He was the only friend I ever had other than you."

"What happened to him?"

"He died in my arms in 1987. AIDS."

Claudia rubbed Jessie's heart. "I'm sorry, sugar."

"Me too. Like I said, you really would have loved each other. I used to talk to him all the time about you."

"About me?"

"That's right. He was the only one I ever told our story to. He used to give me a really hard time—called me a dunder-headed fool for not trying harder to chase you down."

Jessie put two fingers under Claudia's chin and tipped it up until their eyes met. "I did try to find you once."

Claudia gasped and put trembling fingers to her lips. "You did?"

"Hired a private detective, but he had no luck. That was a lot of years ago. I'm sorry I didn't pursue it again." Jessie thought once more about the deathbed promise Lila extracted from her. She imagined that Lila was smiling down on them now.

Claudia shuddered against her. "Claude?"

"I'm afraid I'm fading on you, sugar."

"Let's get you back to bed."

"In a second. Kiss me under the stars, Jess. Let's pretend we can turn back the clock and do it all over again."

Jessie cupped Claudia's neck and closed the distance between them. "I love you, Claude. Now and always."

"I love you, sugar. Always and forever."

The kiss lasted a long time, each of them giving and taking and giving some more, until the intervening time and all that had come between them disappeared. All that was left was the purity of a love strong enough to span sixty-seven years.

Eventually, Jessie pulled back. The stars twinkled above, and the very beginning traces of a pink and orange sunrise shown on the horizon. "It's time for us to go, love."

"Yes, I suppose it is."

Jessie rang the bell to summon Cecily so she could help get Claudia back inside.

When they were resettled in the bed, Jessie looked up at Cecily. "Thank you for making that happen."

"No problem. Everything okay?"

Jessie considered. "Yeah. It is."

"You need anything else?"

Jessie looked down at the woman she held in her arms. "No. I've got everything I need right here."

"I'd say that goes for her too," Cecily said with a smile, indicating the expression on Claudia's sleepy face. Cecily waved at Jessie and took her leave.

For a moment, Jessie simply watched Claudia as sleep took her. She was as beautiful as ever.

"I love you, Jess," Claudia mumbled. "You're my one and only."

"I love you too, Claude. You'll always be my girl." She tucked Claudia's head under her chin and fell asleep.

In her dream, Jessie saw Claudia and Lila together. Together?

"Hey, Jess. You were right about her, she's gorgeous, you old son-of-a-gun." Lila looked young and vibrant, much as he had the night he'd rescued her from the paddy wagon.

Claudia was twenty again and radiant. "Come on, sugar. Join us. It's beautiful here. The skies are limitless and the stars are breathtaking. We could fly forever."

Claudia held out her hands and beckoned, and Jessie gladly took them.

THE END

About the Author

An award-winning former broadcast journalist, former press secretary to the New York state senate minority leader, former public information officer for the nation's third largest prison system, and former editor of a national art magazine, Lynn Ames is a nationally recognized speaker and CEO of a public relations firm with a particular expertise in image, crisis communications planning, and crisis management.

Ms. Ames's other works include *The Price of Fame* (Book One in the Kate & Jay trilogy), *The Cost of Commitment* (Book Two in the Kate & Jay trilogy), *The Value of Valor* (winner of the 2007 Arizona Book Award and Book Three in the Kate & Jay trilogy), *One ~ Love* (formerly published as *The Flip Side of Desire*), *Heartsong*, and *Outsiders* (winner of a 2010 Golden Crown Literary award).

More about the author, including contact information, news about sequels and other original upcoming works, pictures of locations mentioned in this novel, links to resources related to issues raised in this book, author interviews, and purchasing assistance can be found at www.lynnames.com.

You can purchase other Phoenix Rising Press books online at
www.phoenixrisingpress.com or at your local bookstore.

Published by
Phoenix Rising Press
Phoenix, AZ

Visit us on the Web: **www.phoenixrisingpress.com**